THE FRUIT OF LIFE AND DEATH

THE HADES | I | CHRONICLES

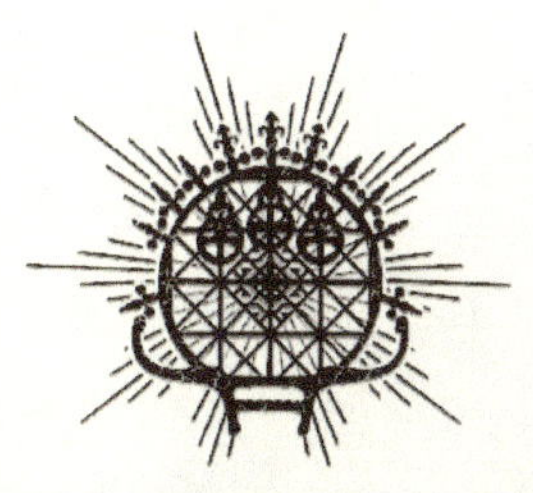

THE RISE OF HADUWAS

AMANDA L. RAUTIO

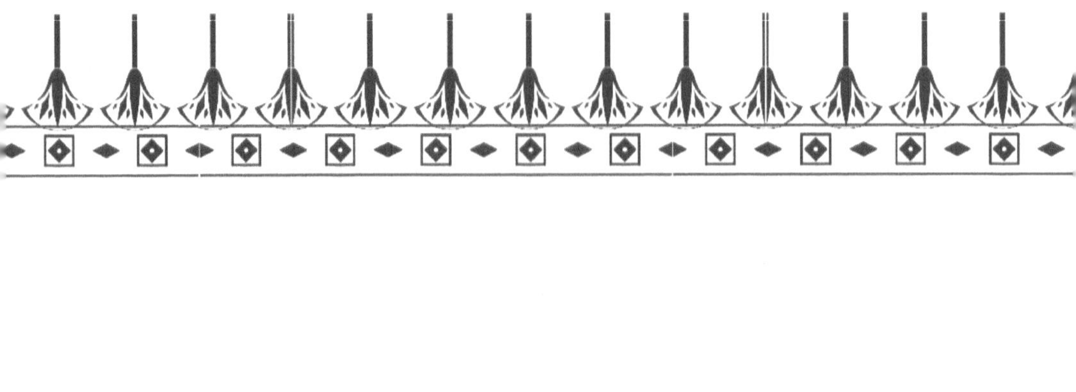

MYTHOSMITH
PUBLISHING

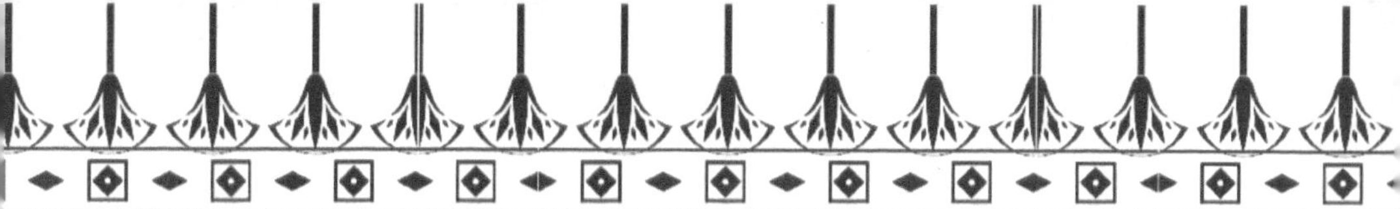

THE FRUIT OF LIFE AND DEATH

THE HADES | I | CHRONICLES

THE RISE OF HADUWAS

AMANDA L. RAUTIO

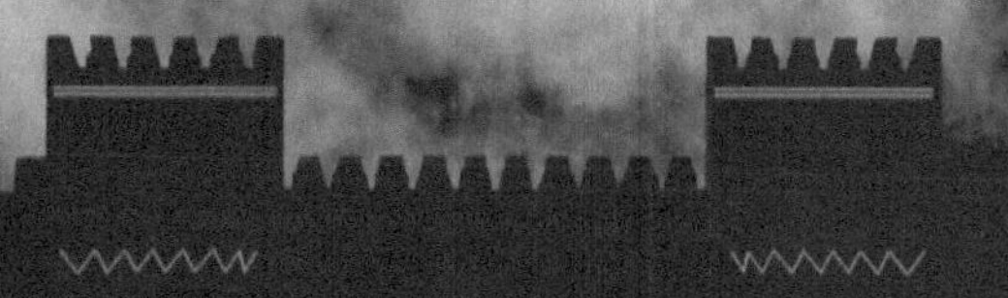

This novel is entirely a work of fiction. The names, characters, and incidents portrayed in it are the work of the author's imagination. Any resemblance to actual persons, living or dead, events, or localities is entirely coincidental.

Mythosmith Publishing
Banff, AB, Canada
www.themythosmith.ca
Printed in Calgary, AB, Canada

Manuscript Evaluation by Samantha Lane
Developmental & Line Editing by Molly Eccles
Proofreading by English Proper Editing Services
Cover, Chapter Headings, and Breaker made by Miblart
Typesetting by Amanda L. Rautio

First Edition Published: May 2026

ISBN 978-1-0693421-5-7 (ebook)
ISBN 978-1-0693421-6-4 (Paperback)
ISBN 978-1-0693421-7-1 (Hardcover)

This book uses Canadian spelling and conventions.

For more information, please visit www.themythosmith.ca
@themythosmith

Also by Amanda L Rautio

The Fruit of Life & Death Series
The Rise of Haduwas (#0.5)
The Tale of Kore (#1)

Non-Fiction
A Fairytale in the Making: a Guided Journal

Short Fiction:
The Mirror of the Lost and the Found

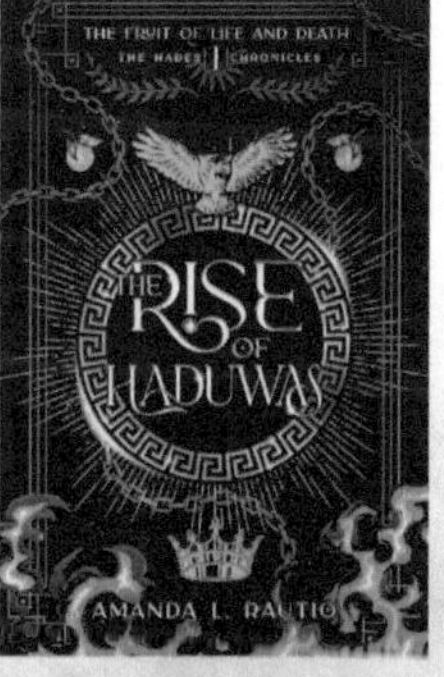

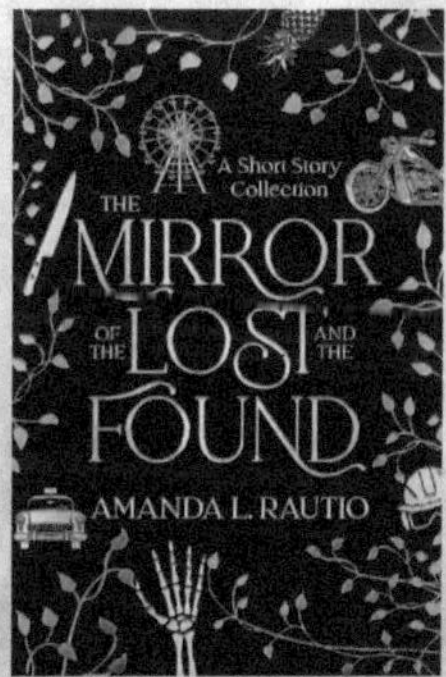

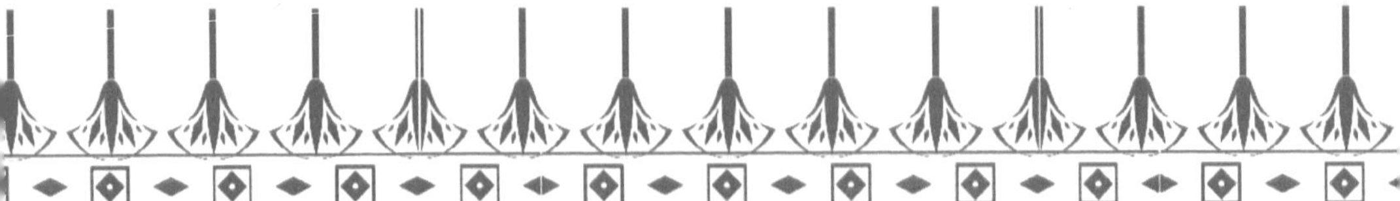

"Humans are born, they live then they die. This is the order that the gods have decreed. But until the end comes, enjoy your life, spend it in happiness, not despair. Savor your food, make each of your days a delight, bathe and anoint yourself, wear bright colors that are sparkling clean, let music and dancing fill your house, love the child that holds you by the hand and give your wife pleasure in your embrace. That is the best way for a man to live."

THE EPIC OF GILGAMESH

(Anonymous)

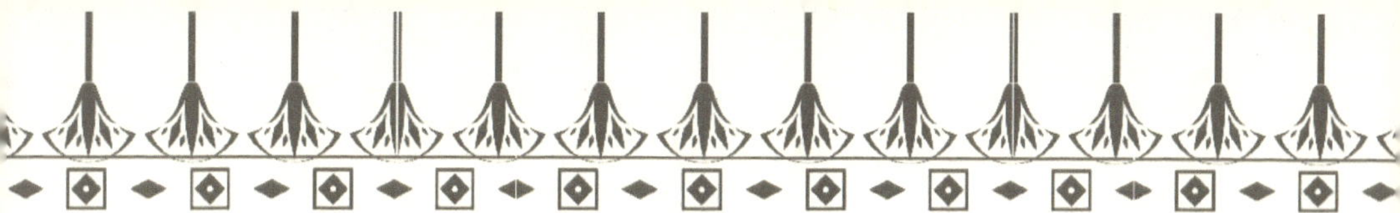

To those who descend
willingly into shadow,
and do not turn back
from what waits beyond the gate—
I dedicate this to you.

The Rise of Haduwas

Left behind in a great migration, a prince is condemned by false omens and sent into the Underworld by priests who are shaping the kingdom's future through a second, favoured bloodline.

In a remote bronze age village at the edge of his father's kingdom, he's spent years cut off from court, orders, and certainty of his father's rule.The King has remarried into the house of priests, binding the future of the kingdom to their chosen line. For the priests, Haduwas is not a forgotten son but the one remaining obstacle to that future.

When Haduwas returns to the city of his father, the priests offer him only one path forward: descend into the Underworld, return with a relic of divine favour, or disappear into obscurity.

But the Underworld does not test strength. It judges the soul. And no man who enters the Underworld is meant to return.

Epic Historical Fantasy meets Mythological Retelling in Bronze Age-inspired political fantasy about a principled heir confronting succession politics, divine law, and a system designed to replace him. Perfect for readers of Circe and mythic Bronze Age fantasy traditions with echoes of Elric of Melnibone.

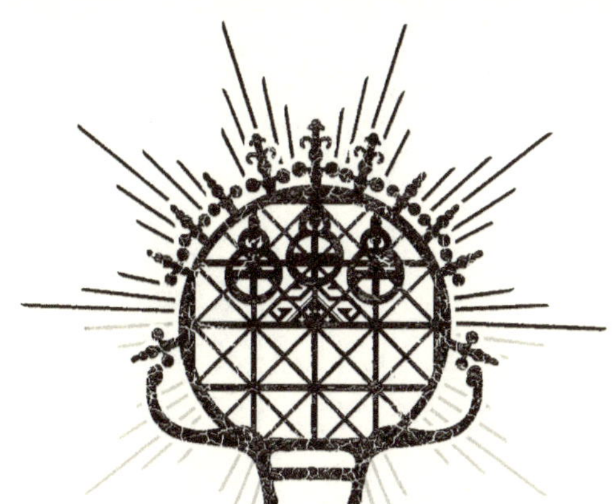

Table of Contents

Dramatis Personae

Prince Haduwas: *first son of King Karuwas; second born.*

Zaza: *an old smith*

Alluwa: *Prince Haduwas's best friend; a hunter.*

Idari: *youngest hunter; son of Huella.*

Mutti: *a hunter.*

Kammara: *High Priest of the sun goddess of Arinna.*

King Karuwas: *King of Kussara, father of Prince Haduwas.*

Huella: *mother of Idari*

Nippa: *a hunter.*

Nipula: *a wise woman with blonde hair.*

Gazaza: *an orphaned child of the tribe.*

Aruna: *a washer woman.*

Belwan: *a young hunter; a scout.*

Sharvara: *a foreign hunting dog.*

Tuwari; Zanpi; Kati; Wadri; Annu; Zuwani: *hunters of the tribe.*

Malla: **an old woman;** *attends to communal meals.*

Annuwanza: *foreign priest.*

Queen Malinuwa: *Kammara's daughter; wedded to King Karuwas.*

Kazera: *the servant of Prince Haduwas; brother to Alluwa.*

Prince Pasaduwa: *second son of King Karuwas; third born.*

Prince Zuwasa: *third son of King Karuwas; fifth born.*

Princess Hestuwa: *first daughter of King Karuwas; first born.*

Askalpusa: *nature spirit in the Underworld.*

Princess Heriya: *second daughter of King Karuwas; fourth born.*

Princess Dameruwa: *youngest daughter of King Karuwas; sixth born.*

Urappi: *a nobleman; owner of a vineyard.*

Kurli; Harli; Puza; Marassa: *the horses of Prince Haduwas.*

GODS:

Arinna: *Sun Goddess.*

Lelwani: *Sun Goddess of the Earth; Goddess of the Underworld.*

Inara: *Goddess of the Wild.*

Kurunta: *God of the Hunt.*

Tarhunna: *God of the Storm.*

Wurrukatte: *God of War.*

Kasku: *God of the Moon.*

Kiase: *Primordial Mother Goddess.*

Upelluri: *God who holds up the Heavens.*

Parasuwa: *God of Foresight.*

Sersuwa: *God of Hindsight.*

Litti: *River Goddess of Forgetfulness.*

Zari: *God of Doomed Might; Cattle Herder.*

Šauška: *Goddess of Love, War, Sex, Beauty.*

Telepinu: *God of the Sun of Harvest and Farming.*

Kumrešepa: *Goddess of Magic & Medicine.*

GLOSSARY:

Hatti: *the term for the native population of inland Anatolia.*

Drink the Gods: *an established Hittite custom of drinking [wine in particular] where the purpose of drinking was to connect with a god or gods, and climb up the vine to become more than you were.*

Gulsarana: *an invented Hittite term for a cleaning, scraping tool.*

Currencies: *Minas, Shekels, and Talents. Standardized weights of precious metals. Associated with tiered values.*

Kyphi & Myrrh: *in the form of imported incense from Egypt.*

Pankus: *a governing body of nobility.*

Heptad: *a term for "the Dark Ones", a group of demons or spirits. Different gods had different Heptads as related to their traits. Often come in groups of seven.*

i

Editorial Note

This book is born from a place where myth and memory intertwine. When I began writing *The Rise of Haduwas*, I set out to tell a story where myth and history *both* fail in practice. History has too many questions with answers which might never be known, and historical narratives seldom venture into the speculative like I do. Myth too is useful, but again, has gaps. So many myths overlap and diverge that there is no single "Truth". However, there are recurrent archetypal themes which stand out stark against both myth and history. Therefore, this story is not so much a retelling as a reconstruction of fragments out of time.

The world of Bronze Age Mesopotamia/Anatolia was one of humanity's earliest centres of urban life, writing, and storytelling—home to some of the first cities, written words, and mythologies which echo through later traditions. This reconstruction is steeped in these stories. You will find fragments of Gilgamesh, echoes of Heracles, of Hades, and the shadows of forgotten deities who once ruled the lands the later Greeks and Romans inherited. I drew inspiration upon cuneiform tablets, fragments of epics, and the surviving rituals of early peoples, but I have woven them into a new tapestry.

What follows is *not* true history. It imagines what might have happened in the *gaps* of history where our sources *cannot* say anything certain. The characters live and breathe in a space between archaeology, anthropology, and imagination. The boundaries of truth and invention are intentionally blurred, but the heart of the story remains faithful to the ancient desire to explain life, death, and the worlds beyond. Where sources exist, I have adhered to the truth, but when there is no source? There is nothing as tempting to this author as speculation.

11

Before the Telling

In the days before parchment was smoothed and letters were pressed into clay, men knew their fathers by memory alone, and the deeds of kings were borne upon the lips of singers. Yet memory fades, and tongues stumble, and what is not written is soon lost to the dust. Therefore I, servant of truth and witness to the passing of ages, have set down the names of rulers and their lineages, lest oblivion devour them.

For kingdoms rise as swiftly as they fall. Stone crumbles, walls sink into the earth, temples are overgrown with brambles, and the bones of kings are mingled with those of slaves. But the word, once fixed, endures. The name of a ruler spoken centuries hence is a second life granted to him; it is for this reason the ancients strove not merely to conquer, but to be remembered. And if they could not shape eternity with their hands, they sought instead to shape it with the echo of their names.

It is said that the first king ruled not by spear, nor by council, but by sheer wonder: men gathered to him because the gods had touched his brow, and his voice held sway as if thunder spoke. Yet the sons of this first king did not hold such divine favour. To rule after him, they needed laws, customs, and armies. Thus the crown, once a gift of awe, became instead a chain of duty. Each generation bore it differently—some with honour, some with cruelty, some with indifference. Still, the line endured, and with it the land itself, as if the earth had bound its fortune to the fates of those enthroned.

But where truth ends and tale begins, who can discern? The old lists, copied from reed to reed, speak of reigns that stretched beyond a hundred years, of kings who conversed with spirits, of rulers who walked beneath the sea or ascended to the sky. Are these mere embellishments of scribes eager to flatter their masters, or do they conceal fragments of a deeper reality, lost to us but once visible to eyes unclouded by disbelief? I cannot say. My task is not to weigh the measure of legend, but to preserve the record entirely, for truth often hides within myth.

Thus I have set in order the names of kings as they have come to me, whether carved in brittle tablets dug from the earth, sung in the halls of elders, or whispered by wandering priests. Some reigns are attested in many places, firm as stone; others survive only in the frailest fragments, a single name half-worn upon a shard. Yet I have not cast them aside, for even the faintest echo deserves remembrance. To omit is to condemn to silence, and silence is a second death.

Let it be known that not all ruled justly. Among the names inscribed here are tyrants who shed the blood of their kin, who despoiled temples, who bartered their people to foreign masters. There are also those who, by mercy or wisdom, bound the land in peace, restored sanctuaries, and fed the hungry. To list them side by side is not to exalt them equally, but to confess that history spares no man from company with the wicked. All are gathered into the same grave of time, and it is for the reader to discern light from shadow.

Nor should it be thought that kings alone matter. Behind every ruler stood the silent multitudes—the farmers, the builders, the weavers, the soldiers—whose hands carried out the decrees, whose sweat raised the walls and tilled the fields. If their names are absent from this record, it is not because they lacked worth, but because no man thought to preserve them. The king's list is but the skeleton of a nation's life; the flesh and breath are lost to us. Yet by the skeleton we glimpse the shape of the living body that once was.

Therefore, readers of distant days, take this chronicle not as the final word, but as a gateway. Question the order, weigh the claims, and consider what lies unsaid. For history is not merely the recounting of who sat upon the throne, but the unending labour to understand what it meant for him to be there.

So I inscribe, with hand unsteady yet resolute, the succession of kings from the first dawn-born sovereign to the latest whose tomb is yet fresh. Whether you honour them or scorn them, remember them. For remembrance is power, and the dead, when remembered, are never wholly gone.

Anonymous

iii

An Accounting of the Discovery

When I first came to the mounds of central Anatolia, I expected little more than the familiar silence of stones and dust. The place was marked on old maps as Kuššara, a name half-conjectural, half-legend, long dismissed by scholarship as a shadow in the annals of the Old Hittite kingdom. Few believed anything of substance would be recovered here; fewer still thought the city had ever truly stood as the cradle of kings. It was said that from Kuššara rose the first sovereigns of the land, men who claimed a dominion stretching across the high plateaus and into the valleys where merchants carried tin, silver, and promises of power. Yet the ground bore no clear witness. Kuššara was less a city than a rumour.

Our initial trenches yielded what one would expect—potsherds of the Early Bronze, the remains of household fires, the detritus of lives long gone. It was the kind of work that dulls even the most patient hand: scraping, sifting, cataloguing. Weeks passed with little to show but a scatter of broken vessels and the faint outline of stone foundations eroded beyond recognition. We were ready to record the site as inconclusive when one of the local workers, while driving a pick into a collapsed chamber, struck against something hollow.

The cavity proved to be the entrance to a sealed room, buried beneath layers of collapse. The air that exhaled from the breach was stale, dry, and heavy with the smell of bitumen. Inside we found a stone chest, its lid cracked but still intact. Within lay a collection of tablets—burnt clay hardened by time's fire, incised with characters unmistakably belonging to the Old Hittite hand. Their surfaces were blackened, some flaking at the edges, but the words endured. The chest was half-filled with earth, suggesting hurried burial, as if someone had sought to conceal these records in an age of calamity.

The tablets themselves contained a patchwork of texts: fragments of royal annals, genealogies, hymns to gods whose names have not all survived elsewhere, and, most curious of all, a narrative of descent and return, composed in a style at once historical and mythological. Scholars may dispute whether these were meant as literal accounts or allegorical retellings of dynastic origins. Yet what struck me was the recurring presence of a singular figure—an unnamed prince, sometimes described as the son of a foreign concubine, sometimes as the chosen heir of an aging king, sometimes as both. He was portrayed as a wanderer, descending into caverns and returning with the favour of gods older than the storm-god of Hatti.

The resonance with myths known elsewhere in the ancient Near East is unmistakable. The descent motif, the bargaining with deities of death, the ascent marked by bloodshed and kingship—these are themes that echo from Sumer to Akkad, from Ugarit to Greece. Yet here, in the heartland of Anatolia, they appear clothed in different symbols, tethered to a different landscape. Kuššara, so often ignored in the grand narratives of empire, emerges from these fragments not as a provincial outpost but as the matrix of a mythic and political tradition.

One cannot help but imagine the scribe who impressed these words into wet clay. Was he recording the memory of his own lord, hoping that posterity might remember? Or was he fashioning an origin story, drawing on the shared mythic reservoir of the East, to sanctify a dynasty whose power was still precarious? We will likely never know. But the presence of such texts in what was once thought a marginal site forces us to reconsider. Kuššara may not have been the silent parent of Hattusa—it may have been the wellspring of its earliest identity.

The work of decipherment continues, but what follows in these pages is a rendering of those fragments into a continuous narrative. It is neither pure history nor pure myth, but something liminal—like the tablets themselves, cracked yet enduring, speaking across millennia in a voice both regal and spectral. For though empires rise and fall, though names are forgotten and cities swallowed by earth, the words remain.

If there is truth to be found here, it is not in the verification of dates or the mapping of campaigns. It is in the recognition that men and women of a forgotten city once inscribed their fears, hopes, and divine encounters into clay, hoping to outlast the silence of the grave. In that ambition, at least, they succeeded.

What follows, then, is no modern invention but an act of translation—translation not only of language, but of imagination, carrying across the gulf of time the voice of Kuššara. May the reader enter as I once entered the sealed chamber: with dust in the lungs, torch in hand, and the weight of the forgotten pressing close.

Mistress of Classics,
Corey Morris, PhD

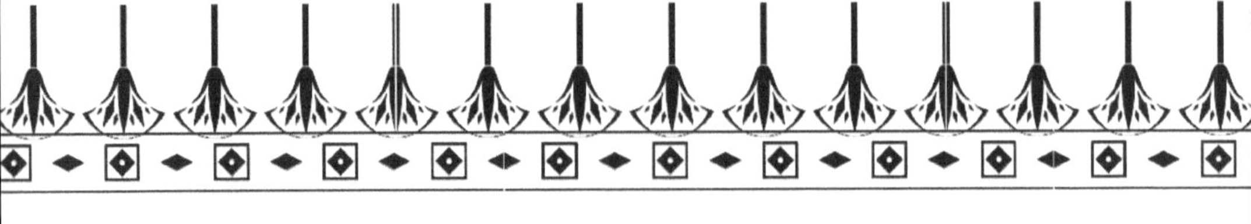

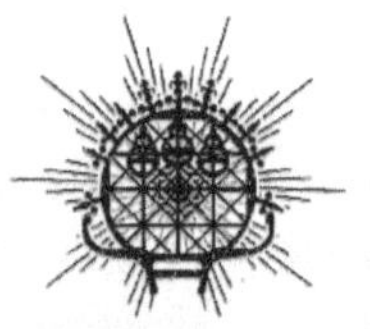

The root of the land lies within the earth,

and the Great Goddess holds the life-force of all things.

The great reed rises, whole and unbroken.

Within her, the heights and the depths.

I
TABLET
THE HOUSE OF KARUWAS

The wind tastes of iron, mud, and livestock, carrying the grit of a late spring thaw. Every step sinks into half melted snow and churned earth. The settlement sprawls before me like a skeleton picked clean with empty houses and workshops standing as reminders of what once was only a handful of years past. Trade flourished with our metalwork desired from all directions; the more delicate and intricate the labour, the more we prospered, but as the trade routes pressed ever south, few ventured as far north to obtain our treasures. Soon, my father had led a great campaign across the grassy sea to a great, fecund land taking with him all the skilled labour and warriors. Left behind to oversee the seasonal migrations, I did my duty as my king and father commanded. I received instructions every year with requirements and vocation requests, and every year I had complied until the commands ceased altogether. That was two summers ago.

We were meant to follow the sun, a long-promised migration, but here, in the shadow of a distant king, I await an order I suspect will never come. To be forsaken by the gods is a tragedy; to be forgotten by a king and father is something else entirely. They say the gods built this place, but they must not have loved it for they've abandoned it, leaving only a crown of dust for a prince whose wisdom now serves only to count the dead and ration the living. We are forgotten, and I've been left to shepherd the shards of my people.

Smoke curls up from a few stubborn fires, rising in thin, grey threads towards a sky mottled with low clouds, the sun weak and pale. What does the goddess of the sun do when she leaves the skies? I doubt I'll ever know.

I pass the old smith, Zaza, who lifts a hammer in his trembling hand, striking at a copper ingot with waning strength. A girl crouches beside him, copying each motion with exaggerated care, desperate to learn the sacred, dying craft. Nearby, goats bleat softly in pens, and the faint tang of their musk floats on the wind. Without having to look, I know the food stores in the stone structure next to the pen are nearly empty. Grains are dwindling, and the dried and smoked goods grow less and less every day. Harvest is still many moons away. The trees bear no fruit in this frigid air, and the bushes and brambles fare no better. Urns of fermenting milk and jars with goat cheese are a welcome change to the anemic state of the people, but it cannot persist. Even if traders *did* venture this far north, there'd be nothing for them–not even hospitality.

As though thinking of my father should summon him, I look to the horizon as I scale the ladder to the fortified wall to stand atop it. There is nothing and no one around. Not for trade, not for correspondence, not for anything. Scraggly branches twitch in the evening light, illuminated by the dying day as they shudder in the wind, but all else is still, and yet, I can smell change.

"Haduwas!"

Whirling around, my gaze traces the wall until I see one of my men, Alluwa, waving frantically. He points to the far gate, one which has been in disuse for many years now, barricaded and overgrown. A muffled skirmish and a yelp is the only hint I get before a priest bearing the garb of the sun goddess drifts into view, struggling between my warriors. His head is perfectly shorn, and with a slight twinge of satisfaction, I note that he shivers in both fear and cold. I descend the wall as my warriors bring the trespasser into the centre of the village. Curious faces look on from homes as they try and discover this utter anomaly. Even the clanking of the old man and the girl in the forge have grown silent. Old Zaza always was a gossip.

"He was trying to sneak past our defences, Duwa," my youngest warrior, Idari, says. He's not more than four and ten. "Tried to cross the backside of the wall to get to the temple." Temple was a nice word for the abandoned shack. Our last priest had died the season before.

Nodding at the boy, I assess the intruder. "Does your sun goddess not keep you warm, priest?" I ask as a violent shudder sweeps through the man.

The priest says nothing to this. Instead, his teeth clack, and I wonder just how much warmer the lands that my father currently occupies are if this mild weather is inducing shivers as such. Granted, the man is not dressed for the region. Instead, he's decked out in a material I have no words for, but the long, yellow and white garment catches the dwindling light in odd ways producing a shimmering effect.

"What message have you brought from my father?" I try, his silence irritating, yet I hold my temper.

"He won't speak," Alluwa says from behind me. He's breathing hard, and in his hands, a bag. "I confiscated this." At the sight of the bag, the priest's eyes widen, and his struggles are renewed as he elbows Idari in the face, but the boy holds fast.

"Don't you dare touch that!" The priest snaps, face growing red, speaking in a foreign tongue only I among my people can understand. Whether from anger or the cold, I can't be sure. Mutti, who secures the other arm, nudges the back of the priest's knee in warning.

"Let me guess," Alluwa says, toying with the bag. "He wants it back?"

"In the presence of my people, you will speak the common tongue, priest," I say calmly, retrieving the proffered bag of linen. Not ready for the weight of it, I nearly drop it, but I clench my fingers on the fabric before it slips free. Tilting my head at Alluwa, who bites back a grin, I give him an unimpressed look before returning my attention to the priest. "Only I am fluent in the words of the Hatti. You will address me with the customs of the land."

"Your authority is not recognized by the sun goddess of Arinna," he snaps at me, still in the tongue of the far west. Sighing, I scratch my eyebrow with my thumbnail, and jerk my chin in the direction of the main lodge where I make rulings—and where the priest was meant to have presented himself to me as a guest.

"Take him to the chair," I announce, and all three warriors, Alluwa, Mutti, and Idari bring the flailing priest to the main lodge while I contemplate the bag in my hands. Without even opening it, I know it for what it is: tablets. Whatever news they bring, I fear it is dire.

My people congregate around the foreign prisoner. He is of the priest of Hatti, that much is certain. Their religious verve is known across the land, and while not one for monarchs or rulers, they are not to be controlled. They control from the shadows with relics of their gods. My father was a fool to ingratiate himself to the priest faction. They pay any price their gods demand no matter how abhorrent the action. It is a fact well known.

The main lodge has seen better days, yet it remains always warm and dry. There is no seat of power, but a great table runs down the centre with benches on either side for meals and conversation, and at the end, an immense hearth with a spit for feasts and festivals no longer observed. Upon the clay walls and suspended from wooden beams, chains of preserved fruits of our labours the season past tethered to string. An assortment of fruits from figs to apples and apricots to berries are pierced and held aloft for circulation, effectively preventing vermin from reaching our stores. Few remain.

Crossing the hall ahead of my people, I take a seat in the furthest chair, not elevated or decorated, yet mine all the same. Seated, I gesture at Mutti and Idari to set the prisoner before me. The villagers pile in and line the seats as they all watch on to see judgement passed.

Mutti and Idari let the man go and the man falls to his knees none too gently, and a squeak escapes him before he stifles it. His brown eyes like the dark earth of spring flit this way and that, never resting long. I stare at him, and the longer I do so, the more his eyes flit about until he can't help but return my gaze.

"You attempted to avoid the attention of the town. It is a fact well known to all messengers who venture this way on behalf of my father to present themselves to me with their business. Were you unaware of this necessity?"

He says nothing to my posed question, and instead posits his own. "Are you aware your father has married?"

Casually, I swing the bag onto my lap and lean forward to inspect the man with my fingers intertwined.

"Is this tablet demanding my presence to pledge fealty anew?"

"No, no," the priest says with a derisive snort. "Nothing of the sort. As I was saying, your father has remarried since your mother's passing." My fingers crumple the linen in my lap before I force myself to smooth the wrinkle out. He continues, "The High Priest of the sun goddess of Arinna, Kammara, was very generous in offering up his eldest daughter as the king's prize."

"Kammara?" I ask, a startled laugh escaping me.

"What is so funny?" the priest demands, and I shrug.

"Only that your high priest's name literally means 'excrement' in my language."

"Why do you think you're still here after so many years?" the priest asks, his tone venom, likely upset I mocked his high priest.

"Because the city is not ready for us," I say, trying not to dwell on how much the excuse feels like ash in my mouth. How many times had that exact question plagued me *today* let alone in the past years? Every reason under the sun has occurred to me. That he was dead, that the messengers were intercepted, that another party was preventing my return, that my father had disowned me, that he'd been overthrown, that he'd named one of my younger brothers heir apparent—even that I was more useful to him here than at the new city for the time being. Dread coils within me, a serpent of monstrous proportions.

"The city has been ready for years now with the most skilled labourers working day and night to complete the task. No. You and the rest of your ilk are not welcome in the city of gods."

"Let us observe what orders from my father," I say, without further preamble. Withdrawing the tablet, preserved in fire, I glare at the priest. Cracks mar some of the words, and where the priest had obviously intended to destroy evidence, there are jagged lines, but the meaning is clear, and when I reach the bottom, my blood runs cold.

My spirit seems to have been plucked from my very body only to be hurled somewhere else far from this room. Surely this tablet is a fraud—a ploy from the group my father usurped who sought to regain their religious power over their lands, and yet, there is no denying my fathers seal at the bottom. No hand could have pressed that seal but King Karuwas. If he has married the high priest's daughter, the faction clearly intends for the new union's child to prevail.

An irritating, staccato laugh escapes the priest. "Like I said," he says, chortling. "I recognize no such power that you lay claim to. Do you not serve witness to your father's seal? Surely no one knows it better than you," he presses, and his mirth only grows.

"What does it say?" Alluwa asks, pressing forward in the crowd, hand on the hilt of his still sheathed sword. My eyes scan the room from Idari and Mutti to every other face in the room. I know them all by name. Every single one. Charged with their protection, our numbers have decreased, yet these faces have been steady for five turns of winter, and every one of them is dear to me. Bundled by the doorway, Huella. My trembling hand is raised in a motion for silence, and whatever Alluwa had been about to say dies at his lips.

"We must evacuate immediately."

The room erupts with chatter not heard in the hall for many a year. Voices clamber to fight to be heard, and I allow it for all of a moment before I raise my hands and the room falls into an eerie silence once more.

"There is an attack forthcoming. We must be gone by morning or we will become bodies for a grave with no one left to bury us." I turn to the priest. "For the crime of conspiring against the kin of the crown, I, Haduwas, son of the great House of Karuwas and ruler of this place, sentence you to death."

Standing from my chair, I look to Alluwa who is already offering me his sword. Nodding at him, I take it and without so much as another word, I strike the priest's head clean off. Shrieks from some of the women and children chill me, but it is necessary. He cannot be allowed to live.

"Gather everything you will need from this place," I tell the room who listens with apt attention. "Gather your flocks and herds. Gather the remaining larders and stores. Bring every vessel we have and let them drink their fill from the rivers. Bring your clothes, your weapons, and only that which you can carry. The sick and the elderly shall ride in carts. The rest shall have to take turns walking. Every mule will helm a carriage and the able-bodied will ride on horseback. Let us hasten away from this place. Go. Now."

At once, the room bursts into a web of action, and all but my closest flee from sight. Mutti, Idari, and Alluwa remain, as do several of my other warriors and Huella, who clings tight to the furs surrounding her too-slender frame.

"Where will we go?" Idari asks, but all I can do is stare at Huella who returns my gaze.

"We must go to the new city."

"What did the tablet say?" Huella asks in the faintest of voices, and I wince. No one on this earth knows me better. I never could lie to her.

"It outlines a direct attack on this settlement with the exclusive intent to kill me and this abandoned tribe in two days' time. The alliances my father has made do not like the idea of his line remaining in power it would seem."

"And yet you'd fling us into the mouths of the lions?" she demands, a flicker of her fiery nature clawing back to the surface. "If they intend to harm us, why would we go back?"

"She poses an excellent question," Alluwa admits, rubbing his lip with his thumb as he tries to follow my train of thought.

"Where else can we go?" I ask.

"What else was in that tablet, Haduwas?" Huella asks, her sombre tenor betraying her thoughts. I cannot answer her. To do so would put her, and everyone in this room, in danger.

Returning to her previous question, I sigh. "We go back to the capital because we must. We are dying here slowly. When was the last child here born?" It's a rhetorical answer. There have been none. "The last ceremony of souls intertwining?" Still no one answers. "The last rite for death."

"The day last," Idari whispers, and Mutti elbows him.

"You're not supposed to actually answer that," Mutti retorts, rolling his eyes.

"Do you trust me?" I ask, and Idari nods emphatically. Alluwa bows his head, and one by one, everyone bows. Nippa and Huella are the last to nod their assent, but when there is agreement, I let out a breath of relief.

"Very well. We all have preparations to make. We leave at first light."

II
TABLET
A STALK OF WHEAT

I will never forget the way my lifelong home went up in flames. At the behest of some foreign power driving the helm of my father, my home was reduced to ash and rubble. There were no casualties that night as I watched from the ridge. My people, led by Alluwa and Nippa, continued with our people at a pace that swept them beyond the reaches of the Hurpa river. Upon my horse, Harli, I rode hard and fast to watch the destruction, to verify the threat was real. It had come not from the West as I'd anticipated, but from the North East. Another desperate clan paid off handsomely no doubt.

Our settlement had been protected by a cradle of curving rivers, providing abundant fresh water and fish. But it came at a cost. Without advanced retreat, it was a bowl you could not escape. It had been imperative to leave as quickly as possible, and had Alluwa not intercepted the priest and found the stashed tablet buried in the muck, we'd all be dead now.

When I'd ridden back, no one asked if the worst had come to pass. My face had spoken more than words. For many days, we'd travelled with a fierceness of an army, though we were a company comprised predominantly of old men, women, and untested children. Grief was heavy upon the faces of the older in the party, but an undercurrent of hope cut through the despair. Our path was quite clear, and to make it to the new city, all we had to do was keep the river to our left until it veered far south and continue west. A stony gorge would need to be passed, and beyond that, sandy grasslands. Once we departed the side of the river, we would come upon a great forest. By day, we traveled as far as we could with the frail and sick upon carriages and the young taking turns walking and resting on carts, and by night, we'd make a hasty camp with members volunteering for the watch. Idari was in control of the main carriage, he himself having a great talent for improving designs, and upon the bench, he sat with leather reins in his relaxed hands.

"He's a natural," Huella says, looking at her son with great fondness when she dismounts the horse Kurli. I follow her gaze to where Idari ties the reins off as he prepares to help everyone make camp for the night. The further south we come, the milder the nights, and yet still, it is wise to be bundled. Fires erupt like blooming flowers in spring as my warriors make communal centres for warmth.

"He is." I dismount, running my hands through Harli's black mane.

"We are taking him to a very dangerous place," she says in a muted tone only I can hear, and my heart seizes in my chest. She leads her horse to me, then past me to water Kurli. The past years in exile had been heart-wrenching and trying, and yet, there had been a silver lining to it. I had not been under a microscope. I had lived with relative freedom, and though I'd never openly shown preferential treatment to Huella or Idari, I had taken Idari under my wing. I'd been left with all leadership in the settlement, to settle trades, to document all accounts and keep track of all agreements with the neighbouring parties, though each year, the correspondence had been less and less. I had been trained in all languages of the area and been taught to read and write. Under this capacity, it had made sense for my father to leave me behind as his voice and messenger for his authority.

"Yes," I say, following her.

"No one can know, Duwa," she whispers quickly, her voice lost in the clopping of hooves on rock. "No one can know."

"I know, Huella," I say, not facing her as we walk. To anyone looking, it would appear as though we were simply walking in silence to water the horses. "I will have to distance myself a great deal in court. You and Idari must stay in the lower town. I can't acknowledge you more than I would anyone else, even here." My words cease when Harli stops walking to lean down to drink. "It's a miracle we've kept it a secret this long," I say, looking at her in the corner of my eye. Turning my head in her direction, I permit myself to look at her one last time with honesty. She had been my first—my only. Now, with the sight of my future, I will never have her in the capacity that I desire.

Shucking her shoes, she steps into the water herself. Crouching, she cups the water in her hands to drink. When she's done, she dries her mouth with the hem of her sleeve before standing and walking directly to me. In the dying light, threads of red seem to glow in her hair even though her hair is a rich brown. Her hazel eyes, trained on mine, burn with an intensity that makes my skin flush, and every instinct I have wants to stride forward, cradle her face in my hands, and kiss her like she deserves—to pleasure her as she deserves, but to do so would put everything at risk, so, instead, with a strength that I am ashamed of, I offer her nothing more than a nod before turning around to be of use to the tribe instead.

I can feel her attention on my back as I walk away while Idari bounds forward with the clinging energy of youth, and it feels like the gods are laughing at my misery. "The camps are all settled, and supplies have been distributed. I've rounded up the horses too. They're over there," he says, pointing to where the horses had been penned into an area with carts and ropes. I reach out and ruffle his hair.

"Excellent job," I say, eyeing the group. The warriors are dispersed among the clusters of fires, attending to the people there with food and water. I take a seat on an outcropping of stone while Idari continues on to his mother. Wild thoughts thunder through my mind, and I try to understand the gods—an impossible task.

It is clear as day to me that the priests are a threat, but their hold on my father concerns me. There are two possibilities that further branch off into more. He either signed it, or he didn't. If he signed it, did my father sign the tablet with the knowledge of what it contained? Had he signed the tablet with his seal without reading it because it was simply placed in front of him to sign. The alternative is not better because if my father did not sign it, either the original seal was stolen, or an impression of the seal was stolen and duplicated for the priest faction to sign off whatever and whenever they dare. I hum, deep in thought, when Nipula, our wisest of women, approaches.

"You are troubled," she says, handing me a hunk of coarse bread. I take it gratefully with a curt dip of my chin. Her long hair like stalks of wheat sets her apart from many of the women whose dark hair coils like serpents. Her skin is paler than most, and her eyes are even more distinctive, for they pierce with the coldest of rivers despite the warmth in her gaze. She sighs and crouches beside me and we stare off in different directions with a shared, solemn silence.

"You fear for Idari," she says, and without meaning to, my head whips to her side, but she does not turn to look at me. Instead, her gaze is fixed on Idari and Huella both. "It is not without cause, Haduwas."

I swallow thickly, the motion a difficult one. I do not ask her how she knows. Either she is observant enough to have guessed, or she sees it plainly with her gift of sight; either way, it does not bode well for me. No one knew Huella and I had ever come to know one another, and after it had happened, to protect the child of the union when she had discovered her monthly bleeding had not arrived, she had married someone else, though he'd died in conflict a year later. There have never been questions into Idari's parentage, and yet, to anyone with eyes, to anyone who *ever* pays attention, the truth is on his face, on hers, and on *mine*.

"I have little choice," I begin, but halt almost immediately. With an angry chuckle, I amend my words. "Of course, I have choices, but only two make any rational sense to pursue," I say, fiddling with the bread in my hands. "Either I reunite us with the rest of the tribe for the sake of everyone here," I begin, "or I don't and we tread a new path and see where the gods take us." She is silent as she listens. "Both are fraught with danger. The roads are perilous no matter the direction we go, so there is risk no matter what I do." My fingers dig into the soft insides of the bread beyond the crust to pinch a piece off. I take a moment to eat, neither tasting or enjoying it. "On the one hand, there is an unknowable danger, and on the other, a knowable one. Am I a fool for choosing the enemy I know over the one I do not? Even if that enemy truly ends up being my father?"

Only now does her gaze seek mine. Her lips part as she takes in the information, for she had not known the true extent of the tablet. I know the moment she leaves me for answers because her eyes glaze over until she stares right through me, seeing nothing at all. Her eyelids slide shut, and her chin dips.

"As you say, there is a danger known and unknown," she begins, "but in truth, both are unknown to you. There is an unknown, yes, but what you believe is known is only a truth you suspect. You will find that nothing in this matter is straightforward, and no matter what you do, the way is fraught with pain and loss." When she closes her eyes, I wonder what it is she sees. I have asked her before how she is in such easy communion with the gods, but the only real answer I have gleaned from her explanations is that how she sees ordinary objects shifts until she sees a symbolic message.

I snort and tear another piece of bread away to plop it into my mouth. I chew aggressively as I watch the grass sway back and forth, back and forth, and suddenly, I understand her explanation in the grass and wild wheat stretching out before me in a sea of pale yellow. I see my own indecision reflected back at me. I am a stalk of wheat in a field trying to control the wind. Shall I sway back and forth until I am shorn from my stalk to be ground up and consumed by a more decisive power? Or shall I decide to plant a new seed? At the precise moment of my decision, Nipula looks back at me.

"You have come to the correct decision."

"How do you know?" I ask, and she shrugs.

"Because your eyes tell me so. The only correct path forward is the one made with conviction."

"Thank you," I say, tentatively holding out my hand to her. She takes it for a moment, nods, and strides away to gather up the laundry. Nodding to myself, I stand up, and make my rounds to ensure all needs of my people are met, leaving mine to die in the field with the wheat. My needs do not matter—only that of my people. My suffering is insignificant because I can handle it, but I cannot handle theirs. The choice, therefore, is easy. I choose them.

"Idari," I call, and he disengages from Huella to look at me.

"Yes, Prince Haduwas?" he calls back eagerly. The term settles over me, a stifling blanket in the scorching sun. Though technically a prince on account of my father's recent status change, it has never felt *right*.

"Walk with me for a moment," I say, and he all but sprints towards me, and despite my previous promise to myself, I greedily drink in the sight of Huella before our son blocks my view, and from there, I allow myself to think of the boy before me as my own son, and I am crippled with longing.

"How can I help?"

"I'm going to be sending Nippa with a message for the king," I say, placing a hand on his shoulder as we walk along the river away from eyes and ears. "He will be going ahead of us with one of my horses to deliver a message to my father. I need your help to discreetly craft this message. Can you help me with firing the clay?"

"I have the clay in your carriage."

"Good," I say, running my fingers over my chapped lips as we walk in the direction of my carriage. *When was the last time I drank water?* "I can prepare the clay and write my message. In that time, can you prepare a way for me to fire it?"

"Yes, Prince Haduwas." Idari chews on his lip, gaze flitting around our surroundings, noting the slope of the land, the river at our back, and the mountain range in the distance.

"What is it?"

"Are we safe here for the time being? The clay will need to air dry of course at which time we can be mobile, but then we won't be able to move while the clay cooks, and it will be very intensive."

"How intensive?" I ask, and his eyes light up.

"I'll build an oven with the bricks we have, and then I'll have to build a blade blower...with six, maybe eight blades, and then we'll have to take turns spinning it to make sure it gets hot enough."

"Here is as good a place as any to make camp."

Idari nods and leaps up onto the backend of the carriage to collect the supplies. Withdrawing a thin cord from a bag, he precisely cuts free a hunk of clay from the mound on the cart, and with a nod, tosses it in my direction to catch. "For the tablet," he says. Snatching it out of the air, I smile, wiggle the clay in his direction, and begin the arduous mental task of crafting a veiled political message as I massaged the bubbles and impurities from the earth in my hands. "I need to find some supplies," he says, jumping onto the cart with his and his mother's belongings beside mine.

With the chaos and intensity of youth, he rifles through sacks buried under cloth and through woven baskets, knocking over linens and displacing neatly stacked bowls. "Your mother worked hard on organizing that cart," I say in warning, and he gives me a sheepish grin over his shoulder before resuming his efforts, more carefully this time. His belly presses into the side, and one leg flails wildly as he attempts to retrieve something too far to reach. I say nothing, but allow a smirk to bloom into a chuckle as his foot points and flexes as he nudges himself closer to whatever object he needs.

My child.

The thought warms me despite the clench of unease I routinely feel when I allow myself to go there mentally. He huffs before brandishing an axe overhead victoriously.

"I need some sticks," he declares, jumping off the cart and landing in a crouch. "And some bark, and then that will have to soak overnight so I can rip it into strands to secure it..." He begins by informing me of what he's doing, but as he walks past me, it's clear he's telling himself what *he* needs to do. With a gentle shake of my head, I watch as he regards every single tree and reed. He seems to settle on reeds because he descends the river bank where they grow in clusters. Returning to my own task, I find a smooth rock somewhat near Idari, and press it flat into a vaguely rectangular shape, and with stylus in hand, craft the most delicate message I've ever had the need to send. It takes me until the dying light to get it just right.

"Nippa!" I call when I see him making his rounds.

"Haduwas," he returns, inclining his head.

"I have a task for you, if you accept."

"Anything," he says, nodding.

Standing, I clap him on the shoulder. "I need you to deliver a message to my father directly. You will need to travel ahead of the group and send word to my father. I have the message, and you must give it to my father, and my father only. Not a priest, not a nobleman, not my brothers—the king."

He nods, resolutely. "When do I leave?"

III
TABLET
THE BIRDS OF DEATH

The undulating grasslands swim in the early evening light, a golden sea waving to the rocky shore of the mountains in the distance. I survey the landscape, determining we are a little over a week's ride to the new settlement in the West. For months we have travelled hard through rocky terrain and endless steppes, cut through arid landscapes and skirted junctions of swift flowing waters. Nippa has yet to rejoin us. Months ago now, I had sent him ahead of our group to deliver the message to my father. It was my hope that he'd have returned by now, but something has held him up. Unease stirs me, and Harli, ever my faithful riding companion, feels it. Time to make camp.

An unfamiliar river cuts through the land, the current mild and not so swift as to be dangerous. Smiling at the sight of the river, I click my tongue and dig my heels into my black mount, urging Harli forward at a gallop.

Once pressed up against the river, the caravans and overflowing wagons rattle to a stop. With the river to our backs and a dense forest looming around us just a little north, we are perfectly oriented for the women to launder the clothes as the men guard and hunt the night's meal. There is sure to be abundant game, especially with our proximity to a freshwater source. The cluster would make any theft attempts more difficult, especially with all the warrior caravans on the outer edge and the women and children protected in the centre.

My scouts herd toward me, and I swiftly unseat myself, landing firmly on both feet. Footsteps sound behind me as I stop in front of Idari who grins at me as he secures the reins and hops down from the manufactured bench. Clapping him aggressively on the shoulder, I share the grin before hopping onto the wagon bench he'd just descended from. Despite telling myself I would keep my distance from Idari and Huella, I have failed, though far more in the case of Idari. Huella has been relatively easy to avoid because her duties do not run directly into mine. Idari has been one of my constant companions alongside Alluwa and Mutti.

"Gather a hunting group, but make sure to leave enough men behind for protection. We shouldn't be too long," I say over my shoulder to my men before entering my caravan to prepare for the hunt. I don't wait for an answer as I slide the panel open to slip inside the small window. The inside is stuffy and too warm from baking in the sun all day, but when the sun fully disappears, the envelope of heat is a gift from the goddess. The space is not large, but it is incredibly organized. Along the left wall is where I sleep on a raised bench with stacks of hides covering straw. On top are piles of blankets that are no longer required in this warmer climate.

Furs line the interior walls including a lion hide—it had belonged to a great beast with eyes and fur of the purest gold. I have a vicious scar from my hip up to the armpit from where it had sliced me in combat as we had traveled through the gorge not a week after I had sent Nippa ahead. I shudder to think what could have happened if anyone else had been leading the procession. The lion had been starving, desperate, and with little choice but to attack, it had. I had taught Idari how to make a hide with it, and even if I could not be his father in any meaningful way, I collected these memories and stored them as close to my heart as I dared.

Wooden shelves line the other walls where various ceramic jars hold precious materials. One jar, in particular, is essential in lethal combat: a concoction of serpent venom and water from the Black Sea to dip arrowheads to poison enemies from afar. Beside it, a belt hangs from a peg on the wall, gifted from my warrior woman, and from the peg next to it, a set of my drinking cups fashioned from bull horns that hang from leather cords.

Some woven baskets on the floor hold various clothing, and stowed away beneath the bench where I sleep is my trove of weapons. Knives, dirks, axes, and arrows for my bow are all neatly tucked out of sight, each comprised of bronze and wood in varying capacities. A small box containing replacement arrowheads sits under the shelving, and strapped to the wall in the corner are my spears.

Pulling on additional armour from the basket of clean clothes, I quickly adjust it to protect myself in case we come across predators. Securing my curly hair at the nape of my neck to keep my field of vision clear, I tuck a loose tendril behind my ear when it falls into my eye.

Looping my bow over my shoulder alongside the quiver, I retrieve a long knife and my shield before withdrawing from my modest quarters. The dying sun beats on my brow as I stand up to my full height, something that cannot be accomplished within the caravan.

Already, my men are waiting outside; some wear bows as I do, and others hold spears, but all hold shields just as I'd asked. Nodding at them, I turn to Idari who is practically bouncing with excitement. At the same age, I'd been in charge of military campaigns, and trained at arms since I could stand. I am glad to know he won't be put into the same amount of danger as I'd been subjected to. At the very least, I have provided him with instruction, and under my care, he isn't ever put into immediate danger—at least not more so than is expected in this life.

"Scouts said they saw signs of a pack of deer," Alluwa says, and I pat his shoulder before walking through the camp towards the river.

"Good," I say. "They should be easy to find then."

Children scream and laugh as they play, chasing each other and weaving through the legs of the adults attending to duties. A little boy crashes into my legs, the momentum pulling him to his bottom. The child cries, and I stoop down to meet his height. Twisting from bum to knees, he places his hands on the ground before pushing himself up, and, with a pout, throws his hands into the air above his head, fingers splaying wide.

"Up!"

Hiding my grin, teeth clamping down on the soft skin of my inner cheek, I pick the boy up before throwing him into the air; shrieking with wonder, the little boy, who is four, clutches at my shoulder with a death grip as he lands. His mother had perished in his birth, and now, everyone in the tribe is his family.

"Again?" I ask, and he nods vigorously. And so I throw him into the air, repeatedly catching him with steady hands. Before his joy can subside, I secure him so he sits on my left forearm and use my right hand to steady his back in case he tries to wiggle away.

Feeling the weight of someone's stare, I seek out to my left. It is Huella, and with the tightness of her face, I know she is imagining the sight she'd been robbed of. She'd had neither I nor her late husband to dote upon her child, to toss him with joy, or see to his needs. She'd had the tribe, but the yearning in her face now as I play with the child is clear.

"Go play now, Gazaza," Huella says at last. "The men have to go hunt and bring back a meal for the group." Dutifully, I put the little boy down. Smiling up at me enthusiastically, he darts off once I have him settled back onto his feet. Alluwa eyes trail after Gazaza who is now tugging on a little girl's braid. The girl smacks his hand away, and he resorts to following her around.

"He's going to be so much trouble," Alluwa remarks with a snort, and I inwardly agree.

"To the river," I say. The ten men around me nod at my instruction. "The deer should not be hard to find so close to the river and the forest." A hum of assent encourages me forward.

Approaching the bank, I pull my water skin from around my neck before unstoppering it. Peering upriver, I watch as horses drink greedily, congregating together as they quench their thirst. If the horses drink, the water is safe.

The women tasked with laundry wash downstream so as not to contaminate the drinking water. Nipula is among them. Their hands plunge fabric into the water, saturating it before they beat the clothes against the large rocks around them, forcing the dirt out of the fibres.

Falling to my knees, I stoop forward to wash my face of the day's effort, and watch as the sweat and grime disperse in the meandering current.

"There. See how the birds cut east? There's a storm coming." Nipula's golden hair cascades over her shoulder, the ends saturating in the river where she leans over. My eyes seek out the birds, and I frown at them. Something on them glints in the sun, and I get the curious sense that they are watching us, though they are not flying towards us. Not a cloud may be found in the sky, for the sun goddess of Arinna has dominion over the sky this day with only great beaming light. The storm god does not claim dominion the air above us, so I tilt my head towards the West and see nothing but skies of blue.

"No storm, Nipula," her companion says, echoing my own thoughts.

"Not stormy weather. *Change.* This land remembers things. It bleeds under the stones, Aruna." Her hands sink into the water, fingers pressing through mud to find a pulse only she can feel. My waterskin slips from my hands as I look over once more, and the two women huddle as they talk. Their hands are idle as they pause their efforts, and the second woman, Aruna, drops the cloth altogether and it soaks up the river again despite her previous efforts to remove the water.

"You see something again?" Aruna asks, and though their voices are quiet, the sound carries on the current to my straining ears.

"A man with no shadow. Carries death like it's part of him. But not for himself." Her eyes lift to me, though I do not believe it is me she sees.

"Omen or warning?"

"Depends what he chooses to bury—and what he brings back."

I'm tempted to join them and ask for more, to ask what else she sees, but my name is called by my gathered brothers, and I've yet to fill my waterskin. Dumping the warm water from the pouch, I refill the skin before securing it around my neck once more. Rising slowly, I pull my bow free before reaching over my shoulder to pull an arrow from the quiver. The women resume their washing and the conversation moves on to a discussion about the best stones for whacking laundry upon.

The men accompanying me are more or less my Guard, and we all grew up together—trained as a unit since we could wield sticks.

Together, we walk to the boundaries of the forest, only a short distance away. The sound of rushing water falls away until the only sound is our faint footfalls and grass getting crushed underfoot. Grass turns to hard-packed earth and rocky soil which houses a variety of deciduous trees, the majority of which are elms. Brambles and shrubs fill up what would otherwise be sparse land.

The silence of the forest is short-lived; screeching courses through the air, a cacophony of utter torment, which makes us all clutch our hands over our ears. Eyes seeking out the culprits, my gaze sweeps over the land, roving higher and higher until I reach the canopy. Birds of logic-defying proportion sit with quivering plumage, shrieking at intervals in unpleasant dissonance. At once, it is clear they are the birds Nipula had pointed out, which in their flight, had indicated to her a storm of change connected to a man who carries death.

Pulling my bow back up with my arrow at the ready, I let it find its target—eye trained on the closest beast to me. The thump as it lands on the ground makes me wince, and it twitches once, violently, before stilling. Arrow protruding from its fist-sized eye, I whistle at the sheer magnitude of it. Never before have I seen a bird like it. With brilliant feathers, it gleams in the sun—a fearsome bird to behold.

Squatting in front of it to retrieve my arrow, I place my hand on its beak to stabilize the bird, but recoil when my skin makes eye contact with it: the beak is made of metal, and I understand why I had seen it gleam in the rays of the goddess. Pulling my dagger from its sheath, I compare the appearance of the blade to the beak. Apart from size, there isn't a great deal of difference. Tapping the beak with the tip of my blade, my brow furrows as it clinks. They are similar in colour and material, and both are sharp enough to easily pierce flesh.

"If they attack," I say quietly so as not to startle the birds in case their hearing is as good as I fear, "their beaks are as strong as our bronze. They're scaring everything away with that noise. There are too many to kill. Any ideas?"

Surveying the bird further, my lips press tighter together as I take in its claws of similar fashion. I rise.

"No sudden movements," Alluwa says, matching my tone.

"What if we scare them away?" Idari asks, and I chew my lips in thought.

"But we don't want to risk them all attacking at once," Alluwa warns.

"And we can't risk them attacking our camp," Idari adds, and there is a moment of silence as we all take this into account.

"Birds normally don't like loud noises," I say, and Mutti snorts.

"Most birds don't sound like death," Mutti says, his brown eyes darting from one bird to the next as he analyzes them.

"Shall we see if they don't enjoy their own medicine?" I ask, not really waiting for an answer. "Shields."

Listening intently, all stow their bow and arrows in lieu of shields and a blade. In unison, we slam blades against bronze shields, creating an auditory competition that drowns the terrible squawking of the birds.

Many of the birds take flight, towards other settlements no doubt, but some eye us with peculiar eyes of winking bronze. They dive straight for us, free-falling off their perch before tucking their wings as they soar beak-first into us. Holding my shield up, core tight, I brace for impact. Gritting my teeth in anticipation, I watch the underside of my shield with bated breath.

The force of impact sends me to the ground, but what is worse than the fall is the beak-shaped dent half an inch from my eye. Scrambling to my feet, I wince as a shout of pain comes from my left. I can only hope it isn't serious.

The birds are disoriented from their crash landing, dazed and unfocused. Sprawled on the ground with great, flapping wings, their heads loll around on overly long necks. The birds are unnatural. Where most birds would display instincts to survive, these have no issues falling to their death.

With a brutal swish of my blade, I slit the creature's throat before it can do me any damage.

I am lucky.

"Duwa!"

The panicked cry of Idari stops my heart. Turning frantically, I spot him; with his shield held out in front of him, he jabs with a knife, but his shorter arms mean he has to get closer to the bird. There is blood on his hand. Within a few strides, I am in line to kill the infernal bird. The bird's head flies off at the force of my swing.

Dropping to my knees before Idari, I examine him and quickly find the source of the blood: the beak must have caved the metal of his shield precisely where his arm held it up. The caved in metal is stuck in his arm even now.

"I'm fine, Duwa," Idari says, panting, fingers turning white as he clenches his knife. Slashing the leather straps of the shield to prevent pulling at the wound where the shield is distended, I drop the shield to the ground as I hold his arm out to inspect the damage.

Pulling my tunic off, I rip a long piece off the bottom hem, and rip the band to make a long strip of cloth. Tying it over the wound, he grunts at the pressure of my knot, but the bleeding is still oozing.

"Mutti!" I call out, and he's at my shoulder before I can even finish the request. "Take Idari back to camp and make sure he is seen by a healer. I will be right there." He nods, and Idari huffs.

"I'm fine, Duwa. I can still walk and finish the hunt. I am strong." Mutti looks between us, awaiting my verdict.

"I know you are strong," I say, meeting his gaze. He glares at me with crossed arms. Sighing, I look into the sky. The chaotic forest is once again calm and peaceful. There is no sign of the birds anymore, apart from the fallen ones, and there won't be predators here for a little while—not after the noise we've just caused.

"Fine, you can stay," I say, grudgingly, "but you listen to my orders. If you disobey, you'll be sent back to take care of the carriages for the rest of the trip." Idari nods emphatically, and I sigh again, hoping nothing lingers out of sight. "Your mother would murder me if anything happened to you."

"Yes," he agrees with a jaunty smile. "I know."

Standing, I examine the area, noting that other than Idari's arm wound, no one is injured. The birds litter the ground. "I don't think we should eat these," I declare. The toe of my upturned shoe moves the bird's head to face me. "Something feels off about them." The earth below its body is foul, and where it had defecated upon death, the ground appears as though it is in the clutches of Lelwani—the death goddess. Another symbol of death.

"I agree, but if they're really made of bronze...should we take the claws and beaks? It seems a waste," Mutti says, and I nod begrudgingly.

"Yes, but be careful. The less these remains are handled, the better."

Everyone makes quick work of severing the beaks and claws, but the silence is broken as Alluwa swears. "The feathers are sharp." He sucks his thumb before shaking his hand.

"I repeat," I say once more, "only the claws and beaks."

"I second that," Alluwa adds, and Idari snorts.

"I followed the instructions," Idari mutters in a petulant tone. I look at him, and sheepishly, he continues working silently as he moves to the next bird.

"Do you think the beaks are truly bronze?" Mutti asks.

"We will find out soon enough," I say, walking to where Alluwa is holding out a basket intended for foraging. A collection of metallic trinkets fill it to the brim as the men toss their tokens of battle inside.

Silently, we continue on, being mindful to give the birds a wide breadth. Once we pass the carcasses, the forest comes alive. Insects fly around as little birds chirp softly, it’s a welcome noise after the screeching birds.

A short distance away, a gentle lapping of water makes me raise my hand to the others, alerting them to the fact that we've found the herd. Quietly, I aim, standing obscured by a tree and downwind, and let the arrow loose. Without a sound of pain or awareness, the stag falls to the ground while the herd, once again, scatters. Approaching the animal, I let my hand stroke his hide as I let out a quick prayer in honour of the deer.

"O, wild-goddess of Inara, ferocious and free are thee. Haduwas, your prince and servant, thanks you humbly for this sacrifice. And you, Kurunta, god of the hunt, are an honoured god. Ever your humble supporter, I bow with reverence to your might with strength and intelligence to overcome all obstacles I face."

As a group, we close our eyes for a few moments to honour the deer. "Alluwa? Can you take over?" I ask, and he immediately sets to work with Mutti, stringing the great stag up over a low hanging branch to remove the guts and entrails to prevent the meat from spoiling in the heat.

Leaving them to it, I observe the group fondly. The group is not quite relaxed after the encounter with the birds, but that is to be expected. It is always a hard thing to wind down after excitement.

Those who were not involved in the preparation of the deer stand idly, but attentively with weapons drawn. Idari, though alert, is tired, his posture slightly slumping. Quietly, I sidle up to him and set a hand on his shoulder; he looks up at me, startled.

"Duwa?" he asks, a crinkle appearing between his brows as he looks up at me.

"You did well today," I say, and he grins.

"I did, didn't I?"

Rolling my eyes, I swat him playfully on the head before hugging him to my side. In silence, we watch as Alluwa and Mutti finish their task. Mutti was the only one who thought to bring an axe, so as the men hold the deer to prevent it from touching the ground, Mutti takes the branch down and they tie the legs over the branch to transport it back to camp.

"I hope the beer is still cold," Idari says as we walk, and I hum.

"Not likely."

"If they hold the urns in the river, they'd be cold quickly—or, at least, not warm. I hate warm beer," he says, and I chuckle.

"Spoken like a high-born. The river is a good idea though. If they did not think of it, take some beer into a smaller vessel, and you can put your own in the river. It would be far quicker."

Idari nods, his eyes far away in that place where he thinks. His fingers fall to the bandage, running along the edge of the fabric on his arm, tracing the wound on his skinny bicep.

"I hope this scars," he says suddenly, eyes lighting up as he looks at me. "Then I'll have a mark of battle like you." My own scar from the lion is tight with slightly mottled flesh. I'd been fevered, but with the help of Huella and Nipula, I'd come through.

Squinting my eyes slightly, I watch the sun and figure we have about fifteen more minutes of sunlight. A single infernal bird flies across the horizon, turning back west, marring the view; a scar on the dying sun.

"It will scar."

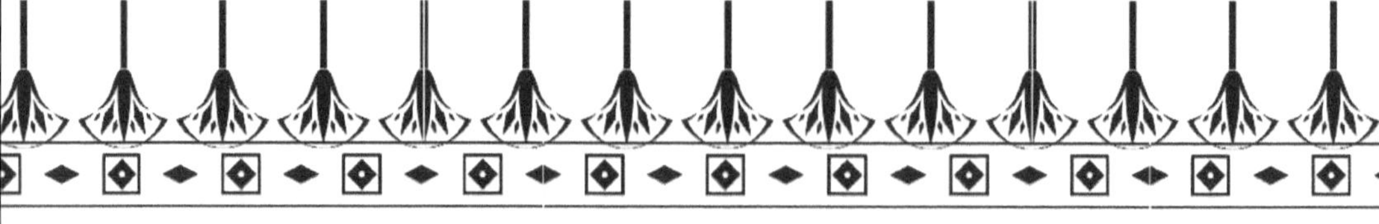

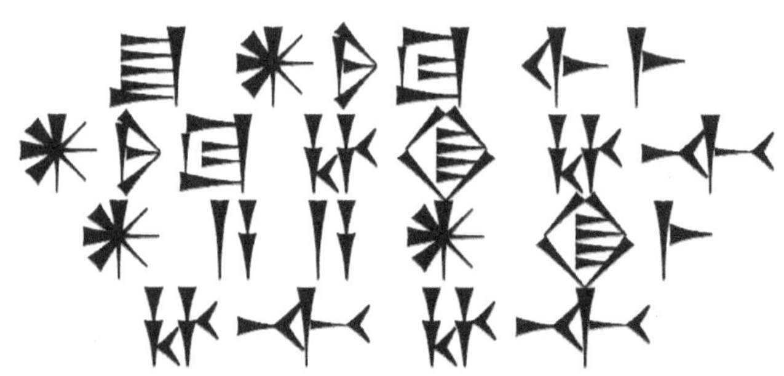

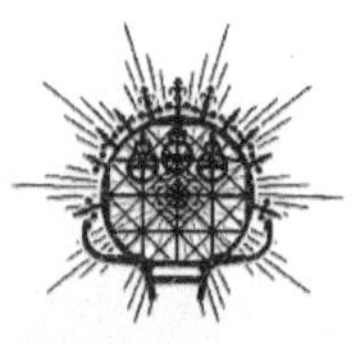

Šauška is present.

The upper bloom is the rising life-force.

Light and movement pass through the sky.

Life a force rising up.

IV
TABLET
THE BREATH OF WAR

Crickets and crackling fire ornaments the silence of the steppes. "First," I declare to my people, holding my vessel of wine above my head, "we drink to the sun goddess of Arinna; then we drink to the storm god, Tarhun; then to the guardian god."

The only light comes from the raging fire at the centre of our huddle. Several such fires surround the camp while scouts remain extended beyond our border to warn of possible attacks.

Cheers and cries erupt as they repeat my vocation in honour of the gods. "Tonight, we drink the gods, as in the custom of my royal house." The group around me, full of familiar faces young and old, grows silent as they listen to my words.

"Tonight," I declare, "drink of my wine and climb up the vine of divinity. Connect with the gods as we make our final voyage across this golden sea to Kuššara."

My blood heats as I take my first sip, and I watch as my people do so too. My fellow warriors are not all with me but divided among the various fires. The stag has been divided between the campfires to be roasted on a spit, and I have not claimed the largest piece. I receive the same portions as each and every other person under my care.

Idari is grinning into his cup of wine, and his eyes are trained on a dancing woman. I tap the side of my cup with his and allow the wine to work its magic on my soul as I take a seat beside him on the ground in a deep squat.

A clay-fired plate is shoved into my hands as the women tasked with the meal disperse the prepared food. On it, a hunk of bread, several slabs of meat, and some goat cheese. The leftover meat from the hunt will be put in tomorrow's stew along with the bones.

Juices flow down my chin as I bite into the rich meat, and when I look at Idari, his face is identical. His head bobs as he enjoys the meat, and he licks his fingers after devouring it. The meat had been rubbed with a spice blend of sumac, salt, and roughly ground cumin.

At another campfire, drums and singing erupt, and the night air crackles with tension and release. Idari beside me whoops, burying his cup with twists of his wrists into the sandy ground before hopping to his feet.

"Come, Duwa! Dance!"

I shake my plate at him where the bread and cheese still sit, indicating I am otherwise engaged.

"Bah," Idari says, slapping my shoulders affectionately from behind me. "The food will still be there after you live! Let the people see the Crown Prince dance."

Exhaling gruffly, I set my plate off to the side in the sand and allow him to pull me to my feet. The group surrounding the fire cheers and more instruments are pulled free.

“I am not Crown Prince, yet,” I remind him, but nonetheless, I do as he requests. Kicking my slippers free to dance unencumbered, I bury my feet into the sand where small patches of grass try to break free from Lelwani's grasp. A hushed silence spreads, the cries and cheers falling away as a quiet drum sets the tempo at the same rate as my heart. It thrums, and I dig my heels in, feeling the rhythm. Beside me, Idari matches my stance, and when two consecutive hits of the drum fall into the air, we begin.

With measured steps and bent knees, we rock side to side in a series of steps, matching the steadily increasing tempo of the drums. The dance, like everything else, seeks to bind us to the divine to climb the vine and enter unity with the gods—particularly as I am of the royal house of

Karuwas. *We* are divine.

Facing Idari, we clasp hands, repeating the steps as we mirror one another, our feet, in turns, hovering over the ground before we kick and cry out with the song.

One by one, members of the circle join the chain, and around the fire we go, spiralling faster and faster. All together, we release hands to kick our left legs into the air, as high as possible, before we break off into partners again.

Idari finds himself a partner in the woman he'd been admiring earlier, and he shrugs not so apologetically at me when I give him a look expressing playful outrage at being replaced.

Idari looks behind me and a grin splits his face. "Looks like you've got yourself a partner too, Duwa," he shouts over the noise, and when I turn around, an easy smile forms as Gazaza, the tenacious child, splays his hands up at me, his chubby cheeks a prominent feature on his adorable face. The little girl he always follows around is with her mother, still eating. The girl's hands are outstretched and every time she gets them even a little bit dirty, she makes her mother wipe them up. This goes for her face too, and I chuckle at the sight.

Gazaza dances on the ground, not following the traditional steps, but to moves of his own creation. He wiggles in place and stomps his feet with superior timing than many of the adults around us. Putting my hands on my hips, I stare down at him with a smile and a shake of my head. I look around the circle for Huella, and when I see she's dancing with Alluwa, I crouch before Gazaza.

"Do you want to dance?" I ask, and he clambers up my leg and jumps up and down while perched on my knee.

"Yes!" he shrieks, his hands gripping my shirt tightly as he balances on my leg. Couples around us hop and shout and shimmy, but I simplify the steps for Gazaza. Setting him back on the ground, I turn him to face me so he can follow the steps. I dramatically stomp my right foot and wait for him to mimic me. When he does, he makes a grunting sound like the other men around the fire are. Huffing a laugh, I nod at him.

"Yes, Gazaza. Now. Other foot." I stomp my left foot, and he follows my directions. "Good. Now," I say, bending low to grab his hands, "follow me. We're going to spin, okay?" Hunched over to reach him as he stretches higher, we begin to spin in a circle, me in something like a squat. "Jump," I instruct, and he does before landing on one foot and kicking his heel forward.

"More!" he shrieks, pouting when he sees the other groups twisting, winding, their limbs moving rhythmically to the drums.

"I see," I say, laughing. Letting go of his hands, I rest my palms on my thighs as I begin to shuffle my feet across the sand. Gazaza giggles as he begins to replicate the movement. His arms start flailing, and I laugh when his hips start wiggling. I copy him, and his laughter grows. I spin in fast circles, crossing one leg over the other and turning on my toes. Gazaza frowns as he tries to do the same, but he falls over. He does not cry as he pushes himself back up, and he tries again.

"Cross your feet," I encourage, showing him again, but much slower. He manages to turn himself slowly, and he grins up at me when he completes the turn. Nodding, I jump up with high knees and land in a crouch. Spinning on one knee, I send a wave of sand behind me and Gazaza claps.

The dancing is cut off when a horn pierces the revelry. Everyone freezes, and I snatch up Gazaza before he can run or find himself in harm's way.

"Wawa?" he asks, and I look down at him calmly despite the thrum of adrenaline rushing through me. He can't say my name yet, so he calls me Wawa.

"Yes, Gazaza?" His hand lands on my cheek, and I gently hold it there.

"Trouble?"

"Not for you," I promise as my eyes search the circle for Huella. I spot her across the fire. I rush to her side where Alluwa guards her.

"Take him, Huella. Get to safety in the centre with everyone else, okay?" I say, pressing a dagger into her hand. She takes it, her eyes wide but she nods and takes Gazaza into her grip. I ruffle his hair before turning to Alluwa.

Idari sidles up beside me. "What is it?" he asks, but I shake my head.

"I don't know yet." But just as I answer, warrior dogs howl, and my skin shivers. "Hunting party," I suggest in answer, standing guard by my wagon. Jumping onto the bench where I have more weapons stashed, I pull the woven bag of dirks free and distribute them to the men congregating around the caravan liberally. Alluwa is doing the same thing across the camp, though he has axes and spears too.

With the back of the camp to the river, and the women, children, and elderly men protected as much as possible in the centre, all of my warriors, fifteen of us, line the perimeter of the camp side to side as we wait to see what happens. Squinting my eyes, I peer into the darkness, but I don't see much of anything. I can feel thumping on the ground, the tell-tale sign of an incoming horse rider, but whether it's one of ours remains to be seen.

"If you have a spear, be at the ready," I call, and about every second man raises a spear.

"Haduwas!" the rider calls, and the men beside me breath in relief. The incoming horse pulls up to a stop in front of me where I stand in the centre of the line. It is Mutti, and he's breathing hard with a serious expression.

"Am I the only scout back?" he asks, eyeing the line-up.

"I'm not sure," I say, risking a glance to my left and right before breaking formation to move closer to him as Mutti slides off the back of his horse. "Why was the horn blown?"

"A band of about twenty or so warriors are coming up the side of the river from the West," he says, gesturing. "They also have a pack of hunting dogs. It is yet to be seen if they're simply hunting for food or looking for a fight."

Nodding, I look around and postulate before turning to look at Idari.

"Go to the centre with the women and children," I order Idari, and his mouth opens in protest, but I power through before he can complain.

"It's not because I don't trust you. If any break through the line, you're the last defence. Your job might just be the most important. Protect our people." Idari slowly nods and turns to join the women and children in the centre.

"How many dogs?" I ask Mutti. "Did you see or hear anything?"

"I can only guess, but anywhere between five and ten dogs from the sound of it." Nodding, I clap him and Alluwa on the shoulder. Alluwa grunts roughly, hands behind his back; he rolls his shoulders in response.

Another rider joins us, and I recognize Belwan, my youngest scout. "Did you see anything?" I ask, calming his panting horse with smooth strokes on his mane as I look up at the boy.

"They have hunting dogs. Is this related to the attack on our home?" he asks, and my mind whirs.

"I can't be sure, but I think we can assume it's related. Do you think they'll attack tonight?" I ask, and he shrugs helplessly.

"I can't say for sure if their purpose has changed. Hopefully, our show of force will be enough of a deterrent but with those dogs...?" He shudders.

"Do you know from where they hail?"

He shakes his head. "They look like everyone else, and there's nothing about their weapons or clothing that stands out to me as distinctly different from everyone else. They might be Hatti or Akkadian, but I couldn't say with any certainty." He nods deeply and urges his horse past the line to the centre.

"Where do you think they'll attack?" Mutti asks from beside me.

"It would depend on their objective. If this was a hunting party, they'd want to avoid casualty, but if they're Akkadian..." I say. "They might not care to survive if they know I'm here."

Another voice jumps in. "I think they'll send most of their forces to one side to try and pull us out of formation and hit us from the opposite side when we're fighting at one end. They may try and kill the women and children, or take the women. I think some might also attempt to cross the river. It's wide and slow, and not too cold."

I nod and slowly formulate a plan. "I need a couple of archers to guard the river to shoot anyone who tries to cross. No one is to break formation. If anyone goes down, fill in the gap. Stand between the gaps between carriages. I'll be in the centre of the line beside you. Let's hope they attack quickly instead of keeping us up all night."

We do not wait for long. As was said before, there are no distinguishing markers, and they have many, perhaps fifty warriors with an additional twenty or so hounds.

"Hold!" I yell, encouraging my warriors. The men approach in a cluster, and as the archers take down a couple in the front, they trip the men behind them. The huddle breaks apart as they avoid trodding on their brothers in arms, and my men steady their spears in front of them. The attackers approach quickly. Dread climbs up my throat. The chasm between us shrinks until it's gone.

My foot crunches on sun-burned grass and sand and then a spear is upon me. Thrusting it to the side, I stab and slice as I create a boundary, bodies strewn before me in a grotesque line as I keep the line steady. The bulk of the force seems to be targeting me specifically, because an unprecedented amount of enemies flock to me. Alluwa falls but stands back up. Blood streams from his bicep as he hacks away at a dog before him.

The dog's jaws are parted revealing sharp canines; if they dig in, he'll lose that limb. Slobber drips to the ground in the torchlight, and as he braces against the dog, I pick up a spear from a fallen foe before me and hurl it at the dog, skewering its neck. The whine it lets out as it crumples is heartbreaking, but I can't stop to feel bad about it because another enemy is upon me.

The world is silent as I mow through the enemies approaching. Five down. Ten down. The chasm in my mind opens again as the dead litter the ground.

"Hold the line."

"Yes!" they cry back.

It could have been minutes or hours before the threat is dealt with, but at long last, with aching fingers that can scarcely let go of the blade from clenching so tight. Wiping it on my tunic before sheathing it, I turn and look at the mess left behind. Bodies are strewn all around, both mine and enemy, and my heart is heavy. Mutti is pacing, eyes on the horizon as he awaits to make sure no threat remains, but Alluwa looks disoriented and faint.

"Brother," I say, stepping towards him. Sweat beads his forehead, cheeks and around his lips, damp hair clinging to his face and neck. His lips tremble, and I see his weapon is nowhere to be found. "Alluwa?"

Stepping closer to him, the god of the moon takes pity upon me, and as I turn Alluwa to face me, I take in the sight of his hand and arm. His thumb, where he'd been pierced by the feather of the dread bird, is black, and from the wound, threads of black weave up his hand, wrist, then arm where the flesh had been savaged by the dog I'd saved him from.

"Mutti!" I call, and enough of my terror must leak through in my tone that he runs towards me immediately. When he sees Alluwa's arm, his face goes slack, and his eyes fly from blackened thumb to the dripping poison and blood.

"We have no healer left," he says, and I snap back into reality.

"Take him to my tent. I'll get Nipula and Huella. I'll meet you there."

I don't await a response as I tear away from the scene and towards the centre cluster of caravans and tents. Crossing quickly through the camp, I note that, while the fires remain, no one has ventured towards them yet despite the battle being over.

"Duwa!" I turn and see Idari standing with a group of women, all armed with daggers.

"Any breaches?" I ask, and he shakes his head.

"None that made it to my attention. But Duwa, I didn't see Huella or Gazaza make it to the centre. I would have left to investigate, but I couldn't leave them unprotected," he says, gesturing to the group behind him.

I swallow over a sudden lump in my throat but nod and place my hand on his shoulder in a comforting gesture.

"I'll find them. I'm sure they're fine. Alluwa was severely injured. Send Nipula to my tent."

Heading in the direction I'd seen Huella and Gazaza last, I reach the other side of the camp, the side towards the river, and a twinge of fear flickers inside me, rearing its head.

"Huella?" I call out, but I don't hear a response if there is one. "Gazaza?" I shout, and I hear a scuffle and a rumble behind the tent across from the fire I'd eaten and danced around.

"Wawa?"

I jog, and my heart nearly stops. The dog gently pants with its tongue lolled out and plays with the sand and pebbles between his legs where he sits. He calls for Huella, likely thinking she's playing a game. She is not playing a game.

Huella does not stir, and her eyes are wide and unseeing. Her lips are parted, but the words died on her lips. Emotion clogs my throat, and any words that might have been remain behind my lips. For what purpose is there to say anything now?

What would her last words have been? A warning for our son, or a word of love? A prayer, or a curse?

Next to her body, there is a dead dog with a knife in its neck—the knife I'd given her to defend herself; there's a strange collar around its throat made of gold with odd patterns on it. I don't inspect it because Gazaza is in the lap of another *living* dog.

"Gazaza? Don't move."

Gazaza babbles, not understanding the predicament he's in. Looking slowly at the dog, not making eye contact in case it becomes threatened, I back away slowly to find a large piece of meat from the spit on the fire which had not yet burned. Slicing a big hunk of meat off, I slowly approach the dog and crouch before putting the food on the ground before it. Its large, black muzzle sniffs the meat questioningly before it takes a bite and it turns its body more fully towards the meal.

As the dog is occupied, I snatch Gazaza from the ground and hold him tightly in my arms. His big eyes are drooping as he starts to fall asleep in my arms. There are dried tear tracks on his cheeks, and I gently wipe away the residue with my thumb.

"Go to sleep, Gazaza," I say, bouncing lightly with him in my arms. I cradle his head in my hand as I secure him to my chest. He falls asleep listening to my thundering heartbeat, and his little body wilts with sleep as I walk through the camp with sombre determination. To deal with the dog, I have to get Gazaza to safety, so I hand him off to the first woman I see by the tents. The men who'd survived the battle mill around the central tent, some taking comfort in their loved ones while others tend to wounds of body and heart at our casualties.

"Huella is dead," I tell the woman quietly. "She belongs to Lelwani now. I'll come see Gazaza in the morning when I've handled everything out here," I say, my hand lingering on his precious face. She nods, eyes keen, and takes him inside the centre-most tent where the women who could not fight are hiding, and I wonder if this was the prediction: if it is about what I will bury?

I stop short when I see Idari. He must already suspect, because when he meets my gaze, his face crumples and he turns into the tent with the women. The sob he lets out is a sound the gods devised to destroy my heart. Ignoring the stinging in my eyes, I turn around and return to the dog to deal with the last of the threat. He sits in the exact place I left him, and he licks the bone between his paws.

When I approach, I meet its eyes, but the dog does not attack. It simply stares right back. I frown as I crouch slowly in front of him. He tilts his head but does nothing else. The dog off to the side of Huella's body is dead and the oddly calm dog doesn't seem too upset about it. I lean in closer to the collar of the dead dog, recognizing the script at once. It is Akkadian. Dread coils in my body. I unfasten the gold chain around the dog's neck and pocket it.

In addition to the dagger in its neck by its shoulder haunch, there are severe wounds that look like they came from a dog. I turn to look at the curled-up beast licking the bone. He hadn't attacked me or Gazaza, and I wonder if, impossibly, the dog protected Gazaza. The dog's eyes are wise, and if I didn't know better, I would say they were almost human.

Kneeling closer, I hover my exposed wrist before him, prepared to attack if necessary, but he only sniffs and gently licks my wrist and his tail thumps on the ground, displacing sand with every swish of his great tail.

Patting his head, his ears perk up, and when he looks up at me, I realize why his eyes look so familiar: they look just like mine, and he has a great spot around his right eye and dappled fur with tufts of light brown throughout the massive rolls of dark fur.

A great hunting dog. If it stood on its hind legs, it would be as tall as me—taller even. With more energy, I ruffle his ears and he rolls over exposing his stomach for rubs. Sighing, I acquiesce and allow my fingers to comb through his fur. He rights himself and licks my face in appreciation before sitting, as though awaiting instruction.

"What are you called?" I ask though I am not waiting for an answer from him. Instead, I wait to be struck with inspiration, but my eyes simply zone in onto his and that spot around his eye.

"Balasi," I say, but he does not react.

I sit cross-legged in the sand as I ponder.

"Namtar." No response.

"Sharvara," I say, and he surges towards me, tongue lolling out. Sighing, I stand, realizing that I can no longer kill the animal.

"Sharvara. Sit." Sharvara sits. "Lie down." He does. "Follow me." I move away, and he rises and trots alongside me. I frown and stop, eyes trained on the gold collar around his neck. "Sit still." Sharvara scarcely breathes as I kneel before him. "You're mine now. You will protect these people with your life," I say, gesturing to the camp. His head does not move, but his eyes follow my hands as though he can read me perfectly despite the fact that his owners speak a different language altogether.

When I'm finished, he stands and uses his nose to point. Raising an eyebrow, I nod, and he trots away while I follow him. He is a pace in front of me, his head continually looking up and back to ensure I'm still following him. The opening to my tent entrance sways in the gentle breeze, so at odds with the violence I expect within.

"Stay," I say, pointing to the ground outside the tent. "Bark if anyone approaches." I can't be sure if he understands, but something in my gut tells me he understands me like no one before him.

Swiping the sheet of woven fabric aside, I pull up to a stop when I see my friend, Alluwa, draped across a blanket on the bed. His arm is a wreck, and his forehead is crowned with beads of sweat while his chest rises and falls in shallow breath; he is pale as the god of the moon. I draw closer, and his eyes ease open in a look little more than a squint. Mutti is not in the tent, but neither is Nipula, the only one left who has a hope of healing Alluwa.

"Duwa," he mutters, and I hold his hand, the uninjured one draped across his belly. "This doesn't feel very good," he says with a strained smile. "I don't recommend it. Not a good way to go."

"You're not dying, Alluwa. Not if I have a say, and I do. I'm the prince."

"Nipula says she can do nothing for me," he says, and a shiver wracks his body. "Mutti went to escort her back to the tents in case there was any remaining danger. She gave me opium," he says, gesturing to his arm with a vague nod. "She says I am poisoned by the gods and that I'll be dead by morning. That woman is never wrong." I shake my head, pulling out my dagger.

"She's not me."

"So, what are you going to do?"

I hover over him and see the black lines have gone all the way up his arm and climb to his chest. It will soon be at his heart, and though I know my efforts to be futile, inaction will not be my curse.

"Duwa," he starts, but he stops. He shakes his head. "There's no point."

"There is always a point," I practically growl, voice low and gravelly with emotion.

"Not this time. This is beyond our abilities. The gods sent those birds—I know this. You must too. Chopping my arm off will do nothing. Even now, the inky fingers of death creep towards my heart. Should have cut my thumb off when I had the chance to."

I am reminded of him hiding his arm before the skirmish, and his grunt. I'd thought it had been a sound of acknowledgement, but rather, it had likely been pain.

"Let me dress the wound at least. I'll wrap it in honey, and then when we arrive in Kuššara in a couple days, the best healers will see to your recovery."

I bring his face up to mine as a tear drops from his eye. He refuses to look at me, silent.

THE RISE OF HADUWAS

"What do you think Kuššara looks like?" he asks, and I sigh. I drag a crate over to the bedside and hold his hand.

"I have been told by my brothers it's the largest city they've ever seen," I say, and I know he must be in significant pain as he takes deep, steadying breaths. As I continue, he squeezes my hand back hard, but I make no complaint nor do I let it show on my face.

"The walls rise so tall that when you stand at the gates, you can scarcely view the god of the mountain beyond the city at its back. There are abundant fields where the farmers work, clusters of homes both stationary and temporary for the evolving needs of the people. Animals on expansive pastures, and a bustling market outside the city walls where fruits, wines, oils, woven ware, baskets, spices, and trinkets can be found. It is a sprawling place," I say, and Alluwa's brow smooths out as he listens to me. His grip is no longer a death grip. His chest moves up and down with slow, uneven breath, so I continue before he prompts me.

"As I said before, the walls rise high into the air; the gods are very active here, not crumbling or easily dislodged as in our once home." I swallow hard. "The gates, they say, are fearsome. Twin lions with wings guard the city walls, their mouths ready to rip apart any who dare disturb the peace of the city. Within, it is not sprawling, but compact." I demonstrate with my free hand despite the fact that the recipient of my words cannot see my gesture. The action feels necessary to showcase the scope. "Having space in the fields is not the same as having space in the city. The streets are so narrow in some places, one can scarcely walk side by side with someone down certain streets, and while the palace and the temples are grand open spaces, the buildings for everyone else are cramped with multiple levels and low ceilings. There are halls of ale and wine run by women."

"Run by women?" One of Alluwa's eyes peeks open and the frown returns to his brow, this time in confusion rather than pain.

"Yes. My brothers say they have strange customs. They drink with kin in their homes, yes, but they also have places where that *doesn't* matter. You drink with whoever might be seated next to you.

"In the tradition of their ancient ancestors, some still hold onto the practice of burying their dead under the lowest level of their homes. Even more strange is the lowest chambers of the palace and temples. What one sees above ground is nothing compared to how the city descends into the earth. For every level you see above ground, there are five below. There are stores there for food and shelter, ceremonial chambers, and even more of their important dead. It is a living crypt. Stone wheels act as doors, and fires in torch brackets upon the walls light the way.

"Brother," I say, cupping his cheek. "The Dark Earth has no claim on you yet. I would fight the goddess of geath with bare hands if I had to. You will not die this night, nor tomorrow morning. I would trade places with you without hesitation, my brother. When the sun rises on your face, that warmth is yours, and you will know the sun goddess is on our side."

"Is it true?" he asks, and I freeze. "Huella?"

My heart thuds once, hard, and my own pain grips me fierce at the reminder. Sucking in a breath, I nod slowly, my eyes pricking at the emotion welling within.

"You should go to Idari," Alluwa says, his grip loosening. "I know, Duwa." He swallows as he looks at me. "I know who he is. He needs you." As he stares at me, his eyes grow glassy and life flees from them.

Tears streaming down my face, I fold my arms over my knees and cry. I can hear Sharvara whimper, and when I feel his face prodding my back, I don't turn him away. Wrapping my arm around his neck, I sob into his fur as I feel my brother pass into the cold earth below and into the cold arms of the goddess of death.

I dig all night. Cheeks itchy with tears and sticky with sweat and soil, I dig. And dig. And dig. When the sun comes up, I do not feel touched by the sun goddess. Her rays do not pierce my skin, nor do they warm my soul. An icy wall has grown around my body overnight, an impenetrable veil of grief which drives me down,

down, down.

Idari and Mutti worked soundlessly beside me. The only sound is of metal piercing earth, and the fall of soil off the shovel as it collects behind us. The mound of upturned earth grows and grows until it is taller than I. Even then, I continue to dig.

"Duwa. We've dug enough." I barely heard the words. Alluwa was dead. My friend, my brother—dead. Many were lost last night. Seven warriors, dead. Seven brothers, and Huella, my fierce Huella. Their bodies were wrapped by the women when the battle had ceased, and the bodies had been washed and clothed. A pile of trinkets, including the bronze beaks and claws, lay beside them to be used for their next life beyond. A hand landed on my shoulder, and I spun to see Idari, his own makeshift shovel lying on the ground beside a pile of dirt fit for a grave of fifty, not for less than ten.

"Duwa," he said, gently prying the crude shovel from my hands, "it's done. We should do the ceremony." Nodding, more to myself than to my son, I take a deep breath and pull myself together. Resting my hand on his shoulder, I nod again, and then pat him affectionately before I regard the hole in the earth. It is absurd in size, and, inappropriately, a laugh crawls up my throat; with an exhaustion which has nothing to do with sleeplessness, the emotion is sapped from me before I can express it. As the strange rush dissipates, I become increasingly aware of the pain in my hands and wrists, the bleeding blisters and aching joints. Weariness crashes over me, but the job is not done...never done.

As the rays of our goddess, Arinna, grace the land, the remnants of my people emerge once more, and while some tend to the fires to get meals ready before we depart this place, others are wiping tears away and clutching objects of their loved ones. In small clusters, they join us. Mutti returns from a tent, and following him, the women and children from the tents. I hadn't even realized he'd left us. Together, the group walks towards the chosen site, and when Mutti meets my eye, he nods at the bodies as I let out the breath that had been building in my burning lungs. Jumping into the pit myself, I turn to receive the bodies of the dead.

Stiff in death and draped in the meagre supplies we have left, six bodies lie in the grave. Two left. The next body Mutti and Idari pass to me is Alluwa. His arm is covered up, but I can still see the black webs of death climbing his arm, seeking his heart. Grunting at the weight, I place him down, steeling myself at the idea of our last conversation. When I look up, again, my son is staring hard at Huella. Mutti has grabbed her under the arms, but still, Idari doesn't touch her feet as he had for every other person.

"I can help," Belwan says, stepping forward to help lift Huella into my awaiting arms. He stands next to Idari, who swallows, shaking his head. Biting his lip, he grabs his mother's ankles and lifts, and Belwan nods, stepping back. Stooping, they pass me the last casualty of war, and in my grief, I allow myself to memorize her face, peaceful in death. Her wounds are covered by the cloth, and now, her soul rests eternally with the goddess below. Settling her down next to Alluwa, I regard the dead, and fix their shrouds. They all look disturbingly peaceful. Gripping the edge of the pit, I pull myself up, allowing the loved ones congregated around to deposit their goods. Some drop locks of hair, and others deposit personal effects. Weapons, flowers, and small canisters of food and wine, small tokens that can be spared, are placed inside. With cloth covering my hands, I pick up every severed beak and claw from the horrific birds before placing them where they belong—with the dead. When all have placed their goods in the grave, I clear my throat, which feels dry and tight. I am not washed, nor am I clothed as custom normally dictated. I swallow hard, and begin.

"Hear me. Earth, who receives all; sun who sees all; storm who carries the dreams of men, and ancestors who have gone below before us. I speak in the place of the one who should stand here. I am not set apart. I am not washed, and I do not speak the words as they were given. Yet, there is no other mouth."

I close my eyes, still not feeling the rays of the goddess. The priests who should be doing this are all within the clutches of the deep earth. To forfeit the rite would be to damn these souls, and I could never allow such a deep transgression.

"I present to you our fallen brothers and our sister. Alluwa. Tuwari. Zanpi. Kati. Wadri. Annu. Zuwani. Huella." I take a deep breath before continuing. "These are the ones who fell when the moon claimed the skies. Their breath was taken by iron, canines, and poison, and the day could not keep them. I return them to the earth that bore them. I set them where feet will not trespass. I cover them so that beasts will not find them, and the living will not follow."

At my words, together, the bystanders scoop dirt to cover their bodies. Some use the three shovels, carved from wood, while others use their hands to sprinkle earth over each person.

"Let not the fault of the living fall upon the dead. Earth, take them into your keeping. Sun, know their names. And let us all remember them as they were." I step back. "I have placed what I have. I have said what I know. May the gods be my witness."

Stepping back fully to let loved ones say goodbye, I meet the eye of Idari; he hesitates before stepping forward, a question and a plea in his eyes. Jerking my head to the side, I gesture for him to come with me. He wastes no time closing the distance to walk by my side. "Idari, come. We will fish." The group pays no mind to us walking away. I had done my duty, and everyone knew we were close, so it wasn't peculiar for me to pull Idari aside in any case. We are silent for a time, and when we walk past the fire where an elderly woman, Malla, stirs a steaming pot suspended over the flickering flames. Nipula is huddled in blankets as she stares at the sky, seeing something no one else can see, though her eyes drift to us for a moment, and I nod at her. She nods back, her eyes flickering between us, and she pulls the blanket closer.

"Going fishing," I say, but I know she understands the truth of it.

"Why are we fishing?" Idari asks under his breath, but when he sees my expression, his mouth shuts. Placing my hand on his back, I direct him towards my caravan where some of my supplies are. "How's your arm?" I ask as I jump onto the bench.

"Fine," he says, subdued. I rummage around for my hooks and some cord. I find them under a basket of spearheads and twine. Feet back on the ground, I jerk my chin to the river, and he leads the way. His arm is bandaged and a sinking feeling begins to grow. When we make it to the river, I set the supplies down on a rock and grab his hand.

"Are you sure?" I ask, dreading what I might find. He'd been hurt in the altercation with the birds, those death-touched birds which had claimed Alluwa's life. Untying the bandage that Huella had fixed up yesterday after we'd returned from hunting, I let out a breath of pure relief seeing no crawling black sickness up his arm. It's angry, and red, but it will heal just fine, although as I'd said before, it would scar. The shield had saved Idari's life, but had dented to cause the wound. A wave of nausea crests over me at the realization that if he had not had that shield, or if the shield had been breached, I'd have buried my best friend, my lover, and my son in one fell swoop. I blink away the thought with effort as I sit on the bank.

"We need some worms," I say, and without another word, Idari combs through the bank with his fingers. The irony strikes me of how this time, he is not digging through the earth to make room for the dead, but rather to gather sustenance.

And so the wheel of life and death turns round and round.

As he looks for worms under rocks at the edge of the bank, I set about tying the cord to a hook made of bone. Silently, he offers me a worm, but I shake my head. I hand him the line, hook first, and settle into the damp bank to watch my son fish. After securing the worm, he casts the line into the water, he wraps the line around his hand and sits beside me. The damp smell of mud and the breeze coasting on the current brings in fresh, clean air. The air is still chilly, but neither of us feels it as we simply breathe in the gentle lapping of the water coasting through the land, carving its path with patience, as we all must.

"Do you want to talk about it?" I ask, and he shakes his head, eyes more solemn than I've ever seen. He gently raises and lowers his hand to wiggle the line in the water.

"It's not your fault, Idari," I say, and when his lip wobbles, I know I've hit the mark. Sliding over to him, I wrap my arm around his shoulders to hug him as his breath begins to come in gasping sobs.

"If I had only done a perimeter before going to the tent," he croaks, his voice breaking, "I could have saved her." His breath shudders, and the tears stream openly down his cheeks. "If I had been circling around, I could have maybe heard her and helped." His arms are wrapped around his knees, tucked close, and he drops his head onto his forearms to hide his face as his cries rip me apart.

"Listen to me," I say gently. "Your mother would not have wanted you anywhere near those dogs." I swallow. "And never, for one second, blame yourself. Understand? If anything, it could be argued it was my fault," I say, and he lifts his head in disbelief, line forgotten.

"How?"

"I gave her the knife, and I gave her Gazaza, and then I left her to get there herself. I could have escorted her to the centre to make sure she was fine."

"But you couldn't have known..." he trails off, and I think he understands.

"No, I couldn't have. I had to do what I thought was right, and that was preparing the men and giving out weapons. You did what you thought was right by standing guard for the women and children under your care. What if you abandoned them and they all got killed?" I let that thought sink in before I finish. "The 'what-if' game is a game of misery. Do not give those thoughts any life by dwelling on them."

My hand makes circles on his back and after he wipes his face with his free hand; only then does he seem to remember we are fishing. He lifts his hand and lowers it a couple of times, when the line suddenly pulls taut. Eyes wide, he looks up at me before a small smile lights up his otherwise dour expression. I smile back and watch as he pulls the carp onto the shore while it thrashes and splashes.

There is little I can do but to hold space for our grief and give him comfort, wherever it can be found.

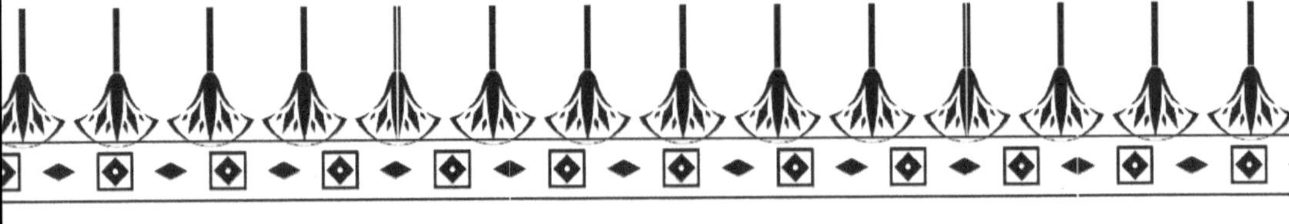

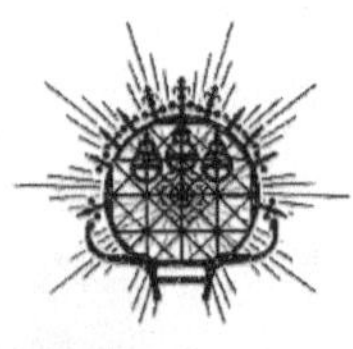

Lelwani descends.

The root reaches into the first earth.

Where light rises, she is cast below.

No light shall follow.

TABLET V

HONEYCOMB

Withholding myself from my people lest they be sliced by the shards of my shattered heart, I survey the scene. I grip Puza's dark mane. Behind me, Idari sits on the bench of my carriage arranged with my other three horses, Harli, Kurli, and Marassa, behind which, the rest of the carriages continue through the grasslands.

Every man capable of wielding a weapon is on horseback for the final leg of the journey. The landscape stretches as far as the eye can see but for the faint path that cuts through the endless sea of pale green and yellow. The grasses get shorter towards civilization, stubby and with shorter stalks. My legs weep with exhaustion, and my lower back bursts with fiery pain, but I keep my back straight as I dig my legs in on Puza's side as I urge him faster on the final stretch. Beside me, my war dog, Sharvara, pants happily at my side, content to run on his powerful legs. He darts ahead of the group and circles back to me in intervals. We are perhaps a week out from the new city.

Gesturing for Mutti to continue leading the group, I fall back to speak to Idari who lifts his brows at me in question. Sharvara takes this moment to depart from us to run the perimeter.

"We are going to a dangerous place," I begin, but abruptly stop. Perhaps I can keep him close in court, say I am personally training him by giving him a place in my personal guard since he has been, for all intents and purposes, orphaned. The alternative is leaving him in the care of

Nipula. "So I am going to give you a choice."

"I want to stay with you," he says at once, and when I slowly lift a brow, he looks down at his hands with a blush.

"Presumptuous of you," I say with a smile. I reach over and nudge him, and when he sees my expression, his shoulders drop and his hands no longer gripping the reigns in tight fists. "As I was saying. I am going to give you a choice, and you must hear both options before you speak." He nods dutifully and pinches his lips together as he awaits his options. I fight the urge to ruffle his curly hair. "Your first option is staying in the care of Nipula and some of the other women. There, you will assist her with anything she may need help with, in particular, because you are strong for your age, and will only grow more so." He makes no sound, nor does he give any indication how he feels about this matter. "She will likely open up her services in the marketplace, and I'm sure you could be of great use to her, especially since she has agreed to take in Gazaza as well. There will be any number of trades open to you, and anything you desire to learn, I will personally see you apprenticed."

"And my other choice?" he asks, forgetting about why he was pinching his lips. I want to laugh, but as I attempt to school my features, a smirk no doubt shows because Idari does not look deterred in any way.

"Your other choice," I say, heaving a deep breath, "is to stay under my care. I do not know the ins and outs of the politics of this new city, and taking such a position could be incredibly risky. It brings attention to you."

He fiddles with the reins.

"What would I do?" he asks, and I meet his eye.

"I'm not entirely certain. Keeping you close puts you in direct proximity to the type of politics I'd rather you stay clear from *and* would be more dangerous. I will have to speak to my father about it, and say I'm bringing you under my wing because of..." I can't finish the sentence. *Because of the death of your mother.* But I don't have to say it because it's clear on his face. I hate to remind him. "Is there anything specific you'd like to ask of me?" I ask, searching his eyes.

He breaks eye contact and his eyes seek out the sky. "I love being outside," he says at last. "Animals too." He swallows. "But I want to be with you."

A lump forms in my throat, and the part of me that desires closeness with him is pleased by the words, but the logic inside me is clawing my insides apart. "Very well. However, if I get wind of anything dangerous, anything at all, I will be sending you to the care of Nipula straight away, is that understood?" He nods.

"Yes, Duwa."

I give him the side eye. "When we're in the city, you'll have to call me by my proper title among others, mind." His cheeks bloom with colour again, and this time, I don't hesitate to ruffle his hair. His eyes return to the horizon as Sharvara barks in warning, bounding towards the group and frightening the horses as he launches himself in my direction. Idari stiffens at him, but makes no other move. My heart clenches for him. Huella had been killed by a dog. I stare in the direction that Sharvara had come from, but I see nothing.

"Are those people?" he asks, pointing to the distance. Squinting hard, I raise my hand to filter out the light, and only then do I spot them.

"Halt!" I shout, and the group rattles to a stop at varying rates. Snapping the reins on Puza, I push ahead of the group to intercept the strangers. But as I get closer, I see they are not strangers at all—well, at least not one of them. Nippa. And at his side, a priest.

"You're back," I say, pulling the reins taut to stop Puza once I'm close enough to speak. They travel by foot, and have little in the way of supplies. Nippa looks pale, not like us who have been scorched by the sun day in and out for months. Something is wrong with my friend. It took him far too long to return to us. At the most, he should have intercepted us a month ago, and yet, he intercepts us here, no more than six days from the capital once we'd already come this far.

"I am," Nippa says, his tone hesitant as his eyes travel to the priest and then back at me. I nod, imperceptibly. "I bring word from your father," he says, and the only bag in their possession, looped over Nippa's shoulder, is brought forth. Stepping closer, he gently places his hand on Puza's side, but he snorts and sidesteps. Hand still outstretched in the air where he'd been petting him, Nippa slowly raises his brows before passing me the bag with the fired tablet and stepping away too. Behind me, Sharvara prowls forward, sidling to my side. I reach down slightly and smile as he extends his head slightly so I can pet his head.

"Who's your new friend?" Nippa asks, eyes widening at the sight of Sharvara, but it is not Nippa's expression I notice so much as the priest's. He seems to claw at his chest as though he's in pain before he says a quick prayer to the sun goddess.

Looking at Nippa, I jerk my chin at the priest. "Who's *your* new friend?"

Sputtering, the priest gives Nippa a loaded expression before turning his attention to me. "I am Annuwanza, a devoted priest and humble servant to our lady Arinna, the venerable goddess of the sun." His affected tone and overzealous bow makes my lip twitch.

"Indeed," I say, leaning forward on Puza's neck. "And why, Annuwanza, have you joined my dear Nippa on this journey? He was to deliver the message to my father, the king, and return at once. It has been many months, and my friend looks unwell."

"There were...delays, my prince," Nippa says carefully. I hum in response, and once again, I pat Sharvara's head.

"I'm sure," I say to Nippa before they slide over to the priest, once again, dressed in that unnatural golden yellow. "Come," I call over my shoulder to the group, clicking my tongue, turning Puza to gesture for the group to begin the slow procession once again to rejoin us. "You carry little with you," I note, and before Nippa can respond, the priest waves me off.

"The sun goddess gives us all the sustenance we require." *Wonderful.* Nippa had fallen into the unfortunate company of a zealot.

The group catches up with us quickly and the priest wastes no time waving down a carriage for him to sit upon the backside of the wagon. "The sun goddess gives him all the *sustenance* he requires, but none of the stamina, it seems," I jest, but Nippa says nothing to that, nevermind laugh, like he would have once done. "What happened to you?" I ask, and he barely covers the flinch. Mutti approaches, and I can see by his expression he's disturbed by Nippa's state as well, for he echoes my exact words.

"What happened to *you*?"

"Where's Alluwa?" Nippa asks, evading the question. Mutti and I share a look before I take a deep breath.

"Alluwa is dead."

"How?" Nippa demands, gaze bouncing between the two of us.

"We were attacked again, two days past...by the Akkadians," I explain. "We lost eight, Alluwa and Huella among them." Nippa says nothing to this, grief evident in his face, and he refuses to meet my eye. My stomach curdles with suspicion and concern; the man who has returned to us is far from my brother, and he looks so incredibly guilty. But for what?

"Where were they buried?" he asks at last, looking at the land behind us.

"Somewhere safe," I say by way of answer. I do not trust this man before me, and when he looks at Nippa, Sharvara growls. "I almost forgot. This is Sharvara." His tongue lolls as he pants in the bright sunlight, dappled fur showing off spotted patterns on his face as the light catches his coat. I hand Mutti the bag with the tablet to put in my cart. I must read it alone. "Have you eaten recently?" I ask, and Nippa hesitates before shaking his head.

"I have been forbidden. The sun goddess of Arinna watches all closely, and only those weak in character require sustenance in her rays."

Scoffing with a look of loathing over my shoulder at the unseen priest, no doubt hiding under the cover of the carriage to stuff his face, out of sight from his *venerable goddess,* I maneuver Puza through the throng of carts, horses, cattle, and goats to the carriage where the priest was indeed hiding under the cover of the back of the carriage. With a flourish, I remove the draping coverings. Honeycomb dribbles down his chin, and resides, seemingly, in equal parts on his priestly garb as in his generous belly. That honeycomb had been foraged by Alluwa not a week past, and the rage brewing in me is barely contained. He gives me an affronted, indignant look as he wipes the honey from his face with the cloth canvas draping.

"You are a disgrace to the title of priest," I say, I grip Annuwanza's fleshy arms tightly, hauling him off the cart with a look of disgust. He makes a feeble attempt at escaping me, but he is no match for me. "You steal what does not belong to you, Priest." Planting my hand on the top of his white painted head, I force him to look into the sky, and he whimpers. "I wonder what your goddess thinks of your devotion to her laws."

We have an audience, but my eyes meet Nippa who looks disturbed at the sight. I lean in to Annuwanza. "You're lucky it is not *I* who will punish you," I whisper. "If I were in the place of our sun goddess of Arinna, I would strike you with an unsatiable urge to eat and drink, and yet no matter how much you gorged yourself upon the spoils of the earth, it would never help, never curb the undying craving within your flesh." The scent of urine wafts up to my nose, and I look down to see a puddle, slowly coursing through the sand and grass before sinking into the earth.

Shaking my head, I release my grip on him and turn back to the cart. Reaching for a covered loaf of bread, I toss the drapings over the priest's carefully shaved head, shielding him once more from his Goddess's eyes —and *mine*. Allowing Puza to trot back to my spot in the front, I pin Nippa with a hard stare. I throw the loaf of bread towards him, and he catches it with a grunt.

"Your priest is feasting on all our supplies, in case you were wondering. Eat your fill."

VI
TABLET

HIGH PRIEST OF THE SUN GODDESS OF ARINNA

Pulling the horn from the cord around my neck to my lips, I inhale deeply and blow, alerting the sentinels and guards on the walls to our imminent arrival. The trail upon which we tread grows ever more prominent, swelling wider to accommodate a road. The signs of civilization had begun yesterday where clusters of makeshift tents had been pitched in a huddle where some farmers camped next to their work to avoid wasting the day travelling to the city. Fields of einkorn and emmer are prevalent in this area, but soon, the sweeping fields of wheat taper off, and other crops take their place. The sprawling vineyards in particular have caught Idari's interest. Carts and mules picked up in frequency this morning, and now, in the afternoon, I see my brothers had not been jesting about the city.

The walls of the city of Kuššara, which rise and recede in incremental units, are lined with archers and warriors on duty. In front of the city walls, staple crops grow in lines and in the sun, every day, men and women both toil to harvest everything they can to last and fill our stores in the arid months.

On either side of the road, camps and stalls cover the gently rolling hillside for all citizens who cannot afford to live within the city walls. During the day, it is a sprawling market where they sell their goods—jewellery of fine metals and painted clay beads along with many varieties of various foods and household items.

Sharvara barks, looking like he wants to run faster but he stays by my side, perfectly trained. I try not to dwell on how odd the dog is. Ahead, a procession of priests and warriors alike step out of sync, though it looks like they're trying to be in unison. My father's sigil, a sun with a geometric grid, wavers on the wind, the standardbearer little more than Idari's age. More of those long yellow tunics adorn the many priests, but these are different from the one Annuwanza had worn. Every step these priests take, their garb chinks with them, seemingly lit by a thousand suns. Hammered discs of gold smaller than my smallest toe nail are sewn onto their saffron tunics, the symbol of their stations as high priests. And if those hadn't been obvious enough, the tall, tapered hats upon their white-dyed heads would have given that away. Their slippers are matching turmeric yellow, with impractical curved toes which loop back around like the tips of ostrich ferns. They shuffle so as not to lose a slipper. Behind them, the warriors wear more familiar items, and yet, still, they are foreign to me. The asymmetry of the leather at their chests is new, as is the linen tunic rather than the customary wool and the tang of lanolin on the bitter air. Their warrior belts are also conspicuously absent, and I fight the urge to frown.

"Eldest son of King Karuwas," the leading priest calls out in greeting, his ears also set with gold. I want his voice to be nasally, weak, and irritating, but it's soothing and pleasant instead; still, his voice sets my nerves on edge. I halt, and the procession follows suit at once. "I am high priest of the sun goddess of Arinna, Kammara. We have heard of the many troubles you faced on the road. My brethren shall aid your people in getting settled while you accompany us up to the palace." His eyes rove over the group, and I can instantly sense his distaste for my people. When his attention falls upon the priest, he smiles broadly. "Ah, Annuwanza. My friend, you collected them so quickly. Very good." He continues looking around, and when he spots Nippa, he nods. "Nippa. I trust all is well." He claps his hands together once and raises them towards us. "Very well! Our priests and warriors shall aid you in getting settled! There is much to go around. Haduwas, you may come with me."

"Idari," I call over my shoulder. "Join me with my carriage and then you may return to Nipula," I say, praying he does not vocalize his displeasure at that. He doesn't, smart boy. I hope he can find it in his heart to forgive me for going against his first wish. He simply nods, guiding the horses through the throng of people to stand next to me. Inclining my head at the priest, who smiles a little too broadly, we follow him up the road to the Gate of the Lions.

The golden lions shine brightly in the glare of the sun, although they share little likeness to the one I had fought in the gorge. Horns blow as I enter a vast courtyard. Crowds of nobility and servants of the inner city approach upon hearing our arrival, and many faces stare up at me upon my horse. All who approach me know who I am, but I recognize very few in return. My father has surrounded himself with all new faces it would seem. My eyes seek him in the crowd, but I do not see him. We pass the throng and into the palace entry which is more or less empty.

"Where is my father?" I call out to the priest, and he bows before me, if not with hesitancy, then with displeasure.

"My prince," he says as he arises. "He is in his chambers. I am sure he will be glad to hear of your safe arrival." His eyes linger on Sharvara who has followed Idari and I into the inner city, and his lips pinch in what I assume is fear. Out of the corner of my eye, I see Annuwanza slink off into a dark entrance of a building, not a temple.

"I would speak with him at once."

"I'm afraid that will not be possible," the priest, Kammara says, feigning an apologetic tone. "The king has demanded not to be disturbed."

I eye the man coolly. Swinging one leg over my horse easily, I land on the right hand side of Puza, and I rub his neck affectionately before I start towards the priest who I can see wants to back up, but though he twitches, he remains planted in place.

"Is that so," I say lightly, my eyes drilling into his face. "I have not seen my father in many years. This is certainly not a homecoming as befits my station."

"Alas, he has taken a wife. I am acting on his behalf at the moment. He shall be glad to see you in the morning, I am sure."

I chuckle without a lick of humour. "Indeed. I got word of the wedding nearly six months ago. Odd that it should occur the very day of my arrival and not when intended. Of course, it was your daughter selected for the marriage, was it not?"

"The gods are just," Kammara intones. "She is Queen Malinuwa to you now."

"Queen Consort Malinuwa," I correct. I am silent for a moment as we stare at each other, all pretense of niceties abandoned. He says nothing because what I say is truth. She has no power, not in any meaningful way. The only way she gains power is if my father dies and she has a son that reaches maturity, and that's presuming she survives the birth.

"Queen Consort," he agrees, though it looks painful for him to say so.

"How you have been rewarded, Kammara," I say, not using his title, walking around him with a blank stare, "for such faithful service. How long though, can it last? Surely those treasured by the gods would not have a name so synonymous with filth," I say, referencing the nomenclature from my language.

"My name refers to fog and mist," he says tightly.

"Oh, yes, in some views, but in others?" I allow my lips to lift into a semblance of a smile, "In others, it is only a scent which attracts flies and filth. I would know, Kammara. I've read everything ever written in our lands, and I have learned the way of the Sumerians before us and the Akkadian. Novices to the art of writing, like yourself, are to be forgiven for misunderstanding the borrowed words." I delight as his face turns purple with silent rage. His eyes glitter, and my smile widens.

"Perhaps we'll be graced with an additional heir should anything imminently tragic occur to you," he says, a poorly concealed threat if there ever was one.

"So much ails children at a young age," I say softly, "especially as an heir to the throne. I wish the Queen Consort Malinuwa well in her endeavour to bring more sons into the world. Afterall, many attempts were made on my life as a babe. I wonder if the dear Queen Mother's child will fare as well as I who seized the serpents and threw them away?"

I ask, feigning concern. I would never make an attempt on a child's life, but the priest does not have to know that. I watch in concealed amusement as his nostrils flare.

I turn away and present him my back. "But of course. You say my father is busy ploughing new fields. My news can wait. Have a pleasant evening, Kammara."

"You should not disrespect me," he calls after me. "Indeed, you should be grateful that he has not asked for a bounty on your head, considering you have, for all intents and purposes, abandoned your father."

Eyebrows flying high, I spin to take a look at him. "What did you just say?" I ask, demanding the priest repeat his words. My heart gallops away from me.

"We think it's rather odd that after all these years of silence, after you were bid to come back, that you should suddenly return. You have no other options, yet return to this city and make demands due to your own failure."

"All correspondence from this city ceased after the last migration was set. I have received nothing and have been waiting for directions all this time." I stalk closer to him. "Indeed, it is curious that every single thing that has gone wrong," I reach out, pinching his tunic and jingle it, "has been attached to those clothed in this godly garb. You may have my father, my brothers, and the rest of the nobility fooled, but not me. You are no more saintly than I."

I leave him there, and upon returning to the forum which I had left Idari and Nippa, I see only Idari being aided by servants with the carriage. Sharvara is nowhere to be seen either, and night will soon fall.

"Idari, where did Nippa and Sharvara go?"

He holds the reins in his hands to bring the horses to the stable, but turns at my question. "I don't know where Nippa went, but Sharvara was taken to the kennels. Didn't seem too happy about that," Idari says with a small smile. "He scared everyone."

"He's a good dog," I say in way of answer. War hounds are unpredictable at the best of times, but I sense Sharvara is a different beast altogether. "You didn't see the direction Nippa went?" Idari shakes his head.

"Did you mean what you said before?" he asks quietly. "That I should go to Nipula?"

I nod. "Yes. I've already been threatened by that priest. If he finds out how much I care about you, you will be in danger. I can't have anything happen to you, you understand?" He nods quietly.

"I will speak with my father on the morrow and see what can be done, but in the meantime, help our people. Yes?"

"Yes."

"Good man," I say, ruffling his hair. He swats me away, and I laugh, but my smile soon disintegrates. We act too familiar, and though no one is staring outright at us, there is no reason to suspect I am not being watched. "Alright. Bring my horses to the stables, and then be on your way. Learn everything you can. Any trade you desire to learn, I will make it happen. Good night, Ari." I use his nickname, and his eyes well with emotion. He nods, guiding the horses away, and I am relieved when he doesn't look back.

The walk to my chambers is unfamiliar. I am grudgingly impressed by the high walls and tight weaving streets. Exploring, I find my way through the darkened passages until I reach what is quite obviously the royal chambers. Torches brightly illuminate the pathway, casting great shadows on the carvings in the walls. The relief carvings stand out in the shadows, marking the entrance to the royal quarters with depictions of my father among the gods.

The sun goddess is featured prominently, as is the storm god. Grazing my hand across the stone wall, the pictures shift and suddenly, I see myself kneeling before a goddess in darkness. Blinking, the image disappears, and instead, I see only my splayed palm pressed against the sun in the wall. Swallowing, I withdraw my hand, trying to push away the feeling that I've connected with the wrong goddess of the sun. The goddess of the dead is referred to as a goddess of the sun of the earth, the divine opposite to the goddess of life.

Footsteps approach me, and I heave a breath to hide how shaken I am. A servant appears at my side, bowing deeply. "My prince. Allow me to show you to your apartments."

"Please," I say, holding a hand out for him to go first. Nothing more is said as I walk through archways and through doorways. At last, he stops before the chamber and bows again.

"I am called Kazera. I am your personal attendant." He opens the doors wide and steps aside for me to enter. Everything has been carved into the sandstone. Pushing open the door, my brows lift. The room is not dark like the hallways, but still full of light. "You have the best view," Kazera says conspiratorily before he shuffles into the next chamber, leaving me to explore.

I drift into the room. Braziers line the walls, flickering with flame, but the light does not come from these. Instead, a giant hole has been carved into the far wall, offering a view of the city from high above, just as Kazera had said. My brothers had not been exaggerating about Kuššara's grandeur. In fact, they perhaps had not quite communicated the extent of it. Approaching the carved out view, I note that the wall is half my height in width. Placing my hand on the stone, I steady myself before leaning my head out the side. It is high enough that I doubt anyone could reasonably scale it. Arrows could find their way inside with a skilled archer, but it would be unlikely for them to reasonably leave a mark. Leaving the sights of the sky, I inspect the dwelling. Woven carpets with alternating patterns of blue, white, black, and red drape the floor. Even the walls hold painted decorations of elaborate geometric carvings and animals on the top quarter of the walls. The room isn't quite level, with chambers branching off with steps and carved nooks where pottery and woven baskets decorate the alcoves.

There is a quiet gurgling, and when I follow the sound into the chamber to the right, there is a natural spring of water where steam rises. Dipping a hand in, I pull back immediately, beside myself with the knowledge they have hot water for bathing. Stacks of linens are in the accompanied alcove, away from the steam, presumably for drying off. Another chamber near it has a simple hole in the ground, and I stare quizzically at it. There are no chamber pots or dug out pits. When I wave a hand over it, I feel a cool breeze drifting from the strange hole. I purse my lips at it.

Joining Kazera in the main chamber, I try not to look out of place, but I must not succeed because Kazera seems to hide a smile. "This place is very different from our once home, is it not?" he asks.

"It is," I say, and I take in my servant once again. He looks so familiar. "Do I know you?" I ask, and he shakes his head.

"You do not," he says, lowering his gaze. "But you know—knew my brother. Well it would seem if the chatter I hear is true."

"Who?" I ask, but the second I ask the question, I know, and before he answers, I close my eyes. "You are the brother of Alluwa." Grief holds fast in my heart. "He lives on in your visage."

"I was young when the expeditions to this city began. My parents allowed him to stay behind with you, but I came here with them. My parents were hoping for something better here."

"And is it?" I ask, gaze seeking his. "Is it better?" He raises his gaze to me, tentatively.

"It could be," he says at last. "How did he die?" he asks, his question candid, assuming, and yet I cannot fault him for it.

"We went hunting, and there were great, foul, metallic birds. When we sought to scare them away so they'd stop sending the game off, some attacked. Alluwa was touched by one of them. The birds were poisoned...tainted. His flesh grew black and it sought his heart. He hid it and by the time we discovered it..." I trail off. I meet his eyes. "We had no more healers or priests from our settlement. There was nothing I could do. I was there when he...when he passed. I buried him myself and sent him with treasures to the beyond."

"I didn't know him well," Kazera says. "I wish I could have."

"I wish that for you too. He was a great man. I am glad that you are with me, Kazera. I think Alluwa would be pleased too."

Kazera's hands play with the fringe on his tunic sleeves. I raise my brows. He wears a wool tunic, long and grey, and the ends which reach for the floor have dozens of hanging strips. "You wear the old style. You're the first I've seen to wear clothing in the old ways." His hands let go of the fringe immediately. He seems embarrassed. "I am pleased to see it." He straightens then.

My parents are sheep herders," he begins, but then he stops himself. "Only the richest servants wear things in the new way, and the nobles, no matter where they're from." He turns and leads me into the chamber to the left. Inside, a great cedar chest. He gestures to it, and had he not seemed so calm about it, I would assume a planted viper or scorpion. Still, my warrior belt is on and tucked away in a leather sheath, my dirk—if necessary.

"What's in it?" I ask, approaching it slowly.

"Your new clothing, courtesy of the king. You can fetch new ones of course, but..." He shrugs.

Lifting the lid, I expect something grimy or dusty, but instead, fragrance slips out, something unfamiliar. Pulling the garments out, fine linen tunic after tunic. "No trousers," I mumble, and Kazera shakes his head.

"Just tunics and decorative belts."

"Very well," I sigh. None of them feature the style of my home, I feel a deep sadness make a home in my chest. The ways of my people are being erased. I straighten, attempting to shake the feeling and return the folded garments to the wooden chest. "My brothers?" I ask. "Are they well?"

"Yes, my prince."

"Please," I say. "You may call me Haduwas."

"That would be most improper, my prince."

"Fine," I say. "In private then."

"Your brothers are next door, my...Haduwas." A rare grin lights up my face, and Kazera's eyes are wide. Poor boy. "Chamber to your right."

"I won't be needing supper this night, Kazera." The thought of eating right now makes me nauseous. "You have done well. I will be meeting with my father in the morning, so please return upon first light. I will require your help."

"I would be honoured, my prince—Haduwas!" Again, Kazera bows. "The servants will be bringing the rest of your belongings up shortly. I hope you rest well." When he closes the door to my chamber, I sigh. I rarely sleep well.

I'm about to step towards the door when it comes hurtling open, and my brothers step into the room. There is a moment where we simply look at one other before they launch themselves at me.

"You need a bath," Zuwasa says, my youngest brother, just as Pasaduwa says, "I forgot what you looked like."

"I just got home after months on the road." Indignance seeps into my tone as I shove Zuwasa's shoulder in jest. "As for you," I say, regarding Pasaduwa, "I'm the better looking version of this fool."

"You're old," Zuwasa says, and he barks a laugh as I swipe at him, and he evades it.

"Distinguished," I retort. "And our sisters?"

"More beautiful every day." Pasaduwa embraces me, but then grunts. "He's right," Pasaduwa says, wincing. "You do need a bath." His expression straightens. "But once you do that, we're going to show you the city." I eye him with suspicion, but he pushes me in the direction of the hot spring and doesn't take no for an answer.

VII
TABLET

THE LANDS OF EVER-NIGHT

Sunlight beams into my eyes as the sun goddess demands I bid her good morning. I had not taken note that my bedroom faces precisely East. My stomach toils in a way it would not have done in my youth after a night of wine and adventure. Wincing at the unfortunate brightness, I peer around, slightly mollified that I am indeed in my own quarters this morning. It will not do to disgrace myself on the morn of my first day at court.

Sitting upright, I untangle my limbs from the numerous furs and fine woven fabrics. Allowing my bare feet to touch the richly carpeted floors, I hum when I find the floor is warm. Sleeping tunic ruffled and clinging to my hips, I gently remove the garment before placing it in the basket for washing. I am struck by the silence of this place. No brothers or friends being noisy as they wake, no villagers going about their toil or asking for an audience. I stand alone.

It is a thing unheard of to room alone. Even as part of the highest ranking family of my people in the old settlement, my father and my brothers all shared a dwelling together. When I was left behind, I still did not live alone, and I had Alluwa, Nippa, and Mutti join my household. That there is so much room in this city for my own private quarters is beyond my comprehension, though my brothers share quarters. When I'd asked them last night why I did not join them, they snickered and asked the woman for more ale, leaving my question to hang in the air like a noxious odour. The lack of an answer had weighed heavy on me for the rest of the night. Though in looks they've matured, they have not done so in spirit.

The natural hot spring still gurgles peacefully, and steam rises, coating the nearby walls with condensation that rolls down the wall to rejoin the pool once more. Beside, the pit in the floor that leads directly to the river running swiftly below. While all others have to defecate in the communal latrine, the royals had their own for private use.

Bare skin delighting in the warm air, I complete my morning business before plunging into the hot spring to remove any grime I may have missed the night previously. Bending my knees to lower myself within the water, I lean my head back, swiping my hands back over my hair to saturate the strands as I relax. Hot water feeds into the bath through a channel in the wall on the far side of the basin, and when a certain level is achieved, the old water finds a path into the raging river unseen below.

"My prince," a voice calls, one I recognize as Kazera's, Alluwa's brother. It will take him some time to grow comfortable using my name. The title makes something inside me twist with unease.

"Come in," I call, and the giant stone wheel obstructing the door begins to turn. When Kazera pokes his head past the stone, he looks around the room until his eyes land on the hot spring.

"How may I be of service this morning?" Despite the light in the room, he carries a torch in his hand. The hallways which connect the royal palace are in perpetual dimness even at the brightest of days unless chamber doors are ajar. Securing the torch in a bracket by the door, he waves his fingers over it playfully, and for a moment, a snake seems to slither across the ceiling before it disappears again into the light.

"I am to address the king," I say, washing my hair further with my fingertips digging into my scalp. "I require my court clothes. And some directions."

"Of course," Kazera says, bowing deeply. "As you were on the road, all your royal dress was made for you and was transferred last night while you were out." He moves to the side room where the chest of clothing had been earlier. "You will need to look your best," he warns, and when he presses his lips together, that slow-churning nausea in my gut stirs up something even more potent and visceral within me: fear.

"What is it?" I ask gently, eyes seeking his, and for a moment, I think he is not going to answer me because he turns from his task to the front of the room. With caution, he opens my chamber to look in the hallway before closing the door once more. He sighs.

"You are not well-liked here."

"I know," I say, but he shakes his head.

"No, you don't." Wordlessly, he sets drying linens on the edge of the pool for when I finish, but I take that as a cue. I wait for him to elaborate. "Your father's marriage was delayed. It was supposed to happen earlier, but there is talk that the high priest's daughter did not want to marry. So, she didn't. When it seemed you were not coming back, the issue was not pressed, and the high priest was happy to allow his daughter some time to warm up to the idea. However, when it became clear you were coming back, the priest demanded it be done. To secure a new line and heir. You threaten the entire order by being here."

My hunches had been correct. Nodding, I stand up and retrieve the cloth which is far too pretty for such menial tasks as drying. Rivulets of water tickle my skin as they seek the floor. My wet footprints follow me as I walk to the table, wrapping the cloth around my hips. "I figured that was the case. The high priest threatened me yesterday." I don't know why I tell him. It's beyond unwise; it's reckless, and yet, in his face, I see my best friend, and perhaps it is Alluwa who loosens my lips. Dragging the cloth over my body, soaking the residual moisture so I don't saturate my clothes, I gently lay it over my hair as I press and scrunch. By the time Kazera rejoins me with the outfit over one arm, I am mostly dried off. Something in his arms catches the light.

"That's not good," he whispers, and he nods to himself. "Then it's even more important you look your best. You cannot give them any ammunition against you."

I grimace at the sight of the gulsarana tool in Kazera's hand. *Months* are going to be scraped from my skin. The flagon on the table looms, and I know what is coming. My entire life, I've had to fend for myself: carry my own water, repair my own clothes and weapons, cut my own firewood, dig the graves, clean the clothes, and yet here, servants cater to my every need, even though I am fully capable of doing it myself.

Tipping the flagon, Kazera warms the oil between his palms—olive steeped with cypress and cedar, and faintly scented with the rare bark from the far east that in the markets might be worth a shekel of silver per handful. The aroma clings to my skin as Kazera coats me with it. My neck aches as my shoulders climb higher and higher, fists clenching as I fight the urge to tell Kazera to stop and let me do it.

"It's a lot to get used to," Kazera murmurs, scraping my arm with the gulsarana before wiping the excess off on the cloth in his left hand. "I'm still not used to everything here," he admits, working smoothly and methodically. As he speaks, my shoulders lose their stiffness, and as he continues speaking, I feel almost relaxed. "Of course, it's even more of a change for you. You're adapting alone." My shoulders hike up again.

"Why *am I* alone in these quarters? I asked my brothers yesterday, and they refused to tell me." Kazera moves onto my back, and the repetitive drag and wipe starts to feel less uncomfortable.

"I hear only whispers of other servants," he says at last, moving to my chest. His eyes remain on his work. "There are two possibilities. One, they want to marry you off ensuring that you start your family here."

"And the second?" I ask, and this time, he does pause his work, but he does not meet my eye.

"If you have others here, they could interfere," he offers, tentatively.

"They mean to kill me in my sleep?" I ask dryly.

"I doubt they'll be that obvious. They will devise some spectacle I am sure. They're good at that." He sounds bitter, but I don't ask. He moves on to my legs, finishing the rest of his task quickly with practiced ease. Sighing, he tosses the rag into a bucket by his feet. "If your brothers are around you constantly, it could just complicate things for the ceaseless schemes. The priests are not concerned with your brothers."

"A good thing," I mutter.

"For them, yes. For you...it means even your family cannot truly be your allies. Your father—" He stops himself, and his mouth parts. "My apologies. I speak out of turn."

"You do not. You do not ever need to fear me. That is not my way." Swallowing, he nods.

"You will not like what I have to say."

"I doubt it, but I will hear it anyway. I doubt you will say anything I have not already thought of myself."

"Your father thinks he's playing them, but everything he does plays into their plans. He's docile here, more concerned with making friends than understanding the truth. Your brothers are...more like your father. They're creatures of comfort now. When the priests demand something of them in the form of a suggestion, they do it without question. They are easily governed. You are not. You are also the oldest. Competent. Strong. Intelligent. A threat."

Laying the items on the bed, he gestures that I should come forward and sit on the stool by the table. Upon the table, a number of tools and vials. Sitting, straight-backed, I watch as Kazera picks up a carved comb of ivory to begin working through my damp hair. He pours something into his hand, rubs them together, and then runs it through my hair. The smell is curious, but pleasant, almost spicy.

"You have good hair and skin. Thank the gods," he mutters. "I think we ought not overdo it with ceremony. No Hattic designs."

"No Hattic designs," I agree. After he finishes with my hair, he brings over the clothing. An ornate white tunic with gold beading on the trim of the neck and the shoulders, it is a sleeveless piece that, when on, would go to the knee. Beside it, a mantle of deep purple, and a golden medallion gleaming with a captured sun to secure it in place. A top the pile, a pair of golden slippers with the gentle sloping toe I am accustomed to—not the style of the priest's then, and I am glad for it.

Nodding at Kazera, I follow him as he approaches the door to lead me to the throne room. "Do you think they commune with the gods?" I ask suddenly, and Kazera frowns at me, pausing. "The priests?" I clarify.

"I do not deny the existence of the gods."

"Nor do I. I do not ask if you believe in the gods. I ask if you believe the priests truly hear and are in the favour of the gods."

"Yes," he says. "Elsewise, our sun goddess of Arinna would have scorched our crops, set fire to our lands, and driven us far from here."

"What if Arinna does not want to harm those in her care? What if she does not wish to punish the people? What if she wants the people saved from those who speak falsely in her name?"

Eyeing me, he hides a smile. "Then I would say be careful, Prince Haduwas, and may she arm you well."

The room is filled with people, most of whom I do not recognize. While my father sits in the throne with twin lions fashioned as arms, his new wife sits in the chair beside him dressed in absurd amounts of wealth. A golden scarf is wrapped about her head, concealing her hair which marks her as wed. Her eyes, rimmed in kohl, follow the movements of the servants before her who pile in with an array of items in their arms. One by one, they present their gifts to their new queen, Malinuwa, who stares impassively at the spread.

Musicians with clever fingers pluck strings and tap rhythmically upon stretched hides, loudly enough to be heard, but not so loud as to overtake conversation. The room is sweltering, and servants lifted woven reed screens to stir what little breeze could be coaxed from the stone chamber.

Toys for the future child of their union are laid at her feet, among them, a rattle with dried beans within, and exquisite clothing. Meeting the queen's eye, her gaze narrows, but even as she turns to my father to whisper in his ear, I am struck with the awareness that she is young. Too young. She could not be older than Idari. No wonder she tried to postpone the wedding. She has yet to live.

My father's gaze flicks up to me, and he whispers something back at her, his expression soft. Standing up, he claps his hands once and holds his palms out to the servants who immediately set to collecting the spoils.

Walking in single file through the nearest doorway, they are to be deposited in their shared quarters.

"We see the gifts you have brought, and they are most fitting." His hand rests on the queen's shoulder, and she looks as though she wants to throw it off, but she doesn't. When she meets my eye, her gaze darts away again. "The queen wishes to retire." She stands, and after a beat, she descends the steps of the dais and the room in unison moves out of her way, parting to allow her to pass. Her eyes remain trained on the floor, and when she is gone, an air of tension fills the room.

"And now, a serious matter. My son," my father says at last. "Haduwas. Step forth."

I cut through the throng to stand before him, and I bow deeply before standing straight. His face is unchanged, though grey is beginning to grace his temple. An ornamented cap of oxblood coloured wool sits atop his head, setting him apart from everyone else in the room. Murmurs explode from every direction, and it takes several moments for people to see my father's raised hands for quiet.

"I desire the truth, and it will be obtained," he says, placating the crowd. When his eyes meet mine, I see whirling emotions: fear and confusion chiefly among them. His eyes flick to the high priest who stands against the wall, Nippa at his side. I don't understand what my father's eyes tell me. Does he look to the priest in deference? Or in warning? I await the questioning and do not presume to speak.

"Nearly three summers ago, a messenger left this city with instructions for you to vacate the settlement with the remaining people in your care and to rejoin us here." He sits down once again and regards me. "No messenger returned. When it became clear you were not coming, another messenger was sent. In total, five messengers have left this city and not returned. What do you have to say for yourself?"

"I received no messengers for four summers. The last communication I received was from when I was instructed to send my brothers and the majority of farmers and smiths. I did as bid. I waited for messages and never received them."

"Was any attempt made to contact us here?" My father's gaze is imploring.

"Yes. One messenger was sent who knew the way. When the messenger did not return, I feared something had happened en route to the city that would make travel unsafe, and I needed every person in our settlement to keep everything running. We did what we could on the settlement, but trade dwindled as routes drove ever south. My most skilled tradesmen had been sent here, and we could no longer reasonably rely on trade as a means of survival."

"So why have you joined the city now when before you deemed it unsafe?" he asks, and the room is so quiet, all I can hear is my thundering heartbeat.

"Because I had no other choice but to take the risk." Nodding at Kazera, who stands in the periphery of the room, I walk to him to retrieve the heavy sack. "We intercepted a priest of this city carrying this." I brandish the tablet which had started everything, presenting it to my father. "This tablet outlines instructions for the destruction of the settlement with the clear intention for my death and all who attempt to protect me. No other expedition between the settlement and this city saw any violence. And yet, the second we left our burning settlement, we were plagued. We were attacked by birds sent by the gods, we were attacked by a lion with a golden pelt, and then again, attacked on the road by a group of Akkadians." I raise the collar which had been wrapped round the neck of Sharvara. "It would seem there is a traitor in the midst, father."

The room erupts, but my father does not seem to notice as his attention is still firmly upon the tablet in his hands where his knuckles are turning white. No doubt he sees the imprint of his cylinder seal denoting his approval.

"Leave us." At my father's declaration everyone begins to depart, except for the high priest whose eyes gleam. Kammara passes by me, brushing his shoulder against mine despite the ample room to avoid me, and steps up onto the dais with zero hesitation.

"My king. What news?"

"What do you know of this?" he demands, presenting the tablet in his lap. It is clear he is referring to his seal. I don't feel the relief I thought I would at the knowledge it was not his doing. Despite the theatrics, the high priest makes a look of astonishment before he schools it. He turns sharply to me.

"Who gave this to you?"

I regard him coolly, and in my bones, I know it was the high priest who wrote this and is looking to pin the blame on someone. I have no way of proving it.

"I didn't get his name."

"Well, where is he?" Kammara demands, and my father looks on.

"In the old settlement," I say, shrugging.

"Well why is he there?" he asks, spittle flying. I do not look at the high priest as I say my next words, but straight at my father.

"Because I took his head for a traitor in the name of King Karuwas." Kammara makes a squawking, choked noise, and I look at him flatly. "He carried the incriminating message on his person, tried to destroy it, and spoke treason to me when confronted."

"Any witnesses?" my father asks, and I nod.

"The entire village."

They both fall silent at that, and Kammara gets a hold of himself. "You did not get his name?"

"He refused any information except taunts. But he was dressed exactly like...you." I drawl, dragging my eyes lazily over his robes, curly, swirly shoes, and towering hat. "Without the hat of course."

"Do not call this a *hat*," the priest snapped, straightening the headpiece. "It is the veil of Arinna. It is the office I bear, not an ornament to amuse the eyes of the *uninitiated*." He says 'uninitiated' like it's a dirty word, and I hide my amusement.

"My apologies," I say blandly. "*Without a veil*." It is a hat—the length of a forearm above his head in yellow and gold.

"Who has left the city?" my father demands, cutting between us without moving a muscle. His attention is purely on the priest who turns back to my father immediately, bowing his head in false supplication.

"We have many mercenaries, but I will compile a list at once, and cross reference who returns, my king." He straightens. "Of course, if your son has executed the errant priest for treason, the problem has been solved."

"Unless he wasn't working alone," I suggest, taking slow, deliberate steps up the dais too. I smirk at the priest when I discover I'm taller than even his hat before I turn to my father and take a knee. "There is still the issue of how your seal was stolen, and of how and why every messenger between us was intercepted. Who was in charge of such communications?"

"Many questions and even fewer answers," my father muses. "I will deliberate, and investigate the matter myself. Kammara, you are dismissed. I wish to speak with my son."

"Of course, my king." Kammara bows deeply, giving me a dark look before retreating from the cavernous room. For the first time in years, I am in the same room as my father. Standing with a grunt, he stands upright, and I analyze him. He's not as tall as I remember, though perhaps it's because I myself have grown. He wears a cap on his head inlaid with gold coins in a connecting spiral to the crown of his head. Over his shoulders, a mantle with alternating red black and gold patterns, and an identical gold sun pendant clasping it together at his sternum. A cream tunic to his shins with a grid pattern covers him past the knees, and a thick gold belt secures it at his waist. From what I'd heard, our ways had been mostly forgotten, but my father's warrior belt instills a hope I fear to read too much in.

"You still wear your warrior belt," I say, and I can tell he's sizing me up as much as I am in return. His stern brow lessens as he regards me. It isn't quite a fond look, but it's about as close to it as my father can get.

"I do," he says at last, and steps closer. "My son," he says finally. His arms are outstretched, and he descends the steps to embrace me. Trying to conceal my shock, I allow him to put his arms around me, and I tentatively return the gesture. He chuckles and squeezes before letting go and circling me. "You've grown taller. A proper man." He laughs again and brings his forehead against mine, and I allow myself to smile good-naturedly at the exchange.

“Congratulations are in order I hear,” I say when he releases me. He nods.

“Yes.” He nods, but he steers the topic away. “I worried you were not going to return. I had thought something terrible had happened.”

“Almost.” I swallow. “I lost many friends.” My father hums in response, his tone gravelly with understanding. “Come. I would have you join me this evening.”

Following the king into a veiled passage behind a tapestry at the throne’s back, I walk through the walls of carved rock and stone. Light from within informs me the floor slopes downward, and I lean back slightly so as not to slip. The air is clogged with mist and smoke, heavy with burning matter.

"What is that smell?" I ask, wrinkling my nose.

"It is incense, my son, sent from Egypt. What you detect is Kyphi and Myrrh," the king explains, and I hum in brief acknowledgement. "Just this way," he says, gesturing to a side chamber which has an incline. Ahead, I can see sunlight coming through a small frame where the wall ceases to let in natural light. The beam of sun hits the Idol of Arinna, casting her statue in a halo of light as it hits precisely centre.

Past the small room where the idol was featured on a stone plinth, a room which descended into the floor from all sides with stairs. In the centre, at the lowest level, a wide floor with cushions, draperies, braziers, and upon the walls, the shadows of our bodies. A bowl of fruit, golden cups, and flagons of wine decorate the table on the recessed floor.

“I am glad you have come back, my son.” My father descends the stairs with difficulty, and I frown at the sight of his gait. He favours his right side. Yet, I do not speak of it. When he reaches the bottom stair, he sighs, and when I descend to join him, he begins pouring the wine. “And yet, you have come at a very difficult time.”

“I can help,” I say. “I am old enough and practiced now.”

He booms a laugh. “Alas,” he says, residual chuckles coax his stiff shoulders into a relaxed posture. “The politics of this city are nothing like anything else you’ve experienced. But, you are right. You are old enough. And *sensible*.” He doesn’t need to say anything for me to hear the unspoken part of his thoughts. *Unlike your brothers.*

"I don't like or trust Kammara," I say, accepting a cup of wine.

"Nor should you," he says, nodding. "But he has his uses."

"He does not mean for your line to succeed," I say, and he pauses, eyes meeting mine over the rim of his own gold goblet.

"Go on," he says, eyebrows raised.

"It's obvious, isn't it?"

"Explain it like it's not."

I take a sip from my goblet. "What were the terms that you initially reached out with?" I ask, shifting the conversation. "What did this place," I say, eyeing the walls and the cups in our hands, "need from *us*? A low-lying trade settlement on the periphery?" I wait for a response, but move on when I don't get one. "I can only assume they required man-power–warriors and skilled trade. That's all they took from the settlement, leaving behind the weak, the old, and the young and unskilled." His lips purse, but I don't let that stop me.

"Now, why would they allow another, foreign chief rise to become their king?" I meet his eyes. "They did not have a king before. They were clusters of villages and temples—ripe for raiding with no military or protection." He nods, almost imperceptibly. "So, you offer to bring your warriors and your labour force here along with skilled trade to protect the city and its people; in exchange, you receive rank and standing. You promise acquiescence to their laws and gods. You promise marriage into their house." I sit back.

"Perhaps you *can* handle the politics of this city," he murmurs, no longer looking at me, but at his wine.

"They did not welcome us as equals even if you obtained a title. They do not trust us. They took the able-bodied, the warriors, the craftsmen, and left behind the old, the sick, and the slow. They gained everything, trimmed what would be inconvenient to them, and still hold the power, and in exchange, you sit in the chair. I'm afraid you drew the bad end of the deal."

"*I* rule," he says sharply, before he swallows and says more calmly, "I rule. The priests tell me of omens, and the Pankus offer their wisdom, they are our nobles afterall, but it is I who has final say." He truly believes he rules them, I realize. He does not see how invisible their authority runs through every act: the law he commands, the bread he eats, even the doors he walks through. They bend the people to the gods, and through them, to themselves. He finishes the goblet. "I have the warriors at my back. I have the loyalty of those who follow the *royal house of Karuwas*," he says, emphasising the title. "*That* is real power. I require no blessing to enforce it."

"Perhaps not," I agree. "Force will hold the walls. It may hold men for a season. But the priests have no stake in your glory. They will make the child of your new union the new heir to the throne, one who does not know our ways or customs and systematically erase us like we never even existed. Not out of any particular evil, but because they are trying to survive. Just as we are."

"You are my heir," he says, waving a hand.

"Unless they stage my death or declare my brothers and I unfit for the throne as deemed by the gods." My father straightens slightly, as though the thought had never occurred to him.

"It won't happen," he says, but I wonder if he believes it. He puts his goblet down. "That's enough talk of this subject," he says, looking me in the eye. "We will be holding a feast for your joyous return! A momentous occasion indeed. There will be games with your brothers, some ceremonies and rituals, and a spread fit for kings..." He claps me on the back, and from the bowl in the centre of the table between them, procures a yellow apple. Contemplating it, perched in his fingertips, he examines it for spots and smiles, eyes gleaming. "And there will be prizes." When he takes a chunk out of the fruit, I have the nauseating feeling that I would not enjoy the prizes.

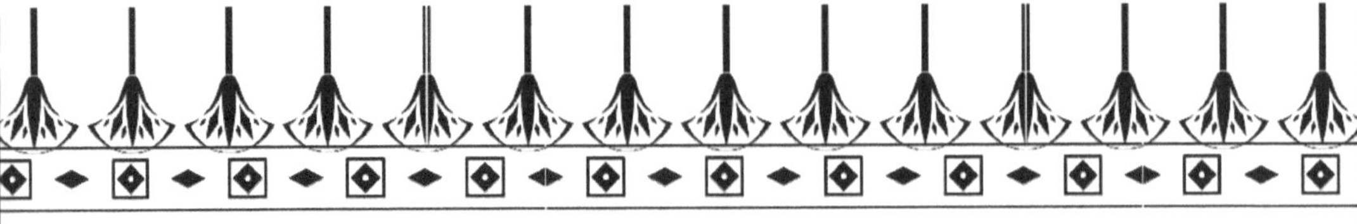

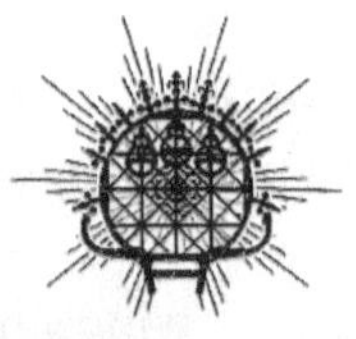

The root is set deep in the earth.

Not by labor, but by balance.

Above and below are placed in order.

Thus the lower realm is established.

VIII
TABLET

THE CONTEST

My father regards the crowds lined upon the square which overlooks a recessed pit filled with sand, accessible by a single descending staircase. Surrounding the pit, the commoners inch in close to the sandy edge to get a better look in hushed silence. Nothing yet stands in the centre, and yet, somehow, I know my feet shall feel it. Beside my father, Queen Malinuwa, and standing in descending order of birth at my side, my brothers Pasaduwa and Zuwasa. Along the wall, my sisters make a beautiful congregation, the youngest just now turning fifteen.

"Welcome!" My father stands to address the gathered crowd. The elevated dais houses the nobility, "Welcome," my father repeats. "This is a very special day for our blooming city. My son, Prince Haduwas, has successfully returned from our outpost city with the last of our citizens, a prodigious deed well done. In addition, as you well know, it is a sacred day to our patron deity, Tarḫunna, our weather god of heaven. Our Prince's timing was fortuitous—most fortunate. Our priests have made communion with Tarḫunna, and our god has proclaimed thus! The naming of the Crown Prince is upon us! He who wishes to be made Crown Prince need only step onto the sand and be the last one standing. I have many worthy sons, so let the strongest of you prevail." Shocked murmurs explode around through the crowd, and I do my best to hide my confusion. Does he intend for me to truly have to fight for it? Or is this for show so that the city can see I am chosen by the gods? If so, this does not bode well for me. As my eyes scan the crowd, I make eye contact with the high priest who looks far too gleeful, which only enhances my fears.

"Does that mean I can skip you, Haduwas?" Pasaduwa asks under his breath, nudging my arm with a sly grin.

"No, it means I can," Zuwasa says, none too quietly. Though the youngest, he is the bulkiest of arm—and laziest of brain.

"It means only," I say, my tone barely above a whisper, "that you may try." I know they hear because they both lean in closer, feral grins twisting their features that are so like mine. It takes only seconds before Zuwasa is tearing away through the crowd towards the staircase down, decorum damned. Pasaduwa snickers under his breath and ambles along after him. I stand still for a suspended moment as I stare at my father, willing him to look in my direction; he cannot resist the glance in my direction to see what I will do. With slow, even steps, I approach the king. Stopping before him, I bow, deeply.

"Father," I say, dipping my chin, before following my brothers through the crowd. While my brothers had raced to get to the sands first, I languish with each step towards my birthright.

Exorbitant amounts of sand have been deposited upon the stone mosaic floor, concealing the symbol of the sun goddess of Arinna—a symbol in and of itself. What was once claimed by light is now claimed by dark; what was once claimed by life is now claimed by death, and to host these festivities here, in this way, the champion will not be for Arinna, but for *her*.

Then, I see him in the crowd: Idari. His face holds a grimace, though I cannot be sure if the expression is because something dire is about to transpire, or if he simply squints hard to block out the vicious sun. Either way, my stomach roils with hard waves of nausea. Nipula is nowhere to be seen, and I lose sight of Idari as he disappears into the shifting crowd.

An overwhelming sense of foreboding floods me, and, suppressing a shudder, I dismiss my fears, allowing them to be felt and acknowledged, but cast away nonetheless. If it is my fate to be claimed thus, so be it. The disconcerting feelings fall away to be replaced with a different kind of stress—adrenaline.

The courtyard has been set up with javelins, heavy throwing stones, targets, and, most excitingly of all, a solid wheel of cheese; every eye who can perceive it is trained hard upon it. For many of the on-lookers, it is more wealth than they will see themselves over the course of a year, and for some, even more.

I note that all of my staples are present, including my own war helm. I also note each of my brothers' top choices are splayed across the centrepiece next to the weapons. As eldest son, I had overseen my brothers' training, so I have an edge that they do not possess accompanied with my level of experience, though perhaps they have trained in the Hattic style since. Of course, I doubt the targets are my brothers.

The thought urges me to look at them, and I wonder if they have stumbled upon the same thoughts I have. As I stare at the pair in question, I notice they're still transfixed upon the cheese, and not on their favourite weapons. They wear only expressions mixed with confusion and excitement.

"Why is there only one wheel of cheese?" Zuwasa asks under his breath.

"Hardly customary," Pasaduwa agrees, brows furrowed. I've heard tales from my brothers about it. Traditionally, there are two teams and each has to capture the enemy wheel and bring it back to base.

"Today, let us prove our princes' valour! A game of physical prowess! Our festivities shall have the high priest judge each performance and they shall, in the order of their rankings as deemed by the gods, attempt to steal the cheese from the sun goddess Arinna!"

All moisture within my mouth vanishes leaving my mouth with the feeling of the driest wine known to man, armed with the most bitter of aftertastes. If that slippery leech is judging, I have to fight that much harder to be the obvious crowd favourite—or hope my brothers aren't even half as competent as I.

"To begin our ceremony, our young princes shall drink the gods to honour them. A trial of force and a trial of strength, and in the order of their prowess, a final showcasing for the gods! The prince who most honours the gods shall be named Crown Prince of Kuššara! Let the games begin!"

At the announcement, three servant women shuffle across the sand with ornate goblets; they are careful not to spill a single drop. At once, my brothers and I accept their offering and with a moment of thoughtful silence towards the gods, we begin the process of draining the goblet. It is not a quick task. Instead, it is an earnest intention to climb the dangling rope towards god-hood—to be more than we are presently. Although a powerful rite, most don't have the sincerity to make the connection. *I* never have.

With each sip, I dedicate it to a new god or goddess. The first sip goes to the goddess Arinna, and the next, to her consort, Tarḫunna, the god of thunder. Next, I pray to the goddesses of fate. Another sip is dedicated to Kurunta, god of the hunt and then one goes to Wurrukatte, the god of war. But my mind, for the most fleeting of moments, thinks of the sun goddess of the Earth—of Lelwani—and the second my mind grazes the thought, I am struck.

Sick with a whirling sensation, like I am but a spoke in an ever-spinning wheel riding into battle, time loses all meaning. No longer am I a man, but a wielded piece on a game board. Fever sweeps over me chasing the chills away only for the hunter to become the prey as the cold climbs back up. Gasping, I barely cling to the cup as dizziness overtakes me and my sight sparkles and fades, dimming until only the barest hint of colour can be seen in the centre. Did I just get poisoned?

When again I am conscious of myself and the world around me, I am somehow still standing, and by a miracle, still clutching the now empty goblet. The last sip has gone to the goddess of death—and she has answered. My movements don't feel like my own, and one moment I am looking at my brothers, the next into my cup, and I don't remember moving.

Beside me, my brothers have finished their cups too, but they look just as they had the moment before. I look into the bottom of the glass where the sediment has made its home, and then, so slowly, I look up to see the high priest staring directly at me with pinched lips. Though he looks displeased, I cannot ascertain whether the look is as a result of his natural dislike or because he understands a little more. Perhaps his goddess whispers on the wind or speaks through the rays of light which strike his severe face to tell him who has claimed me as her champion. When he moves, his shadow slithers towards me as he steps into the sun.

With a long breath, I let go of the shock only to find that my body feels...different. My limbs, though the same length and size, seem to swell with newfound power, though surely it is an instance of pure imagination. I can't have truly touched divinity and been bestowed a grain of her power...? I try to remember what her powers are, other than death of course, but I can't touch it. It's as though since connecting with her, she has retreated to see how I will act.

The goddess of womb and tomb, I think. The being who resides over our souls. She is not a banned goddess of course, and she is exclusively the deity who presides over death and funeral rites, but she is an unmentionable, one you do not want the express attention of lest you be pulled into her lands prematurely. I fear it is too late for me. I am going to die in this event. I am certain of this, if I am her chosen champion.

A drum beats, and while Zuwasa and Pasaduwa cheer and pound their feet in unison with the chanting crowds, I do my best not to upturn the contents of my belly, meagre as my breakfast had been. Instead, I breathe hard through my nose, forcing my nausea down. Three guards stride towards us, and my attention falls upon the sand, so easily displaced by heavy footfalls. Digging their feet in deep as they stand at attention, my gaze meanders up the body of my opponent, and as I meet the hard stare, I am aghast. It is Nippa—my friend—my brother. I suspect he is neither any longer.

The shouts of the crowd are no longer audible to my ears. Instead, all I hear is the frantic thumping of my heartbeat and the blood pulsing up my body to rush to my head.

"Nippa?" I start, but then, the horn is blown and our fight begins. At once, my brothers begin, but it is all I can do to stare. Father had declared he'd hand-selected his personal guard. Had Nippa truly defected from my service and without a word about it? The boy I've known since childhood?

In the man before me, nothing of the boy remains—not his humour or easy grin or the air of friendship. Instead, his eyes hold only contempt for me, and a promise of bloodshed. It is years of our forged bond that allow me to see his tells, still loud as ever despite his attempt to mask them. His hands twitch and his ever-shifting weight shows me he is anxious to go, and it is only because I know him so well that I am so easily able to evade his first swing.

Sliding over the sand to the right, I duck as his fist arcs around, and I stick my leg out to trip him, but he easily hops over it. As easily as I can read him, he can just as soon read me. He advances, I retreat. I advance, he retreats. It is a dance of danger, one honed through years of practice. Still, my vision swoops and heaves, and my limbs feel heavy and detached. While the crowd roars in approval at the brawls no doubt orbiting mine, mine is only fraught with tension, but no violence...yet.

"Why?" I ask, and in response, his lips curl.

"Because of *Alluwa*. You disgraced him in death. I shall not follow you to reap the same ill-gotten reward."

"Disgraced? How?" I demand.

"Your death rite on that mound! We found it! They said you performed improperly! No sacred words! And their resting place was marked!"

I snort in derision. "You would listen to the priests about anything concerning souls? I myself arranged the rites being performed." He strikes my cheek and it lands, snapping my head back.

"You had no priest! And you killed the one who came to us! How could you possibly have performed it properly?"

Licking my lip, my eyes hone in on his, and I drop all pretense.

"And whose fault is that?" I demand, swinging at his chin, but missing.

"Yours."

"You're a fool, Nippa. What should I have done? Left their bodies to rot under the sun and be taken by scavengers?" When I swing, I catch his nose, and it crunches. Grunting, he steps back, cupping his nose. I advance to kick him in the gut.

"If you had allowed us to turn back and visit the grave, the priest with me could have *done* something!"

"If we had done as that priest had said," I pause to swipe sweat from my brow, "his soul would surely have been doomed. I saved his soul."

"You have been corrupted, Duwa. So now I serve the priesthood.."

"And when I'm king?"

He snorts derisively. "You shall never be king." I shiver at the finality of his tone. "You have no idea the enemies you have and the lengths they shall go to prevent your crowning and ascension." Slowly, I nod.

"And so, my *brother*," I spit the word at him, returning the unkind gaze he'd levelled me with. "You've joined my enemies and now you're a warrior of the faith? A little piece in the game of priests? I always thought you were smarter, Nippa, but you're eating their poisoned rhetoric without a second thought as to the grave effect of it."

Nippa hisses through his teeth. "You openly mock the gods if you slander their mouthpieces."

"I do not mock the gods. The *priesthood* does this by using abstract omens and portents to suit their narratives."

Nippa shakes his head. "You condemn yourself with every word you breathe."

"So be it. It is the truth, and if Kammara thinks he can usurp my throne through his daughter, he's got another thing coming."

"And you openly shun the divine queen?" He laughs in shock.

He moves to strike, but I block the blow with my forearm. Snatching his wrist, I yank him in close and send another blow into his belly that leaves him wheezing, and I don't allow him the chance to recover. I rain blows down on him, all restraint having vanished, and it's all he can do to cover his head. Rage like nothing I've ever felt floods me. Bitter with betrayal and hurt, my strength is at an all-time high.

Briefly, I wonder if the feeling is channeled through the goddess of death—this anguish, sorrow, and wroth, is a snapshot into how Lelwani feels. If it is, a sympathetic ping for her hits me hard as my fist connects with flesh. Nippa goes down with a grunt, and when my gaze falls upon my fist, a small, snaking trail of blood runs over my fingers from where I'd broken Nippa's nose earlier.

The horn blows again signalling the end to the event.

"Very well," the king declares. "Well fought, well fought. I shall now turn your attention to our high priest who has made communion with the gods and been shown the gods favour."

"Your Grace," the high priest says, bowing low. His voice grates on my ears. There is, in truth, nothing wrong with his voice, but just knowing it is his makes my gut and fists both clench. "After much deliberation, the gods have seen fit to declare the ranking thusly. In first place, Zuwasa. In second place, Pasaduwa. In last place," his eyes flick to me with triumph, "Haduwas. The challenge set forth by the gods was to land a blow to the opponent on the crown of the head for that is where the gods live. Through their divine directive, we have all seen the speed at which Zuwasa met this condition. Haduwas must not have been told the objective by the gods for he did not manage a single blow to the crown in the entire round. Therefore, he is in last place. In this order now, we shall proceed to the throwing of the stones."

Nippa had gotten back up during the speech, but as he left with the other two guards, he had nothing but hatred in his eyes. Servants carry the three stones, each rock approximate in their size, though judging by the look on the servant's faces, they are, perhaps, not all the same in weight. A line is drawn in the sand, and with the statue of the goddess at our backs, we are marched to our starting places where our stones are already in formation for us. Zuwasa is directed to the left, I to the right, and Pasaduwa to the centre.

"To prevent advantage, our princes shall all throw at the same time," announces the high priest as we settle in. Eyeing the polished ball between my feet with a frown, I glance at my brothers who both shrug.

"By the honour of the sun goddess and her consort the storm god, I hereby insist the second festivity commence. Pick up your stones." In unison, we bend and retrieve our stones, and I grunt with effort. Studying my brother's expressions as they consider the weight, I notice no tells in their faces, though Zuwasa's muscles don't bulge. With furrowed brows, Pasaduwa tosses it between his hands with confusion. Even still, my strength seethes through me making me hot and slightly irritable, although the latter could simply be the result of Nippa's collusion with the high priest and the smug face the priest sent me presently.

"The rules are simple. From where you stand with your toes at the line, you shall cast your stone forward from your shoulder."

It's too easy. The weights must be different. Mine is the heaviest which means I'm at a disadvantage in distance. They've given me a faulty stone in the hopes that I shall not surpass the advantage of my brothers' stones, twice—possibly thrice lighter.

This is no contest. It is a rigged pageant, a showing to the populace to publically shame and disgrace me to try and sway the populace who has always been heavily in favour of me.

The reality of my situation truly dawns on me, the fact that they may very well succeed in usurping my throne by fraudulently citing "the gods" as their source of power, just as I'd suggested to my father. I can't see his face, but I wonder if he thinks upon my words too. My wroth turns icy. No longer is it explosive, bursting forth like a mountain of fire. Now, it is creeping and cold, bringing everything into fast focus.

With the stone at the ready upon my shoulder, when the horn blows, I send it flying. Comically, my brothers' balls fall short, even with the advantage of far less weight behind them. Mine, however, lands, bounces, and then rolls and rolls and rolls. It cuts through the shocked bystanders who move out of the way as it approaches before stopping in the middle of the mob.

Turning to face the priest, ecstasy coursing through me, I falter at his glib expression. He is...pleased by this outcome. Dread sinks in. While my ball had gone on and on, both my brothers' stones had stopped no more than two bodies' length from them. The sand before my brothers is deep, but as I look in front of me, it barely covers the lines in the stone floor.

The high priest holds his hands high awaiting silence to destroy it with his pronouncements. "The gods have spoken once again, as clearly to my ears as glass is to eyes. To rule, a king must always be in proximity to the gods. The divine relationship between king and god is the pillar of our kingdom's wellness, wealth, and stability. To shun the gods is to shun our people. Therefore, it is the opinion of the gods that Zuwasa wins, yet again, for his stone is closest in proximity to that of the statue of the goddess. It is a clear sign of her favour.

"Again, it is plain to see, our Prince Haduwas is not in the favour of the gods. His stone lies in darkness and shadow, and ill omen to be sure. He's been led astray, and if allowed to rule, he'll bring about our ruin, isolation, and fall from divinity. We shall lose our connection to the sun and the rain, doomed instead to be in communion with only death and destruction.

"Heed me, my people—my brethren—Zuwasa is favoured by the gods for the title of Crown Prince. For the final test, the princes shall throw spears. No doubt, the gods shall view the outcomes similarly as they have thus far."

No doubt, I think darkly, finally realizing the extent of this forged contest, rigged by a predetermined winner. No matter how I play, the priest shall smear my name. He clearly wants Zuwasa to rule, notably because he is young and naive, but also because he is reckless and has no desire to truly rule. He is exactly like my father, an ornament and nothing more, with excessive appetites which can be controlled by the priests. I cannot be controlled, and therefore, I am dangerous to the priests because their newfound power would be stripped away. Zuwasa is uniquely unsuited to the role.

Meanwhile, Pasaduwa, while he wouldn't be a bad king, would not be a good king. His desire, though he has never said it out loud, is to travel—to explore the world. He cannot do that if he's forever on a throne. What is power if you can not exert your will? There would be no power for Pasaduwa here.

I am the only one who can do this. I have both the head and heart for rule. I understand the intricacies of ruling and I care about the needs of the people. I am responsible, able-bodied and able of mind and spirit. My brothers would put the crown in ruin.

It is this knowledge that gives me the strength not to throw my spear into the high priest's ample belly which grazes upon the crown's resources as though it were his own. With my father his puppet, he practically is, and yet, somehow, I am the only one to see it.

The three servants who had brought the stones over now bring the spears. Each decorated with a different coloured tassel. From Zuwasa's, a red tassel, from Pasaduwa's, a blue, and from mine, an ominous black.

Grasping the spear, I wonder exactly how this will be judged. Will it be about the target, or something symbolically asinine instead seeing as Kammara seemingly has a gift for the contrived? We do not wait long for the explanation, vague as it is.

"For the final task, our princes shall throw the spears, one at a time this time. Prince Zuwasa shall begin followed by Prince Pasaduwa...and so on," he says, omitting my name and title entirely. "In the cleared space," he indicates the sandy patch leading to a temple I have never entered, "each shall direct their spears and throw. Only the gods know what shall be deemed an ideal throw."

When he finishes speaking, the horn sounds, and Zuwasa, spear in tow, steps forward. Before he throws, he sends me a confused stare as if wondering what I've already figured out: why is he winning, and how? The priest had spoken of divine connection, but Zuwa didn't have a religious bone in his body by any stretch of the imagination. For show as a prince, he has of course perfected the art of appearing pious, but that iss all it is.

Finally turning, he holds the spear, just as I had taught him, and eyes the distance of the general target. There is nothing specific to aim for, so Zuwasa's guess was as good as mine—in fact, with the trends displayed, he can truly do no wrong. Lining himself up, he takes three large steps back from the line before racing forward and hauling the spear.

It arcs high in the air, nearly grazing the stone ceiling high above us, and I do not think he intends to do this because his curse is audible. Pasaduwa smirks before sending me a grin, one which I only half-heartedly return. The spear descends rapidly and clatters on the stone where the sand is not so deep. Pasaduwa goes next, and his throw is smoother and goes further than Zuwasa's, though that doesn't necessarily matter.

Sighing, I take my place. Testing the spear's balance, there is nothing off-kilter or unfair in the design of it, so I shrug, hoisting it high by my ear. Several paces behind the line, I take a deep breath and go. With as much grace as I can muster, I throw the spear higher than Pasaduwa and further than Zuwasa to hedge bets—a hunch which pays off.

The horn blows for the final time for these trials, and the high priest and his brethren amassed around the hole in the ceiling clap politely. Briefly, I catch Idari's gaze, and he's never looked more worried. The crowd moves, blocking my view of him, and he does not reappear.

Kammara makes a grand show of communing with the gods with his eyes shut, chin tucked, and hands clasped at his chest. I sincerely doubt he is doing anything but deliberating if there is a way he can put me in last place without making it obvious to even the citizens what he is doing. He must come to the conclusion he can't because the sour expression tells me everything. No matter what, I am in second place for this round.

"As I said before," the high priest declares at last, "Prince Zuwasa is the chosen of the gods. In this round, the gods were looking for how high the spear went in the air rather than the distance or direction. They foresaw the respective height of the spears as a symbolic glimpse into the heights each prince shall reach in their lives.

"In a surprising turn of events, Prince Haduwas comes in second place in this round leaving Prince Pasaduwa in the last place, though it must be noted it is not enough to raise Prince Haduwas from last place overall. For the cheese fighting attempt, the order remains Prince Zuwasa, Prince Pasaduwa and finally, if the other princes fail in the objective, only then does Prince Haduwas have a final chance to prove himself worthy of the crown." His tone indicates how unlikely that seems to him.

Sneering, I watch the same three guards approach again, and together, they form a barrier to the wheel of cheese. As they do, Kammara provides the crowd with further instructions.

"Each Prince shall have a chance in descending order provided the preceding prince fails. The time allotted shall be determined by how excited the gods are by the spectacle."

My scowl increases with this information. It, of course, means my time shall be cut short while Zuwasa will be given an egregious amount of time to fulfil the task. It also means the guards are absolutely in league with the priesthood—that they'll go easy on Zuwasa to ensure themselves and their makers a victory. So much for the warriors being in father's control...unless my father means for this, but somehow, I do not believe that to be the case.

Additionally, the winner will greatly endear themselves to the citizenry for it is the privilege of the winner to distribute the cheese personally to every man, woman, and child in attendance as a blessing from both the gods and the crown.

Standing in silent vigil as my brother steps up to take his turn, I tamper down my anger. To place blame with Zuwasa would be unfair. The high priest and his ilk are the true problem. There are no weapons, so I wonder how much Zuwasa wishes he had his bronze dagger at the moment. It was a gift to him when he'd left our settlement, and it was always his weapon of choice. He'd once confided to Pasaduwa who then relayed the information to me that Zuwasa admitted to feeling naked without it with him. Apparently he slept with the thing below his pillow, much to my and Pasaduwa's amusement. In times like these, though, perhaps I should do the same.

Presently, Zuwasa stands tall and regards the obstacle before him. It isn't complex, but is challenging for the simplicity of it. The odds, while unfair, are not impossible if you use the formation against them, picking them off one by one.

Musicians line the walls creating an echo effect within the enclosure as the games come to a head. Watching my brother, I never want him to truly fail, but the baser part of me is in control; I want to do what I was born to do. For my entire life, I've been trained to be king. For this to be happening at all is evidence enough of the fraudulent hold the cult of Arinna had over the monarchy. The role of my father in all of this troubles me greatly. Whether he truly believes Kammara or if they are in league together, hatching plans remains to be seen, but with the marriage to the priest's daughter, it's difficult to ascertain the truth of it. So enmeshed are they now that they are seemingly becoming one entity, something that cannot be allowed to happen.

So lost in my thoughts am I that I scarcely see my brother's defeat. It brings me to joy to watch as two fight him off while Nippa remains dutifully guarding the wheel of cheese. It is only because I am watching Nippa so closely that I see it. The sand shifts ever so slowly, a small, cresting current surfing below the surface towards Nippa. Squinting, I try to sharpen my focus, and when I do, I curse.

"Nippa!" I shout, catching his startled attention. "Viper behind you!" He scoffs, not believing me, but several people spot it too and gasp in horror. When corroborated by others, he swings around, causing the viper to emerge from the layer of sand veiling it. Cursing, Nippa stumbles back, trying to keep the snake at a distance while trying to still protect the wheel of cheese.

Zuwasa flees. His terror of serpents is not well-known, so if the planted serpent was a trick of Kammara's to provide Zuwasa with an easy opening to steal the cheese, it was a grave miscalculation...for him. I fear no creature more than I fear man.

Lifting an eyebrow at Pasa, he shakes his head vehemently. "I don't tangle with serpents."

"It's just a viper," I say, shrugging, and he scoffs.

"Growing up, it was always whispered that you threw snakes out of your cradle, and I wouldn't have believed it if it weren't for the fact that you've always been fearless."

"What's there to fear?"

The chaos of my brother Zuwasa's flight and the guards congregating around the snake without weapons prompts the high priest to try and salvage the situation.

"It seems our champion has failed. Next, it is Prince Pasaduwa's turn to steal the cheese of the sun goddess, for only a hero favoured with her blessing can achieve such a feat."

Pasaduwa clears his throat before sending me a look. "I concede my right to the title of Crown Prince. I forfeit this challenge. May my eldest brother, Prince Haduwas, prove himself more than equal to the task."

To the credit of the priest, he hides his panic and anger well. "Very well. Prince Haduwas." He stretches out his hand, and while the guards, Nippa in particular, tries to tear their attention from the viper, a few more spring up.

No more than a foot and a half in length, they are not large specimens, but what they lack in size they make up for in ferocity. The behaviour is most bizarre. Fairly timid creatures in nature, they are known to attack only when provoked.

Stalking forward, I prepare for a fight, but none comes. The guards are far more concerned with the vipers than they are of me. Nippa can only glare as I stroll right through the path set before me. The snakes barely glance my way, focused entirely on the guards. There is something...preternatural about it. Atop the wheel of cheese, another viper is coiled, basking in the ray of sunlight striking through the hole in the ceiling. Lazily, it lifts its head to stare at me, but it neither hisses nor makes a move to attack. It simply regards me casually. I approach, unperturbed by its presence. Snatching its body, close enough to the head to prevent any unintentional bite, I fling it away from my prize towards the guards who shout and flee, seeing as I have won the challenge. Not bothering to watch them go, I seize the wheel and lift it above my head in victory.

The three male servants who had been in charge of the weapons now approach to prepare the cheese for dispersal. I know I should feel victorious, yet all I feel is dread.

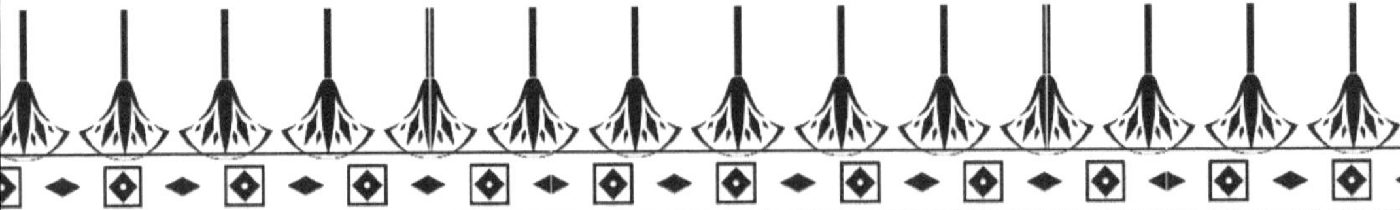

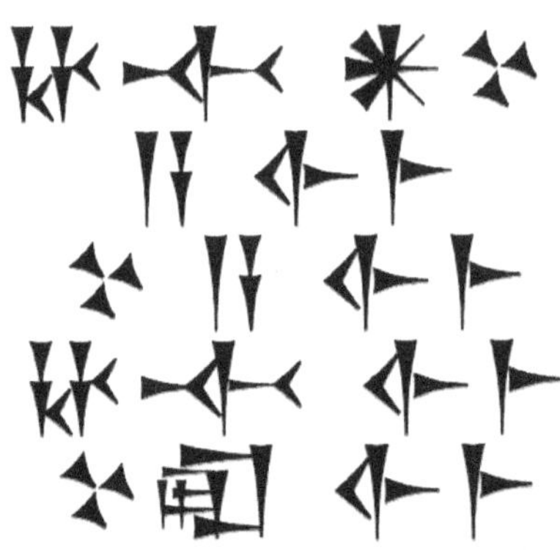

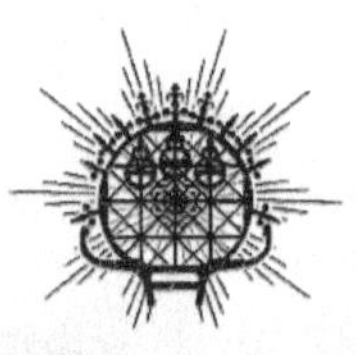

The lower realm is her dwelling.

No sun reaches within it.

It is as it has been set.

The root endures there.

IX TABLET

THE FEAST

Soothing melodies of string and reed flute circle the room, cutting through the chatter of the royal banquet hall. At the centre of the raised table, my father. I sit in the honoured spot at his right, and further along by order of birth, my brothers and lastly, my sisters. To my father's left, court officials, dignitaries, and the high priest and his ilk. Along each side of the room, great tables form a U, filled by the heads of households with wealth, title, or both. The tables are so stuffed that each man brushes shoulders with the next. Servants of the royal household circle the room waiting for glasses to fill while the musicians play for our pleasure—though no one seems to be listening to the lyre and flute. Behind us, lined up against the wall, the entirety of the royal guard—Nippa included. His stormy eyes met mine once before darting away as I entered the hall, but I can feel the weight of his eyes upon my back even now.

My father nudges my foot under the table. "I did not think you would be right," he murmurs with his glass by his lips to cover his mouth. "They nearly succeeded in passing you over."

I lift my glass to respond. "Indeed. Someone should have made Kammara aware of Zuwasa's deadly fear of snakes. Shame." My father's mouth twitches. He places his goblet on the table, hard enough he gets the attention of the high table, and when he stands, he claps once to garner the attention of the room.

"Welcome!" The lyre and flute taper off into silence. "We celebrate the official naming of the Crown Prince! Prince Haduwas succeeded in the trials set before us by the gods. It is a momentous occasion, one that promises a fecund future for us all. We will proceed with the breaking of bread."

Two servants enter the hall, one with a loaf of einkorn, its flavour no doubt nutty and rich, and the other with a great bowl. In order, they approach the head table to stand in a line before me. Without speaking, I stand, slowly, as does Kammara who speaks for the whole room to hear. "We consecrate this bread in honour of the sun goddess of Arinna and her consort, the storm god Tarḫunna. Let the prince crumble the loaves so we may bless them and eat it with Her imbued will." The board with the bread and the bowl are placed on the table in front of me.

Reaching out to retrieve the first loaf, I deliberately break the bread in half, offering my own silent prayers to the goddess before breaking off pieces enough for the whole room and deposited into the awaiting bowl. With unhurried steps, the high priest waves the servants off as he rounds the table to pick up the bowl with his fingertips, and raise it above his head in presentation to the goddess who is saying goodbye for the day as the light dwindles on the horizon. Meeting my eye, his mouth twists as he places the first piece on the wooden plate in front of me. He moves to the king next, and then down the entire row on both sides. The lyres and flute pick up their melodies again, but this time it has shifted. The tone hints at something out of reach, something ominous.

The scent of caraway and sweat fills the room, coasting on the flowing sounds of gentle murmurs and soft melodies. Cloying perfumed oils clash in the room and the faint tang of smoke from the offering to the gods mixes to produce a truly pungent room. There are bells on the swooping toes of Kammara, and they jingle with every step as he makes his way back to his seat, though he does not make a move to sit down. Instead, he lifts his own piece of bread into the air. "The gods have breathed their essence into this bread. We eat it so we may share in their wisdom, their power, and their strength." At once, everyone picks up their piece of bread to receive the blessings of divinity. The piece is little more than a collection of crumbs, and my throat aches with suppressed laughter at the knowledge the high priest had gone out of his way to give me the ugliest, smallest piece. With an amusement I cannot shake, I chew the bread slowly, relishing in the nutty, rich flavour of the einkorn.

Another round of servants enter the room, this time armed with bowls. The soup placed before me possesses an oily sheen which catches the dying light. Peering discreetly at my father's bowl, I note his appears identical. The sheen is therefore not likely that of poison, though, truth be told, poison could still be present. In fact, eyeing Kammara over the edge of my glass, it is with great effort that I allow my shoulders to fall back to their resting place when I see the glint in his eye. Or perhaps it is simply the candle light casting his eyes into something manically bright. Paranoia churns in my belly, a seething, frothing tumult which desires freedom. It would be very easy to blame the cooks if I were to keel over at my own inheritance ceremony. I force myself to pick up the bowl—which feels cold in my hands despite the steam rising from its carved interior.

The room falls into silence as they watch me, and with trembling hands I hope no one can see, I bring the rim to my lips and drink deeply. Rich in a way I can hardly describe, and hot despite the cool stone bowl, I gulp it down until I find lentils, onion, and carrot alongside various herbs suspended in the broth. The room in unison lifts their bowls to enjoy their soup as well, and as quickly as my bowl had arrived, it is empty again as I scrape the final bite with my carved spoon.

The hall is silent of speech, but the noise of the music, eating, and scraping of wood on stone grates upon something in my soul. All I want is the peaceful dark quiet of my chamber. I had very quickly accustomed myself to solitude in my room, finding it refreshing rather than lonesome. Too many people, too many opinions, too many schemes to feel at ease here. Tossing a casual glance to my right where my siblings sit, Pasaduwa looks relieved and confused while Zuwasa looks ashen and forlorn. Meanwhile, my sisters, one being my elder while the rest are younger than my own Idari, are quiet with gazes on the table as though the grain direction was the most fascinating thing in the world. As though sensing my gaze, Hestuwa, my elder sister, wipes her mouth with a cloth and mouths something at me, but I can't make it out. She tries to communicate with her eyes, but it's a language I do not know. It has been too many years since we'd conversed, and though her eyes hold knowledge, to my sorrow, I am unmatched to the task.

As the night progresses, the room grows dark and further rituals and ceremonies are followed; and yet, for the majority of the night, I fall deep into my own clouded thoughts. The Men of the Bronze Bowl distribute beer, and then more wine is presented to me by the chief of the guard, showcasing my integration and oversight of these different units of the city. At last, my father stands and the hall falls silent. He gestures for me to stand, and guiding me, he brings me to the front of the dais and bids me kneel. With a look of pride, he smiles at me and then the room at large. The stone bites into my knee, but I show no sign of my discomfort as my father retrieves something from the table at the side of the room in a brilliant chest with hammered copper rays, beaming from the golden emblem of the priesthood.

Without the aid of a servant, he grips the handles of the chest himself, hauling it to his seat of honour before opening it with his back to the rest of the room. Inside, a thin band the width of my head that he presents with a raise of his hands. "The crowning of the heir," my father booms. The room swells with breath as every head turns to see this moment, and with a stilted breath of my own, I incline my head to receive it. The metal is cold upon my brow, a vice encircling my head with the most weight I've ever held. "Prince Haduwas. Rise."

I rise, slowly, smoothly, and when I meet my father's eyes, he nods before addressing the room once more. "And now, the Crown Prince must be blessed in the temple of Arinna and given the goddess's blessing. Our high priest will guide the prince and show him the way." Alarm floods me, but I bow despite my rampaging heart and rise again to meet the eyes of the priest whose expression instills only dread.

Rougher than necessary, hands grip my arms, leading me from the hall. With a raised eyebrow, I turn to face the guard who had grabbed me, and I'm almost shocked to see it isn't Nippa. When the guard sees my expression, he lets me go, but his expression is not a kind one.

"Keep moving," the guard mutters. I sneer at him, but say nothing. Flickering sconces lead the way through the halls and through the courtyard, blanketed by the early evening and a chill seeps into my skin. I had not yet seen the temple of the sun goddess, but if I had to make a wager, I'd wager it's the building that is even larger than the palace, looming closest to the mountain.

The walk is silent, and I keep up, endeavouring to not give them any reason to be arbitrarily punitive. The steep steps of carved stone lead up to an entry terrace high above us, and as we begin the ascent, the sound of uneven breath echoes around me by the halfway mark, something that almost stops me in my tracks. How can the guard be winded by some mere steps?

It makes me want to sprint up the stairs to make an example of them, but I resist the urge and instead allow my features to fall into a pleasant expression as we near the top. The priest is the first to reach the top, and when he whirls around, I almost smirk because I can imagine just what he sees: the royal guard panting and sweating with effort while I walk up the steps like I'm on a pleasant stroll in the gardens.

Kammara turns around and strides through the open terrace to enter the temple of his patron. Bypassing the struggling guards, who had likely been doing nothing but standing around, I follow Kammara into the atrium. It glows within with inexplicable light, and though my mind tells me it's the hundreds of candles, my soul is not convinced. It feels like the resting place of a goddess. Mouth parting, I take in the vast room, the candles sweeping across the floor in a long aisle, the stone pillars supporting the high, vaulting ceiling, and of course, the iteration of the goddess on the raised floor, deeper inside the mountain. Fashioned from bronze, her image takes on the flickering lights of the candles and braziers, and even in the night, it appears as though her skin, her hair, her eyes glow.

"You feel her," Kammara says, observing me with a tilt to his head. I nod, no snark or tension in my body as I agree with him.

"I do."

"This way," he says, frowning at me, and he casts his eyes back at the royal guards who had stopped at the entry way to prevent anyone from coming in. With a sweep around, his priestly garb arcs with him, brushing my shins, and I follow without hesitation. The candles frame the way to the statue of Arinna, but before we get close, he picks up a stray candle and cuts through a pathway to the left, between two stone pillars, making no move to check if I follow. The turns are disorienting, and if I had wanted to escape, I'm not entirely certain I could replicate the dizzying pathways and corridors he leads me through until at last, we stand in a chamber which overlooks the city below.

"It's a sheer drop," Kammara says as he lights the room with the candle in his hands. "Don't be entranced by the view." I want to say something sharp, but I refrain. It doesn't feel like something that should be said in a place like this. Indeed, Kammara seems a different person here in the temple of his patroness. "You have a great task ahead of you. A task your father himself had to do before he was truly king." I raise my brows, but say nothing in response, waiting for him to lay the cards down. "As you know, the goddess is our patron deity here. She is mother to all things good. But, she has another side. The side which disappears during the day to be our guide at night."

"Guide?" I ask, not following.

"Into the earth."I shudder, and he nods, catching the movement. "Yes. It is a chilling aspect—so devoid of the light we're so accustomed to seeing in her. And yet, it is her in all her glory."

"You say I have a task," I say, redirecting the conversation.

"Indeed. You must first show that you are blessed by the goddess. After you have proven this, you must venture into her lands to retrieve a relic of her domain. It's different for every person."

"My father was the first king among you. This must be a very new tradition," I drawl, but he shakes his head.

"Ah, but it the oldest of traditions, from the Sumerians before us. Your father tells me you are well versed in Sumerian texts."

"The ones which have survived, yes." My fingertip circles my thumbnail, putting pressure on my cuticle as I try to understand the meaning of this conversation. "And what will I do with such a great gift?

Return it here?"

"Yes," Kammara says simply. Weaving the threads together, I try to fit the pieces together. Such a gift could not be allowed into the hands of the priesthood who would, no doubt, abuse it. "We have a great library here. I'm sure it would be of interest to you." He turns his back to me as he continues to light the candles. "You must first be ritually pure. After that, you must ascend to the roof and watch the path of the moon until she rises again. If you can lay there all night without moving, you have earned the right to walk her passage."

"That's it?" I ask, and he smiles.

"It's not as easy as you would imagine. Time will seem to stop, each minute will feel an hour, and every second an age. You must not move, not for thirst, not for appetites, not for relief."

"Then I shall not move."

At the doorway, more priests file in, some carrying pitchers of water, others carrying implements I know all too well. Hiding my grimace, I straighten as I await instruction from the priest. He turns and smiles. Another carries a box.

"We shall see. Come," he says, taking the box from the hands of his disciple. "Follow me." There are no windows further into the room, but the floor is covered in sand, and the blazing torches cast the room in an orange glow. The priest reaches into the box quickly, snatching something within to toss it in the corner.

A horned viper hisses, shuffling away with undulating, sliding motions to burrow itself in the sand, but I see its eyes and head protrusions still. Kammara claps his hands. "The gods have spoken! Indeed, you shall leave at the next opportunity. If the snake had fought back, it would have been a clear indication to hold off, but it burrowed into the earth—as you must do, Haduwas. It is an excellent omen. You will leave at first light."

He steps closer to me, and plucking my newly acquired band from my forehead, he clicks his tongue. "You shall get this back if you succeed. And not before. Now," he says, his eyes feverish, "into the cleaning chamber."

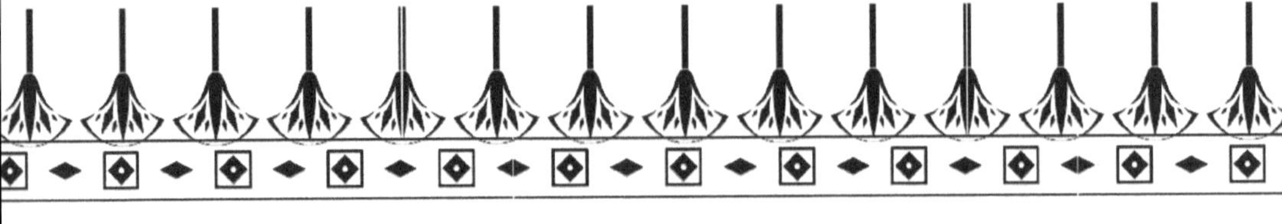

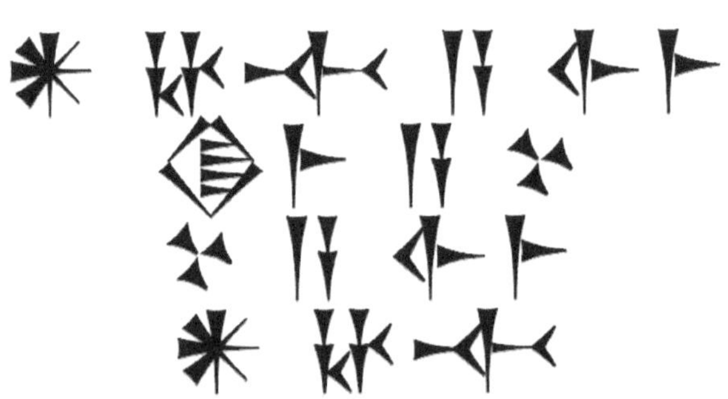

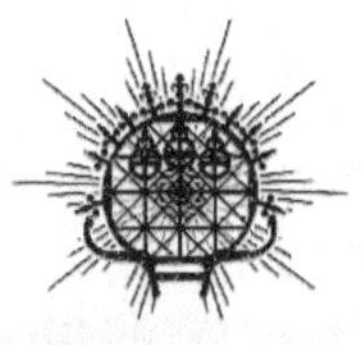

Affliction comes into her realm.

Storm and turmoil gather there.

Her land is formed in suffering.

Yet it stands.

X
TABLET
SCOURED BY THE MOON

The moon hangs low in the sky, full and bright. My skin weeps from the brutal, efficient regiment the priests had forced me to endure, and my smarting skin from the whipping of branches to "purify" me pulses uncomfortably.

Alone, I lie on a flat overhang on the roof of the temple, awaiting the return of the goddess to the sky above. From the vantage, I can see the entirety of the city, see the river wrapping around the southern border and the great plains spreading out beyond. The moon hangs low in the sky, and at my head and feet, potted jars of beer and wine, the libations intended to curry Arinna's favour as I shiver and endure the rough stone beneath my skin. I had not been afforded so much as a thin layer of cloth. My flesh is exposed to the skies, and a chill seeps into my bones. I dare not move, though my skin in particular weeps for relief.

The priests had not been gentle in their ritual cleansing. First, had been the water, slightly too hot, scalding, but forgivable under the pretense of ritual and the scrubbing with a mixture of oil and ash. Next had come the two rounds of scraping with more oil, the tool digging in mercilessly. Then came the whipping from the plucked branches, and even now, I can feel the welts upon my skin, but I hadn't made a sound. The priest's face had been stony as ever, but somehow I knew he was displeased; he wanted me to break, to complain, to give voice to my pain, but I kept it locked down. The icy water had been unpleasant too, dumped over my head with no warning, and finally had come the smoke, more of that fragrant smoke my father had called myrrh. I was no more fond of it this time than I had been for the first, and even when I held my breath, it cloaked me as it was intentionally wafted in my face. Fighting coughs, I'd been pushed through the halls, naked and shivering, still wet, and guided up through another antechamber which connected to steeper stairs than even to the entrance of the temple. At the top, I'd been left with vague instructions, and yet they were clear: settle myself between the pots and loaves of bread, and do not move.

The stars are bright tonight in a way I seldom appreciate. Kasku, the shining star, our god of the moon, who once fell from the heavens to land in a common street, now stares back at me after his restoration to the skies; whether it is my own internal strife or a feeling passed onto me by Kasku, my limbs seek freedom, movement. Beyond anything, I want to stand, stretch, *run*, and yet I cannot. Frustration laces each of my muscles as they bunch, and when I return by gaze again to the moon god, I wonder what he thinks about the world and those who dwell within it.

By my face, the scent of the two loaves of bread, enhanced with nuts and caraway seeds, floats to my nose. Had I not already eaten the oily soup, surely I would not have succeeded in my task. Regrettably, the little bowl of soup had done little to staunch my hunger, but having gone so long with sparse meals, I struggle to persevere.

Breath unsteady, I fling my desires away, and when I breathe out, I find it does get easier as I focus on the rhythmic drawing up of air—so much so, in fact, that I forget entirely about the smell of the food before me. Eyes closed, I block everything out and continue to focus on my breath, steady under the direction of the moon. Images bloom in my mind, and though my eyes are closed, somehow, the moon is still visible with his silvery light piercing into the heavens above. I am like a bird, soaring high through the night with the mountain and the temple stretching before me. I soar across my city towards the sweeping, steep steps, then the roof, and—my eyes fly open and ahead, the gentle glide of wings flitting about on the currents of the weather gods, blessed in a way man never can be. For a moment, I had seen myself prostrate upon the cold, rough stone, which even now, leeches all warmth from me. With the loaves of bread by my head, I'd looked like the perfect sacrifice, a veritable bull with horns, laid open for the gods to do with as they would. And I had no doubts in my mind that they *would* make use of me.

My mind skirts the final words I had heard from my father, passed on through the lips of Kammara. I don't *want* to acknowledge the task set before me, don't want to accept it, and yet, tilting my head to the side, all I can see are the shadows of the bread, reaching towards me by the will of the moon. Shadows, darkness, death, things from the land below. Rapidly, the signs I'd been picking up fly through my head. First, the bronze birds which had so decidedly left their mark of death upon me by stealing my brother. Then, the dark dog which had claimed the lives of Huella and my other brothers in arms. In no uncertain terms, the goddess of the earth had been encroaching upon my life. Then, there had been the moment when I had thought of her for the slightest of seconds, but it had been enough. I had *felt* her, and from there, my fortunes had gone from bad to worse because I'd made an enemy of one of the most influential men in the city, one who could orchestrate legitimate ways for me to die in the eyes of the city, and he was sending me directly *to* her.

Whether the words had been my father's or those devised by the priest, it mattered not. I was to travel to the lands of ever-night and procure a sacred artifact, one only disclosed the moment before the trap door to the roof had swung shut. I would have to retrieve a fruit from the tree of immortality.

All the times I had prayed to the sun goddess Arinna, my prayers had been seemingly neglected—remaining unanswered. Perhaps...my prayers were in fact not able to land on her alters before they were being snatched by the goddess below. And all the snakes...

The moment the sun rose once more, I was to descend, without aid, and not deign to return unless I was successful. In one moment, the priest had won. Either I would fail in the lands of darkness and perish, rendering me not a threat, or I *would* succeed, and that fruit would be used in a way which would betray the gods themselves. I could not fail. The lives of my brothers and sisters were in danger, not to mention that of my father. Idari's face flashes in my mind too, and as I stare at the moon, I allow him to witness my grief as my cheeks itch, and my tears collect in my ears. He'd already lost his mother; I could not allow him to lose a father too, and yet, hadn't he already lost that? My failures weigh heavy in my mind, mounting with the fear of what failing in my task could wreck on my family. There was only one option: succeed.

Succeed, and weed out those who wish my family harm. To willfully allow the destruction of my family could not be a permissible option—could not be entertained. My mind bounces from one face to another—father, brother, sister, brother, sister, son, sister, and back. I see their faces shining in the moon above, and queerly, I see the face of the dog I had claimed, Sharvara, and my chest bursts with aches. I would not see any harm come to them—could not. The sky darkens, dawn nearly upon us, and Arinna begins to chase Kaska from the sky. The sky, locked in battle, one that occurs every day, hues of red, orange, and yellow chase the dark blue from the sky, and when she suddenly tears into view, her rays stretching over the mountain, I know it is time for my descent.

There is no warmth in the greeting of the goddess. She rises, and when she turns her sights upon me, there is only a bone-chilling coldness which seeps into my bones. Ignoring the stiffness of my joints and the burning pain between my shoulder blades from the seam in the rough hewn stone below me, I eye the carved tunnel into the mountain from the roof of the goddess. It is a slice through the skin of the mountain, a deep carving which plummets deep into the earth. I have been given no supplies nor weapons, and as I stare the darkness down, I resolve myself to swallow my fear, that acrid bile clawing up my throat. I do not chance a look behind me into the city—don't allow myself even a moment to second guess the task ahead of me. I take one step, then another, and before I even realize it, I am out of sight of the goddess.

XI
TABLET

PROTECTION OF LELWANI

Inside the chamber is a set of clothes. Hurriedly, I drag the trousers up my legs, and don the tunic over my head. There is still a chill deep in my bones, but it's something of a reprieve. Beside the clothes lay a pair of drawstring shoes, and I find myself grateful that the priest had at least done me the courtesy of supplying me with clothing for this task. In addition to the items worn, my warrior belt is present, as is a simple traveling cloak. It helps, and the moment I have it on my teeth cease chattering. There is no light by which to see, but the longer I stare into the cave mouth, the more my eyes adjust. Crude stairs are carved into the sandstone, irregular and steep, and it takes time to descend. By the time I can no longer see the light from above, my eyes have somewhat adjusted. The grainy walls trail beneath my outstretched fingers as small granules of the ancient structure collect on my fingertips before falling to the floor.

All that can be heard is my heart and my breath, but as I descend, I feel another's presence. "Who's there?" I call, but no one responds. I hear a rhythmic clicking noise, like something sharp clicking on stone, and with no light, it strikes a fear I can barely quell.

"I am the Crown Prince of Kuššara. I ask that you show yourself," I call out, my voice betraying none of the turmoil warring inside me. *Panting*. Quick, panting breaths from below me, and as I cock my head to the side, eyes open and seeing nothing, I rely on my ears, but they do not tell me enough. "Sharvara?" I venture, unsure how, if it was indeed my dog, he had gotten into these passages. Perhaps the priest, who had so feared him, had released him for me to bring him back to his home below.

There's a soft rumble, and when I reach my hand out, there he is. Stifling a gasp, I bury my fingers in his fur. If it had been a malevolent creature, I could have been dead already. Sharvara snorts, guiding me down with him in the lead; worry begins to creep into my thoughts.

Fear has gripped me with his taloned hands, for a good hunter does not stew in the sensation but sets it aside to do what must be done. But as fast as I sidestep one thought, another bombards me. For instance, how far down does the cavern go? And just how is one to find the entrance to the Dead? Surely no one would seek such a thing out, and yet, here I am, ever the fool dancing to the whims of my father and king.

And, upon my remembrance of my father, my thoughts turn ever darker. Surely he knows the mind of the priest he follows? If he doesn't... then possibly my father is the fool, and yet how can the king be a fool? More likely, he *does* know what the priest intends, but that would mean, devastatingly, my father wishes me dead. But this does not make much sense either as there is no guarantee my father will ever sire another child, let alone a son, and the stability of our people is paramount.

My mind goes dark with grief and confusion, and I do my best to bury it as I walk with Sharvara. His muzzle nudges my hip, and my hand finds comfort in the soft fur of his head between the ears. He barks playfully before trotting ahead, my scout. I've been here long enough that I can see the outline of Sharvara ahead of me out of the corner of my eye. His tail wags happily before me, hypnotic in the back and forth sway, and time loses meaning as I walk, and walk, and walk.

Eventually, I am able to secure my mind, but it is a battle hard-won. These questions will only be answered as I fulfil the quest, and therefore, I must proceed like the warrior and not with questions like the philosopher.

There is a time and place for both, and now is a time for nerves of steel, so I stoke them hot into the flame of my chest and beat them into submission with the hammer of my will to forge a blade of my fear.

I can hear Sharvara sniffing something, but the reach of the torch is not so strong the further I go, despite my eyes adjusting to the dark. By the time Sharvara barks in warning, I am in control of myself once again. His growl as I approach the wall lifts the hair on my neck and sends a shiver through the many layers of my clothing to settle in my bones.

Ruffling his fur as I pass, I pull up short when I feel the wall under my outstretched hand. I ignore Sharvara's quiet snarls and frown at it. Embedded within the stone is perfectly chiselled cuneiform—a sign. Pressing my fingers into the ridges of carefully carved stone, noting the shape of each relief in stone, I read it aloud with a weary sigh as my fingers catch on a sharp edge of stone, slicing my finger.

kuiš anda ešzi, apēl kuit maninkuwan ešzi
anda Arinna katte ešzi
kuiš egir-an pai, pa Lelwani kuit paiš

Sucking on my finger and cursing in my head, I return to the message again, mindful of the sharp stone. "Whoever enters here, let him know what lies within. Here, he is beneath the sun goddess of Arinna. Whoever goes further goes under the protection of Lelwani," I say out loud, and as I go to press my hand to it a third time, I find the wall is not solid, and my hand surges through the stone where coldness licks at my fingers beyond.

I step through, the stone nothing more than a false image like a desert mirage. Sharvara follows easily, not hindered by such a thing as blood sacrifice...or perhaps I had paid the price for him. As I stand on the wretched bank in darkness, I cast my shielded gaze out beyond, but I can perceive nothing.

The cavern in which I stand houses no natural scents nor sound apart from my own rapidly beating heart and whistling breath. If I had light enough to see, no doubt my breath would be visible in the air, but as it stands, I can only imagine it floating on this cold, dead air which plunges sharply into my lungs.

Sharvara presses his body into my side, but he remains silent and alert, and I wonder if his eyes can see where my own cannot. Where before his claws had made sound, he now kept them sheathed, silent on the stone. Were it not for my fingers on his head, I would not know he was moving at all.

With my right hand buried in Sharvara's fur and the other outstretched to ensure I don't walk over anything, we walk slowly forward, ever forward, and I am certain Sharvara knows I cannot see for he does not try to escape my touch so he can lead me.

There is a serpentine cavern, one which discombobulates the senses, and my sense of direction has fled from me; my gratitude for my dog's presence grows with each unfaltering step he takes forward.

At last, the passage through which we walk narrows and my hand brushes upon something cold and wet which I can only surmise is stone, and the slow trickling of water in the distance tells me the environment shifts with every step forth, though I still remain blinded by the blanket of night which is the natural state of the Under earth.

But it takes only one single step for everything to change.

Where there was darkness, blinding light suddenly appears. It hurts the eyes to behold, and I shield my eyes with my outstretched palm to acclimatize myself to the hateful, colourful brightness. Upon the air drifts the cries of suffering, of the moaning and groaning of despair. Where there was naught but stone and cold air, in the distance, a shore where hundreds of bodies mill about, each choosing a different path. Some sit, some lie down as though asleep, and still others are curled up on their sides. Many walk around in groups while the rest roam on their own; some edge towards the water while a few trail along the jagged wall, looking for an escape which shall never be found.

Sharvara pulls me aside, making for a rocky outcropping to hide behind; I don't understand how he knows to go there and why, but when I make to turn around, Sharvara bites my pants and pulls me back behind the rock. It is only just in time for me to see a figure paddling across the water towards the unsightly dead, paddling so swiftly, no current can be seen.

I duck quickly, understanding at once: I had looked upon a god of the underworld, the boatman, and he must not discover I am here. Somehow, Sharvara understands—had sensed the approach and brought us to safety. I pat his belly as he lies at my side, head on my knee as I sit down.

"Good boy, Sharvara," I say, and quietly. I can't be sure how long we walked, but it felt like a long time. Now is as good a time as any to rest, especially if we have to wait for the god to depart once more.

Perhaps an hour goes by, and still, the god of that water stands, wading through the crowd with his hand outstretched, apparently looking for those who have payment to cross. Few do. Hidden behind a wall of rock, we doze, passing the time for us to make a move across the water. With the boatman present, we are not at leisure to explore the surroundings, and, by extension, our options. With nothing to do, we wait.

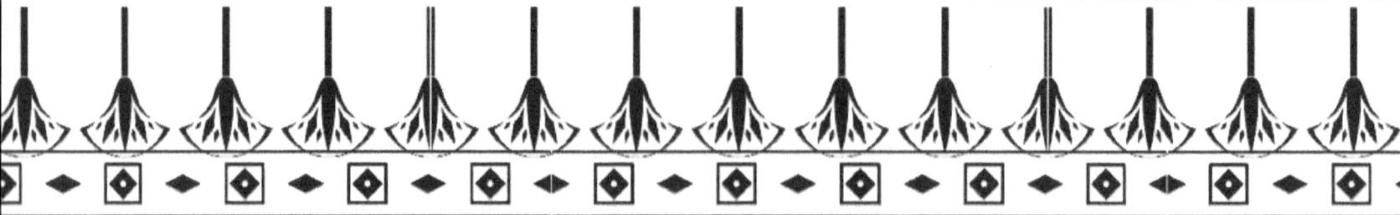

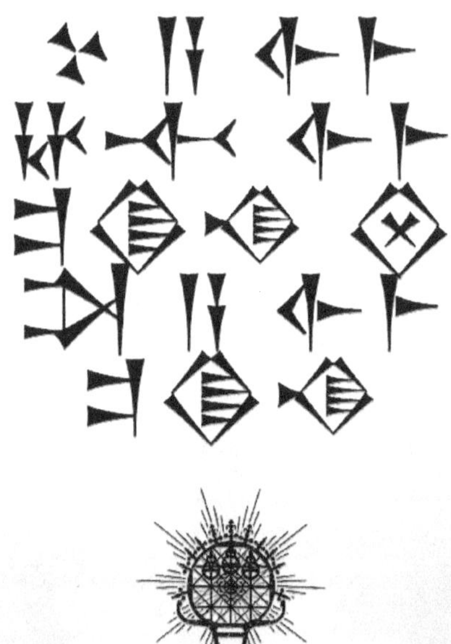

The heart of the lower realm is breached.

Its life-force is stirred.

The sickle is set in the hand.

The blade is lifted to strike.

XII
TABLET

THE RIVER OF SOULS

Noiselessly, Sharvara draws himself up to peek over the edge of the protruding boulder we hide behind—an action altogether too human. I join him, watching as a few souls congregate on the skiff before the boatman pushes them off the bank to deposit them on the other side for the ultimate judgement.

Waiting to ensure the boat was well and truly out of view, we creep out from behind the slab of obsidian, drawing towards the black shores of the dead. The wet sand clings to my shoes as we walk through it, and the fact strikes me as odd. The waters appear dead with no current or tide to speak of to dampen the granules of the beach, and yet the sand is wet as though the water levels have just retreated.

Beads of trickling water splash on the rocks as water from above finds its way down and condenses on stalactites high in the ceiling. The wailing of abandoned souls helps conceal our slow advance to the water's edge, wrapping around the right-hand side of the large lake. Keeping my hand pressed to the wall, I allow Sharvara to lead because of his sharp nose. We skirt the water carefully, taking pains to avoid it. In legends, it is a water of death, of *hate*. Sharvara growls lowly, and I pause for a moment before I smell it: a gust of sulphur coming from some natural vent in the black, rocky cliffs, hemming us in. Upon my skin it feels pleasant, but the stench is foul.

Ahead, Sharvara stops, nestled between a family of stalagmites, and turns his head to face me. He pants lightly while I crouch beside him, catching my own breath. His ears perk up as he faces the water again. Cautiously, he approaches the water, great nose sniffing, but his tail is still. He lowers himself to the damp sand, claws just a hair's breadth away from the surface.

"We shall have to swim then," I say, nodding to myself, "but it is too wide here. We have to keep going to see if it gets narrower."

Sharvara whines, but rises nonetheless and continues, his tail moving slowly again. The rough texture of the rocky wall bites into my injured hand as I carefully follow Sharvara, no doubt leaving a bloody trail on the stone face as I had done to enter this place.

Greatly disadvantaged by the lack of light as we stride away from the congregation of souls, I rely on my hands and ears to guide me. Lagging only by a few strides behind Sharvara, he sets an easy pace for me to follow, and before long we stop at an odd outcropping where the bank sharpens into a point.

My eyes adjust gradually to the darkness, and I can see just the slightest indication of water before us, evident only by the faint shimmering of distant light catching on the treacherous surface which promises death. Shedding my cloak, hiding it behind the outcropping of rock, I bury my hands in Sharvara's fur for a moment to gather my courage.

"Come on, Sharvara," I whisper as I edge toward the shore. Sand parting quietly underfoot, the frigid water soon licks the soles of my feet, even through my treated, hide slippers, and yet still, I push forward. The water claims my calves and my thighs, and then my belly as I press on, determined to see my task through.

Unseen, the slope of the bank steadily grows steeper until my feet touch nothing at all. Pitching forward, submerging my body to the neck, my lungs clench painfully as all my breath is expunged. With a sharp inhale, I attempt to ignore the cold as the lake seizes all semblance of warmth from my body, leeching me.

Sharvara passes me, trotting into the unrelenting water with little difficulty while my own teeth chatter as I tread water. Sharvara whimpers as he looks back at me. Together, we cross where the lake begins to turn into a river. The narrow passage is ideal, and yet, the current is a factor I had not considered.

The strength of the river is considerable, and with every stroke, my power seems to dwindle. Sharvara is fine, and in fact, it's as though his huffs are not from exhaustion, but rather intended as encouragement for me. Trying not to be discouraged by the distance still before me, I force myself to continue despite the onslaught of water below me trying to drag me away and despite the sluggishness settling into my aching limbs. As cold as it had been initially, the water grows warmer; the realization is enough to keep me alert. Below, a ticklish sensation on my calf shoots my heart into my throat, and I clench my eyes shut.

It's just seaweed. It's just seaweed. It's just seaweed...

The phantom feeling returns, but this time, it is firm, and it's not letting go. Thrashing wildly, I kick and pull in an attempt to dislodge the thing, but it holds on tight despite my every provocation. It pulls me under, and I suck in a short gasp of air before I am fully submerged.

Lungs on fire as I fight the overwhelming urge to breathe, I scramble for purchase, but I can't get a grip on whatever is holding me. It seems to have claws, and yet each time I reach for it, it's as though my hand passes through it.

Opening my eyes, I squint—not from trying to see in the darkness, but because it is surprisingly bright. A spirit is pulling me *down, down, down,* into the depths; the soul is pale green, and there isn't just one. Hundreds lay on the lake bed and while most are seemingly at rest, many are beginning to look up with interest.

Kicking again, using the last of my force to pull myself away, I struggle with everything I have, but it isn't enough. *I have failed my people. I have failed my father. I have failed my son.*

I am close enough to discern the faces of the souls; most have dazed expressions, vacant from their endless patronage to the rivers of death. I see hands, reaching, teeth gnashing, and still, the distance between me and the surface grows more and more distant until I can no longer tell how deep I am.

More hands reach for me, and I know I am doomed. Two hands,

then four, then countless, I am suddenly swarmed by raging bodies. The one dragging me snarls and is kicked away, and then, collectively, the group of souls around me do the impossible: they guide me back in the direction of the surface. Lungs burning, my confusion rises until I catch a glimpse of one face, then another, and my mouth parts in horror. There, among the listless, unclaimed dead, the poor souls who had lacked payment and patience alike, who had resolved to live among the river spirits, my best friend and my love. With fiercely flashing eyes and souls bared, they are brighter than the other souls who had begun to fade in the currents of time. With effort, they drag me higher and higher, fighting against the will of their brethren.

Had Nippa been right? Had I doomed them to this fate? Did the priests have the right of it? No longer do the souls of the river possess the gift of speech. Huella, frantic as she cups my cheek, tries to pat my face to get me to focus, but I cannot. Nippa's mouth moves, but I can hear nothing, and he and Huella stare helplessly as they thrust me higher. Other souls have caught on, and where I had been protected, cocooned by my chosen family, I find myself alone as they are ripped away.

But the pressure building in my lungs is too much, a ravenous fire, and at last, the water rushes in, filling my lungs and leaving me with a searing pain in my sinuses until it finally dulls and peace settles in.

High above, a dark shape disturbs the bright lights, descending fast toward me. Reaching with lethargy towards the being, my hand trails above my head in a moment of awareness. With incredible speed, the shape becomes known to me and as my blessed companion tears through the soul's grip on my ankles, I am suddenly free, but I cannot do anything with that new-found freedom for I am tired to the bone. Blinking is a feat too much for my aching body, let alone clawing my way back up to the surface.

Sharvara bolsters my ascent, dragging my listless body by the sleeve back up to the surface, where, upon breaking, I am barely conscious. Somehow, Sharvara manages to drag me the rest of the way because I feel the sandy bed and the heavy air before a treacherous cold rattles me to the bone. Pulled up high enough on the bank to avoid the turmoil of the frothing body of deathly waters, churning from the excitement of ravenous souls, Sharvara climbs on to my chest.

My eyes fly open once more when Sharvara bounds on my chest with his paws in fierce repetition. Gagging and choking, I turn my head to the side as a torrent of water dribbles from my near-dead lips. At long last, the river purged from my lungs, I cough hoarsely before rolling to my side, fingers dragging through the sand and Sharvara's fur; I grimace at the acrid blend of bile, and salt, and muck.

Focusing only upon my breath and the fact that I had so narrowly escaped death, I allow Sharvara to wiggle in beside me, providing me with such necessary warmth before succumbing to a haunted sleep where I watch my friends die and fall into the river's clutches from the banks to drown.

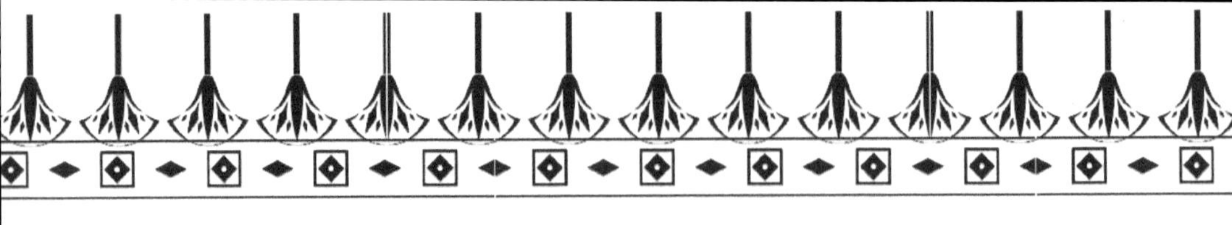

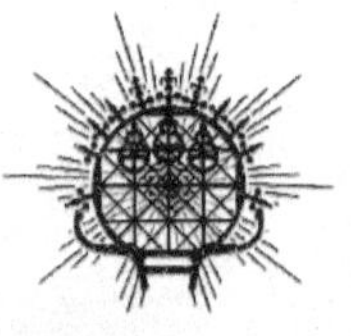

He comes in pestilence.

His sharp brother guides his hand.

The earth is made to yield.

The blade begins its work.

XIII TABLET

WALLS OF FIRE

I had heard tales of wounded soldiers who'd lost something intrinsic only to be later gifted with something else once healed—a spiritual recompense for such a sacrifice. What I had done to warrant such elevated senses, I cannot say, but to be sure, my senses are overwhelmed, even with closed eyes.

What before had only been the slight stink of sulphur is now a cloying, suffocating thing, and it does not stop there. Now, I can sense the souls from below, watching me from the depths, ravenously incensed that they had not claimed a prize in my stupidity, for this quest was in no uncertain terms, a fool's errand.

When again I peel open my eyes, everything appears sharper. I can discern droplets of water tracing grooves within the rocky ceiling high above and further still. I watch in fascination as they drip on the cavern floor, a sound as loud and obvious as speech in an otherwise quiet room. Though I can distinctly hear each rivulet, a nagging sense tells me I wouldn't have heard it prior to my brush with death.

I can see the path to the palace where dread Lelwani dwells, and see the place she likely treads over and over in her boredom in this wasteland, and further, I can see the souls who have paid the boatman's toll; they mill about looking vaguely lost as they wander and wander with no destination to reach.

Rising to my feet, Sharvara nuzzling my thigh as I do, I feel like I could hold up the weight of the world. Patting Sharvara's head affectionately, I stare hard into the water where the souls reach for me from below, but they do not breach the surface. I want to believe I had imagined seeing Nippa and Huella, but I know I had not. I want to drown in that knowledge, suffer for the pain they'd endured after improper burial, but I have to push forward.

From behind me, Sharvara's low, menacing growl sends the hairs on the back of my neck up, and, whirling around to discover the reason, I come face-to-face with a demon climbing down the rock face towards us. The distended limbs support a gangly, emaciated body, its skin dark as the underbelly of the earth with a tint of blue and grey. Matted hair hangs in clumps around its rigid face and razor-sharp teeth grin at me. It is not a tall creature, but what it lacks in size, it makes up for in its terror-inducing design. Sharp nails chink on stone as it climbs down the rock face-first, using long-fingered hands and long-toed feet to grip in its descent.

Despite my awareness of it, still, the creature approaches us, and yet again, Sharvara growls low in his throat. It is not enough of a deterrent to the creature because one moment it regards me with cold calculation and the next it launches itself at me from the wall, limbs flailing as it lands on me with a shriek.

Bracing myself for impact, I grip its bony body to send it away, but it is far heavier than it looks. Striking the ground hard, I land painfully on an outcropping of rock, and the creature attacks from above. Raining blows down on me, my adrenaline pumps so hard I can hardly feel the onslaught, try as the creature might.

Its sharp nails rake my skin and its rancid breath escapes from its gaping maw as its mouth descends to rip a chunk out of me, but before the creature can try, Sharvara clamps his teeth on the arm of the creature and throws it away from me. Gasping for breath, I scramble to my feet to face the creature again who now circles Sharvara and me. It is weary of Sharvara, but its mouth opens and closes like a fish out of water as it stares at me, and saliva drips from cracked lips and bared teeth.

It launches again; a mindless, desperate thing. This time, I don't hold back and I pummel it back to the ground. Scowling up at me, reproach in its eyes, it skulks off with a pitiful whine before returning whence he came, scaling the nearly vertical face of stone with ease. Shuddering with disgust, I try to shrug the matter off, but I still see its crazed, large eyes, desperate for flesh.

"Why did it retreat?" I ask aloud, despite knowing Sharvara cannot reply. Perhaps it retired because it realized I was alive and not among the dead of the realm? Or perhaps it was because we fought back and the creature possessed a modicum of self-preservation? The questions trouble me.

Sharvara nudges my backside in earnest, prompting me to follow the rock face around the realm. I cannot discern which direction is which, but I decide this does not matter any longer. The rules of the netherworld do not resemble that of the world above. Besides, even if I did know which direction was which, I had no way to employ that information seeing as I had not a single clue as to the direction of my objective. Sharvara seemed to know, however, perhaps my saving grace.

Without a word, I follow Sharvara's prompting and make my slow trek around the palace of Lelwani. The realm all looks the same: lots of dark stone, muggy air, sulfur deposits and vents to the world above, and looming high, visible from every direction, the Palace of Lelwani where gate after gate prevents intruders. The thought of her watching my progress as I enter her abode doesn't bode well for me. To my right, having passed the lake and river, water gurgles gently, and it's all I can hear. Not even Sharvara's breath is louder than the water, which, to my ear, does seem to be getting louder, the current growing swift as we make our way deeper into the land. Truly, it is a grim place, though, to my eyes, there is a natural beauty here, even if macabre—a deathscape.

Sharvara cuts in front of me, leading me away from the now rushing water. An archway emerges from the stony face of the wall, but a boulder stands blithely in the way. Lifting himself onto hind legs, Sharvara mimes pushing the rock out of the way with his front paws before falling back to all fours, tongue lolling as he waits for me to do his bidding.

Without hesitation, I do as he suggests. Planting my hands on the boulder, I barely push before it rolls out of the way, cascading down the slight slope before tumbling into the dread waters a little ways to my right. Before I can so much as cross the threshold, a cry echoes around me; a sound of pure exaltation followed by a choked sob. I look down to see the boulder had been meticulously placed so as to cover a recess in the ground, a pit of small proportions. Within, a man. With a stiffness that hints at the length of his stay, the man slowly stands despite the unadulterated excitement on his face.

"Oh, thank you! Thank you!" the man cries, falling to his knees before me with hands outstretched as though in prayer. "You have no idea how long I was down there."

"How long?"

"So long that even I do not know how long I was down there."

I regard the pit. There is no air flow, no water, no food. My eyes trail over the man, his bones a prominent feature on his thin body. I meet his eye, wary of the stranger. "Why were you down there?"

He shifts, avoiding my eye, and swallows hard before responding. "Because I told the truth. I was a bearer of bad news to ears who wished not to hear." When he finally looks at me, I can see the truth in his face. A voice can hide a tremor, but the eyes ring true. The man is peculiar, but perhaps it is the result of perpetual loneliness and the slow creep of madness when left entirely to one's own devices for too long. He seems pleasant enough, and if Sharvara has no problem, then neither do I.

"What is your name?" I ask the man, who even still, crouches before me, though it is likely equal parts inability to stand as it is gratitude.

"I am called Askalpusa," the man wheezes as he gorges on air. I am not certain the man is alive. If he was down there as long as he suggests... Perhaps he is not a man at all. While he is malnourished, certainly, he does not have the swollen belly of true hunger, nor the feral gaze of someone who had gone without for as long as I fear he may have been trapped there. Despite the questions I have and the gaps in my perception, I somehow trust the man.

"I am Prince Haduwas," I say after a weighted moment.

"A prince." Askalpusa gasps, bowing his head yet again. "Forgive me, for I did not know."

"Rise, Askalpusa, if you are able."

With difficulty, Askalpusa does rise. "Whatever are you doing down here? Do you understand this is the place for the dead?"

Eyeing him warily, I nod when I glance at Sharvara; I can imagine him shrugging. "I am here on a divine mission to obtain a fruit of immortality for King Karuwas, my father."

Askalpusa barks out a laugh which ends in a cough. "I see. And how do you suppose you shall accomplish this feat of folly?" I wonder at the same thing.

"However I may."

The man nods, sagely. "Very well. I'm in."

I stare at the man, who has yet to see Sharvara, but Sharvara does not react ill towards the man which bolsters my hope and drive. I briefly make introductions. "Askalpusa? Meet my hound, Sharvara."

Askalpusa, to his credit, barely blinks. "Your hound," he muses. "He's rather large."

"And loyal," I retort, a warning in my tone. Askalpusa simply raises his hands and nods.

"Do you know where you're going?" he asks, and I shake my head.

"I do not, although, Sharvara seems to know the way." Askalpusa seems to find this statement humourous, although he doesn't feel the need to explain why. I do not press him for the information. He regards me and Sharvara for a moment before taking a deep, exaggerated breath.

"Let us strike a deal: if I help you find the Sacred Orchard and help you fulfill this task, in return, you shall allow me to return with you back to the surface."

Not seeing anything wrong with the proposal, I seize his outstretched hand and shake him on it. "Very well."

Clapping his hands, he gestures beyond the boulder and the pit he'd been relegated to. "The way is that way."

“Lead the way, my friend,” I say, and he beams, clapping me on the shoulder.

Along the way, he regales me with tales of his youth, of swimming in his father’s river and a time when he spied upon a maiden in the orchard his mother tended to.

"You see, she was not meant to be in the orchard at all. I did not want to say anything to get the girl in trouble, of course, but then she ate of the sacred fruit, and I had to tell someone what I had seen, even if nothing came about it."

Upon informing his mother of the maiden eating the fruit, he was punished by a goddess and forced to remain in the hole I had found him in.

"You were punished to a lifetime in the Underworld?" I ask, confused about how he came to be here.

"Alas, that is a curse of birth, I'm afraid."

The words sink in, and it dawns on me he is of the immortal race. "Who are your divine parents?" I ask in shock.

"My father is the river flowing yonder." He points back the way we came. "You might have heard the woeful cries of the souls of the dead upon thy entrance. My mother was a tree spirit, long passed by now." He trails off, descending into memories both pleasant and painful by the look upon his face.

"So you're immortal?" I ask, and he shrugs.

"As far as I can tell. I haven't died yet." He chortles and nudges my arm. "A mortal me would have long ago perished in that cursed hole, claimed by the demon who gorges on flesh of men." I wonder then, if he refers to the crawling creeper whom Sharvara and I had fought off.

"How is your life line secured? Do you not age? Are we all not, in a fashion, nature spirits?"

"Ah," he says, raising his finger over his shoulder as he walks, "but I am a spirit of the eternal oak. Therefore," he declares, "as long as my tree remains, so too do I."

"If you're tied to the tree...what happened to your mother's tree...?" I question, and he sighs.

"Her tree was destroyed for my declaration against the maiden."

"Who was this goddess who punished you thus?" I demand, and his whole being seems to quake.

"The goddess of the earth."

"Lelwani?" I ask, and he shakes his head.

"Lelwani was the maiden. I speak of her dread mother above." I freeze in place. He speaks of a time when Lelwani was but a young maiden? When she took her place as guardian of the dead? I look at my companion anew, regarding him in a new light.

The man smiles wanly, shrugging his shoulders, and before I can give life to any further questions, he takes off at an unbelievable pace, eager to help me complete the quest to leave the Underworld. Setting aside my curiosity, I follow him, skirting the pit which had housed Askalpusa. We emerge through the archway of rock on the other side, where, to my eyes, the light seems to be ever-increasing.

"Do my eyes deceive me," I ask, "or do my eyes detect more of this infernal place the further we descend?" My query is answered in short order.

"They deceive you not. The Darkness, while perpetually existent, possesses degrees which wax and wane throughout the earth. We approach the titan Ubelluri where he holds up the weight of the world as punishment for taking the side of Kiase."

"The god lives here?" Shock seems to permanently cloak me in this temporary exile here.

"Indeed, he does."

"Why do we approach Ubelluri?" I ask, nearly tripping as I follow him even despite the increasing brightness.

"Because, my new esteemed friend," Askalpusa says, looking over his shoulder with a grin, "his daughters guard your prize." My mouth opens in wordless understanding. "You will have to trick him to grab a fruit for you. Then, once you have your prize in hand, we can leave this place, and you can claim your title and I may begin my life anew."

My stomach clenches at the idea of tricking a god—an elder god, no less. I nod, but non-committally. If the task had to be completed through trickery, I would do it; to secure my throne and the future of my people, I would do just about anything...but. *But*, if I did trick a god, he and others could punish me and my people—severely. If I went about it wrong, I would not be the only one to suffer. There had to be another way to do it.

"Up ahead is the river of fire, an open vein into the hell below, and its waters are lethal. We will not cross it, but we have to skirt it, rounding its frothing, bank of fury to get to the place betwixt worlds. You mustn't touch the flames. The waters are deadly. You will never leave this place if they leave their mark upon your skin."

"I heed you, my friend. We shall be cautious of the river of fire."

Resuming our walk, Sharvara runs ahead of me, nose turned high in the air at frequent intervals as if he smells something intriguing and seeks to find and follow it. It was all but confirmed by Askalpusa that Sharvara was a dog of death, a hound bound in service to the dread goddess of the underground—of darkness—of death. Tail wagging, he looks back to me to ensure I follow before resuming his playful inspection of the trail.

Despite the exhaustion I know I should feel, there is none to be found. At some level, this journey has already changed me, morphed me into something more than I had been. The only sensation akin to how I feel now is the moment I drank of the gods. I had seized the vine of Lelwani and ascended her divinity, soaring to heights normally barred to mortals. It occurs to me that perhaps my presence here, in her realm, has strengthened that connection and thereby, increased my capacity for strength and stamina because I easily keep up with an immortal nymph and Sharvara and my breath comes easily, even as we jog through the rocky landscape.

We run for miles, and as we traverse through the twisting path—wary, I spot more of the soul-eaters looming in crevices and cave openings above us. They do not attack, nor do they descend, but their opalescent eyes gleam, picking up on the minute light, a flickering sheen in the darkness. Like a sky of many little moons, reflective eyes guide the way through the cave system pathway, shimmering brightly only to wink out in apparent disinterest.

Ahead, I can see the frothing river of fire; its body rears up in gushing torrents to spray the bank, and small fires burn at the side as ghost grass burns before turning to little more than ash. Still, the moon-eyed demons watch, and follow us, evidently hoping for a misstep to capitalize upon.

"The river I told you about," Askalpusa warns, pointing with an outstretched finger. "Do not let its waters touch you. Not only will it be painful, but it can kill you or change you."

"Do we need to cross?" I ask, trying to see the direction, but it's unclear to my eyes. The remnant of a crumbled bridge is the only method I can see, and even then, it is a treacherous one. I'm not sure I can make the leap.

"Alas," he says, turning to face me with a grim expression. "That bridge was once whole. I do not know if we can get to where we need to go with the bridge gone."

"It's too far to leap?" I ask, and he nods gravely. "And there's no other way?"

He hesitates. "There is, but it is not in your best interest to travel that route."

I look him in the eye. "I cannot return to my father empty handed. I either succeed, or I die trying. No terrain is too difficult, and no problem is unsolvable."

"Very well." He stops and stoops to the ground. "Do you have anything I can use to show you the way? A blade? A stick?"

Before I even have a chance to pull out my blade, Sharvara is off, trotting away to find a stick. Grinning at him as he pants and sniffs at the ground, it is only a short while before he comes back bearing a sizable stick.

Askalpusa laughs and rubs Sharvara's head in thanks. Squatting, he begins to draw a map. "We are here," he says, drawing a rudimentary depiction of our current location. "The first river is behind us," he adds a line below our circle, which curves up to our right and above us, "but continues up to intersect with the river of fire ahead of us." He draws a curvy line above our position. "The location we seek is way up here." He draws another circle, but this time, it is far above the line and to the right. "You must have crossed the first river to get here. It would have been far easier if you had not." He squints at me. "Although, I suspect it has benefited you already to have crossed it, so perhaps it was wise after all."

"Are there any other important landmarks that you can remember?" I ask, and he nods.

"Here," he draws a triangle, "is a mountain. It's not visible from here because of the darkness, but it's to our right. Upon it, the great Titan Parasuwa where he is bound like I was."

"Then I shall free him too," I say, and he shakes his head.

"I strongly advise against this course of action. As grateful as I am, I am a small matter. To free a trapped god, that is to declare war on the reigning gods themselves." He draws two more lines. "You have two options from here: either we go back the way you came and you cross back to wrap around the Eastern side," he demonstrates with his drawing, "or we continue curving to the right here and hope there's a bridge intact, or a narrow enough gap to go through."

I study the drawing. I had a great deal of luck crossing the way I had, and I had only survived because Sharvara had ensured it. I don't want to press my luck with more of the Soul-Eaters or the beings in the water. I never want to touch that water again.

"What are the odds the bridge over the first river is still intact up ahead?"

He considers the question. "The bridge over the river of fire is the oldest bridge, and considering the heat, it was bound to crumble eventually. The second one? I'd say the odds are slim, but not impossible."

"Then we forge ahead," I declare. "If it is no longer there, then we shall reconvene, but I'd rather move forwards than backwards."

"Very well. The way is steep."

Nodding, I stand as does Askalpusa, and after Askalpusa returns the stick to Sharvara who chews on it with a fearsome strength, we continue on our journey. The crackling of fire is audible as we grow near, and the heat emanating off it is remarkable. Drenched in sweat, I pump my arms in time with my steps and work to keep my breath even as I match the pace set out for me. At long last, Askalpusa comes to a halt, and I see why. The bridge is intact, but calling it a bridge is generous.

"You still wish to proceed?" he asks, and I nod, though a tremor of fear thrums my heart into motion. "As you wish, my prince."

Together, we approach the bridge. On both sides, stone walls cage us in along a thin, crumbling path of stone, though wide gaps emerge on either side of the walkway with walls of flame rising to lick the stone. Steam rises, and as I peer over the edge, cautiously, I see two rivers converge in a messy tumult. Black water meets fire, and they hiss and spit at each other as they battle eternally. The effects of this war is the alternation between columns of steam and torrents of fire rising from the riverbed.

"We must time it correctly. We will sit and watch to see how long each lasts. Do not attempt to go while there is fire. Only steam. Now may be a good time to lighten the load of your pack." Settling in, the three of us observe the task at hand while we eat. There is no pattern. There is only luck. Sensing Askalpusa has come to the same conclusion, we rise.

"Who shall go first?" Askalpusa asks, and I nod.

"I shall. Should I fail, there is no sense in you attempting to go in my stead." I approach the bridge. The thinnest of walkways, I have barely a foot in width to go, and the way is far. "I shall see you on the other side," I vow, and without waiting for a response, I begin.

Behind me, Sharvara barks, but Askalpusa holds him back. It is a journey that must be done one at a time if any of us have any hopes of success.

The heat once I step onto the path is ferocious. All around me, the sweltering steam scalds my skin and under my feet, I can feel the stone's persistent thrum of power. Carefully, I keep in the centre of the path, trying not to veer too close to either side where the steam collides with the air, but it can't be helped. My elbows, feet, shoulders, and face take much abuse, scalded brutally as I make my way across—and not quickly enough. As I make it towards the centre, the heat below my slippers increases with terrifying quickness, and my scorched feet protest immediately.

The soles of the slippers smoulder at once. Hopping from one foot to the other in anguish, I take off with a sprint, stretching my stride to be as wide and quick as possible. My carefulness costs too much. The steam hisses in my ears, coiling and swirling, blocking my vision. Blinking furiously, I don't risk a quick glance to the side to see if the fire shall come. Instead, I focus on just running. I don't see anything. I only feel pain.

A shout behind me warns me of the oncoming fire. I dash, and as I do, I grow off-kilter. Wobbling, I make a wild lunge for the end of the bridge, and collapse on the other side as a burst of flame billows up from the depths, missing me only narrowly.

Heedless of my injuries, I look up to see Sharvara's tail wagging, his piercing eyes locking on mine. Whining, his paws skitter on the ground as he works up the courage to cross to my side. Moving side to side, he watches the flames lick the air, but as soon as the columns of fire die off, he takes off towards me.

Truly, Sharvara is a marvel. With caution, speed, and precision, he sprints across the bridge, and before the fires return, he is already at my side. Pummeling into me, he knocks me over in his enthusiasm, tongue licking every injury and burn he can reach. Between pats, rubs, and scratches, mixed with a gentle voice, I reassure him and settle him down as I turn my attention back to Askalpusa, who looks as frightened as I had been.

"You do not have to cross!" I shout, but I wonder if he can hear me because he does not respond. "I shall continue, and come back this way!"

He must not hear my words, elsewise, he ignores them because I watch him take a sprinter's position down low, fingers perched on the rocky floor as he awaits the return of the steam. The flames recede, and he's off, but it was a false retreat of flame. It returns with a mighty gust of flame, and Askalpusa screams in pain before crumpling to his knees. Before my eyes, he shrinks, arms and legs receding, and his colouring shifts, darkening, and then his skin molts, revealing feathers, wings, and ominous, yellow eyes.

With a shrill cry, Askalpusa, who is no longer a man, but a great bird, soars high into the air to escape the heat before diving straight towards me. Wings outstretched, he slows his flight, but he is not yet used to his form, and he too barrels into me. His beak is sharp as it collides with my chest, and with a grunt and a cough, I fall back, cradling him as much as possible to prevent injury to his wings.

Head swivelling around, his large, golden eyes stare me down, unblinking.

"You're an owl, Askalpusa," I remark, and a demoralized hoot answers me. He tucks his head under his wing as if to hide his visage from me. No longer can we communicate with language...unless. "Can you still understand me?" I ask, and the answering, pitiful coo stirs my heart. Two weak trills call back.

"Do you still seek to aid me?" Two trills. "Very well. I will do everything in my power to restore you to your true form. I promise this. In the meantime, what direction do we go?"

His head emerges from his wing, and his taloned feet dig into my forearm where the burn is. Adjusting his grip on me so his sharp claws don't scrape my newly injured flesh, he perches on my outstretched hand. Testing his wings experimentally, they flap, but he doesn't lift from my grip. Releasing him, he flies off and swoops around, arching high into the air in fascinating loops. From his vintage point, he must see much.

"Show us the way!" I shout up at him, and screeching, he does.

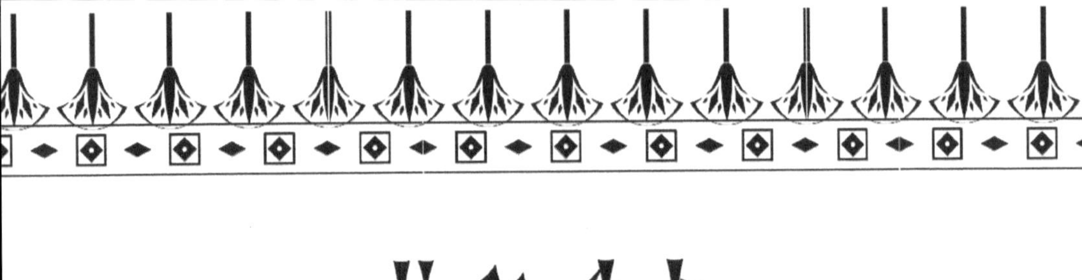

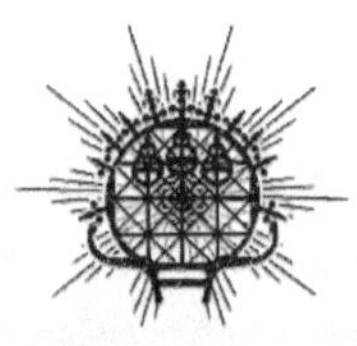

The brothers go down into the lower realm.

Life is summoned there.

The goddess of death is bound in root and bloom.

The living hand is lifted against her.

XIV
TABLET

THE ENSLAVED GOD

With Askalpusa as my flying guide, and Sharvara at my side, I easily navigate the terrain. My muscles burn with power, and my sight sharpens with every step I take towards the looming tower of unhewn rock. The path, now having passed the obstacle of the bridge, is far easier now.

The usual suspects are to be found: bats flutter about while the occasional snake slithers blithely past. Stalactites descend from above while their siblings on the ground reach high to greet them. Water drips from the ceiling unseen, splashing my head and trickling into my eyes, while mineral clusters catch the dwindling light.

Having passed the bridge, the gates of Lelwani can no longer be seen, but I have no doubt that they remain close enough to be concerning, and though I am hiding in plain darkness, I still have a creeping suspicion that Lelwani must know of my presence here. Even in the wild, reclusive beings always know when their home has been invaded—goddesses should be no different. These thoughts spur me on faster, and Sharvara huffs beside me before taking off at a sprint.

"You want to play?" I gasp, forcing my body into a sweet burn as I run flat out in the direction of the mountain where Parasuwa resides. Askalpusa had warned me not to interfere, but the more I think upon it, the more I realize his imprisonment cannot stand. He must be freed.

For the crime of aiding man, lending to us knowledge stolen for fear of our divine power when united, he has been strung up to endure the eternal torment of the storm god and his symbol.

Askalpusa screeches, landing softly upon an outcropping of rock high above me. Sharvara bounds up the rocky terrain, and I follow. The way is steep, and as I walk, a noise rises up to my left. I cannot see what causes this sound, but when I close my eyes, it sounds like the grinding of stone, and the heaving, breath of effort. Sharvara barks at me, returning me to my present purpose. I begin moving again, scaling the side of the mountain.

For some time, naught is heard but my ragged breath and the crunching of stone, until a shriek of sorrow fills the air followed by a ground-shaking collision. At once, I straighten, turning to see what had caused such a disturbance, but Sharvara's bark of warning brings me once again back into the present. High above, the disturbance causes shards of stone to crumble and descend the mountain side. Rocks the size of my fist and bigger fly past my face, and I seek cover just in time to see a boulder land the precise place I had been only seconds before. Wide-eyed, I wait for the tremors to cease before rising once more to fulfill my mission.

With renewed vigour, I scale the side of the mountain, sloping ever steeper and ever more precarious as stable stone turns to shale and scree. Mist collects on the top of the mountain, concealing the god, but I know he's there because Askalpusa has disappeared into it. For the duration of my climb, Askalpusa had flown ahead, finding comfortable perches to wait upon for me, and every time I'd get close, he'd take to the air to repeat the process. Sharvara too is a far more efficient climber than I, able to bound and leap and keep pace with the owl apart from one exception: the sheer wall of stone that prevails.

I come to a sudden stop as the mist gives way to the solid stone with only the barest of cracks and texture to it. There are no handholds to speak of, and I daren't scale it. Sharvara nudges me, and I turn to see Askalpusa sitting on a rock. He extends his wing to the side where a path curves over the mountain side to descend around the wall. Leading the way this time, I allow my hands to brush the jagged stone. Metal clinks, and I pull up short as I see a man in chains, forehead stooped low on the ground. It is the god Parasuwa. The man turns slowly, head raising from the ground to stare up at me, and confusion marks his face. Slowly, I step forward, and behind me, Sharvara plunks down to sit, panting. I do not see Askalpusa.

"Who approaches?" the man croaks.

"I am Prince Haduwas," I declare, "a mortal prince of Kuššara, and I have come to free you."

The man chuckles. "And how will you do that?" he asks, holding up his raw, fettered hands, whereupon shackles of gold keep him in place. "That cursed eagle will follow me no matter where I go, so even if you do somehow release me, it will be for naught."

Eyeing the sky, I hope Askalpusa has evaded the notice of the eagle, for while the owl is a noble hunter, it is no match for a divine eagle. "And if I kill the eagle? Would you aid me on my quest?"

The god eyes my lazily, and he gives me a once over. "You seek the apples guarded by my nieces." I nod in response. "I can give you information. That is all."

"Knowledge is a great deal," I say, stepping forward. "I will free you, even though I may turn the attention of the gods upon myself in doing so." A hoarse laugh climbs out of the god's throat.

"You will certainly gain the attention of the gods, there is no doubt about that, young prince."

"So be it," I say. "I find your state to be most disagreeable, and I cannot, in good conscience, allow you to remain so."

"I too find it..." he looks down at his abdomen where blood had flowed, dried, and caked over the years, "disagreeable. Alas, I knew what my actions in the mortal realm would result in, and I knew this day would come. You may think knowledge is a fine thing now, but when you truly understand what is to come, ignorance is truly a bliss."

"And yet I would rather live as you do than your brother."

"Which? The one who holds up the weight of the world? Or the one cursed to always be a step behind everyone else?"

I consider his words, tilting my head to the side. "I suppose neither is ideal, and yet it is your twin I refer to, your brother, Sersuwa, who is cursed with belated epiphany. I would rather make decisions with clarity even if the outcome is destined to be grim than to always understand after the fact and be plagued with regret and a desire to do things differently."

"Remember your stance on that, young prince. I see your future. Are you sure you wish to be cursed with such knowledge?"

"I need not know my future," I say, "though I seek more practical knowledge. How do I obtain the apples of immortality."

"I would say free me first, but I see your soul, Haduwas, and I know you shall keep your word and free me. You must seek out my brother, Ubelluri, and he shall obtain the apples for you. You must convince him of your quest, however, because he will not steal those apples lightly; his own daughters are tasked with keeping them safe."

"I hear you, Parasuwa. And how do I free you?"

"You must slay the eagle of Tarḫunna. It comes this way now. Every day, it attacks and steals my liver, whereupon, it regrows within me; I must watch each time as he gorges upon it."

"You shall never see it again," I vow, and the shriek of the eagle echoes and bounces around the stones. From around my body, I extricate my bow and pull an arrow from my quiver.

"Do not miss," Parasuwa cautions, and I smile lightly.

"I've had practice killing birds these past months—ones with poisoned beaks, talons of bronze, and sharp feathers of plated gold." The bird soars high above us, circling us. "An eagle should be no problem."

"You say that now..." Parasuwa says, but he does not finish his statement. When the god of foresight says something ominous like that, it's hard not to take it to heart, and yet, I've never felt stronger, or more sure of myself. Sweat trickles down my brow, as I take aim directly above me. The eagle is watching me with interest, but he does not dive yet. With the casual grace of a predator, it simply circles and circles above me, dizzying in effect and sickening to the eyes, but still, I keep my eye on my target. I feel nothing in my arms, and yet I know they should be trembling with strain, and I feel nothing in my legs even though they should be aching with effort.

Pulling the string taught with my notched bow, I exhale and let the arrow fly. The soaring eagle screeches as it is pierced true, and its body spirals to land before me, feathers fluttering in the aftermath while its broken body crashes to the rocky ground. It all feels too easy. Surely there's a catch? I nudge the bird, but it remains still and lifeless.

"My fetters, if you would," Parasuwa says, jangling the chains as he shakes his wrists at me. His skin, rubbed raw from the countless years spent in this abysmal state, has deep grooves where the restraints had left a long, nasty impression. Stepping over the broken body of the eagle, I approach the enslaved god and yank on the chains with my bare hands. The gold bends easily, and I wonder, briefly, if perhaps Parasuwa had not even tried to escape, but I had seen the impressions upon his skin. Marks like those had to have been earned. Chains released, I work on the bands secured to each of his wrists. Crushing them with my grip, the hinge snaps on the left, and then on the right, and they clink, uselessly to the ground.

Blinking, Parasuwa stares at his broken bonds hard before looking up at me. Gratitude shines in his hazel gaze, brown curls falling in waves over his forehead.

"You have done me a great service," he says, rubbing his angry and swollen wrists. "One day, far from this one, you shall reap a reward beyond your wildest dreams. You will not want it, but you shall have it regardless, and the world shall be better for it."

"What is this reward?"

"You shall need to go to my brother, Ubelluri," he says, avoiding my question. "There, he shall aid you in your cause. Tell him you have freed me." He looks up, and above, I see Askalpusa in the owl form descending from a hiding spot. "Your friend knows the way." His eyes fall to Sharvara who sidles up to my side, grumbling. "Apologies. Friends."

"Where shall you go?" I ask, and the smallest of smiles emerges on his young yet weary face.

"Away."

"I wish you the best, Parasuwa."

"And I you, young Prince Haduwas. We shall see each other again.

Not soon, but in time. Go now, and succeed in your quest."

Both Sharvara and Askalpusa urge me forward, yet something roots my feet to the ground. Nothing in the physical sense stays me, but something unspoken—something moral. "Have you any request of me before I depart, great Parasuwa? Any way I can aid you?"

The way he looks at me makes me think he knew I would ask, and I wonder if that gets depressing, always knowing how something will play out and being a slave to it without the ability to alter the course of fate. "There is nothing you can give me, but I know you'd do it if it were in your power."

"Name it," I say.

"As a god, I do not require sustenance," he says, casually, "but I would enjoy the cooling, quenching powers of fresh, flowing water, the gust of breath-taking air through my hair and robes, and soothe the gnawing pains of my belly with a common feast."

Stepping forward, I kneel before him, forehead bowed. "If I succeed in my journey, it will be so. In your honour, I will provide you fresh spring water, a common feast, and all the fresh air you could possibly breathe. It will be a rite I sanction alone. This I will do."

Parasuwa gently leads my face back up by the chin, and when I meet his eyes, tears of gratitude shine back at me. "Your graciousness has no equal. You shall deserve your reward like no other before, and be the only one to do it justice in all my time. Go now, Haduwas. You shall do great things, and if no one ever says this to you, I shall: I am proud of you and who you will become."

Heart pattering in my chest, I nod, my own eyes prickling with unspoken emotion. My voice is gravelly as I thank him. Rising, I offer him my hand to stand, and gratefully, he takes it.

"It is here we must depart, Haduwas," Parasuwa says, standing on shaky legs. "I shall take my fate in my hands from here. You have freed me, a debt I cannot repay. You shall fail in this quest, but win at the true game." And then he disappears.

Whirling around, I seek him out, but Parasuwa is well and truly gone. On that ominous note, Sharvara nudges me with his nose, ushering me in the direction of the passage through stone where the steep incline descends through the mountain in a carved tunnel with steps. Minding my head, I descend deeper into the realm of death to find the god who holds up the world.

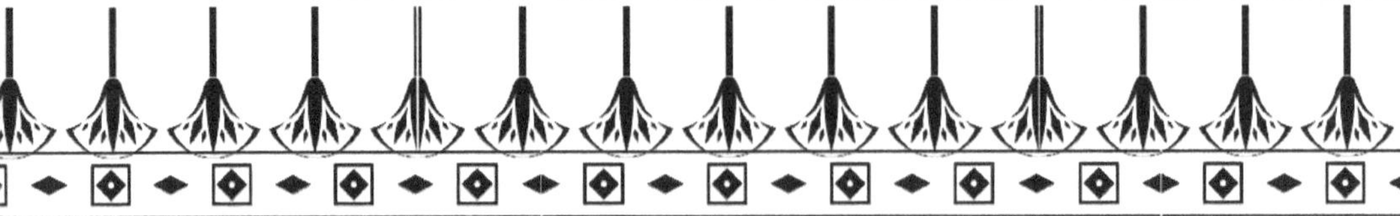

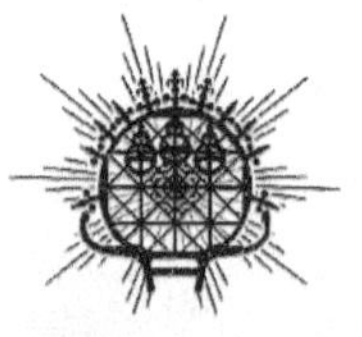

The axis and the earth are established.

The instruments of life are set in place.

Then life is turned downward into her domain.

They have broken the order of the earth.

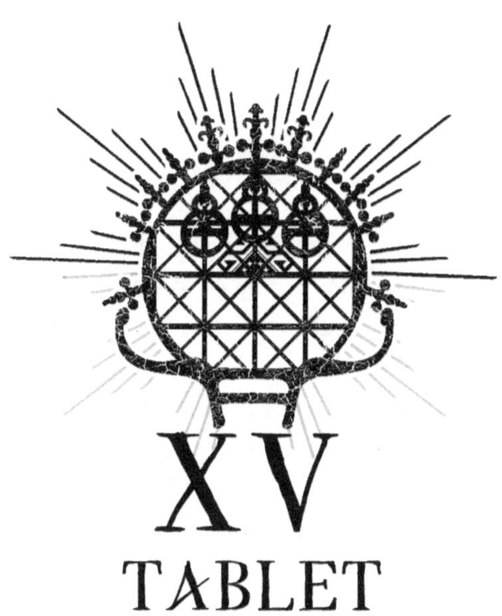

XV TABLET

WEIGHT OF THE WORLD

Each step down the stone-carved tunnel feels heavier than the last, the weight of my decision settling deeper into my bones. Parasuwa is gone, his cryptic words still echoing in my mind, but I cannot shake the feeling that this moment marks a turning point—one that will ripple through the heavens. The gods will know what I've done soon enough, and their wrath will be swift. But in the stillness of this descending path, I find no regret.

Freeing Parasuwa was no mere act of defiance, nor a rebellion born from pride. It was a choice—one that bound me to something greater than fear. The fire-bringer's suffering was unjust, a punishment too cruel for the knowledge he had gifted us. If the gods see me as a fool for risking everything to free him, then so be it. I would make the same choice a thousand times over, even if it means their fury falls upon me.

Sharvara presses his nose to my hand, his silent companionship grounding me in the moment. We press on, deeper into the heart of the mountain, where the shadows cling to every surface like memories long forgotten. My thoughts wander to the task ahead—the descent into the unknown, into the very depths where death itself lingers.

Yet, even in this place of stone and silence, a flicker of hope remains. Parasuwa spoke of failure, but in his final words, I sensed a deeper meaning. There is another game at play—one that even the gods themselves may not fully understand. Perhaps it is not the quest that will define me, but the unseen forces I've now set into motion. The gods may seek to break me, but I am no stranger to burdens. Let them come.

With each step forward, Parasuwa's words sink deeper into my mind —into my being—into my soul.

I will fail at the quest, but win at the true game.

The words rebound in my head, over and over, and along with it, questions begin to gnaw at me, clawing with feral swipes to gain purchase. What part of the quest do I fail? Do I fail to retrieve the apples? Do I get captured by the dread goddess? Do I make it above ground and still lose the throne? Do I perish?

The questions siphon off, starting as a deluge, but gradually, it slows to a trickle, and the only thing I can think about is one last final question —the most vital of questions: will I ever see my son again?

A shudder courses through me at the idea of an existence in perpetual darkness, and yet, it would not be the worst fate in the world. There is a brutal beauty in this haunting place—a sense of comforting finality. It is still and lacks the scheming and swift pace of the upper world. Even burdened as I am by this quest, I feel no particular rush, and I do not feel the time trickling by.

The pressure of this impossible task weighs on me in ebbing waves, and an unfamiliar feeling rises inside me. It is a phoenix, stoked back to life from ashes. Its black eyes open, the first embers ablaze, and from there, the wings spread, speckled in dancing coal and flame. It rises up to my chest, and I gasp, as though my fury is truly alive in the form of the mythical bird. It burns, acidic hot, and I clutch at my throat, half believing that if I try hard enough, flames would replace breath. For a moment, I loathe my father. Loathe him for making me do this task. Something inside me, something treasonous, threatens to be acknowledged. Doubt and wroth combine, and suddenly, I am certain my father had never done this. His limp was not caused by any journey to these lands or any other. I am certain of it now.

Askalpusa still circles high above us, still leading the way. Pockets of precious stones glitter in the perpetual night, shards catching the limited light, and even as a prince, one accustomed to sights of obscene wealth, the careless existence of these stones, neglected and forgotten, makes me pause. With the sheer amount of precious stones and metals, this landscape could be utterly transformed into an opulence not matched by the gods above, and yet, here they remain—untouched, and in their natural state. The goddess of death is surely the most wealthy of all, and yet, she does not display it.

"I suppose she does not need to display it," I mutter under my breath, and Sharvara huffs ahead of me. "There is no one to show it off to." His great head is turned in my direction, but still, his body faces the descent through the stairs, though I don't move—not yet.

I take the time to inspect the walls—the carved steps weave in and out of solid black mineral walls, and trickling water forges new paths through the walls, tiny reservoirs burrowing deeper into the earth. I continue, slowly this time, and as we crest the next corner, the steps smooth out into a sparkling floor, and to the right, a milky-white river, ambling around at such a leisurely pace, it may as well have not been moving at all.

There is no movement within, nor any smell. It is, in every way, lifeless, and I know to approach it would be death, and yet...I want to. To look at it is to desire it. It's a promise, a wish fulfilled...a dream that never ceases to deliver...but it is a lie.

Barking and shrieking sound behind me, and though I hear it, I disregard it—not because I am enthralled, but because I am conscious. I don't know how, but somehow, I know what this river is; this winding, lethargic, mindless river. Looking behind my shoulder, I shake my head slowly at Sharvara and the barking stalls. Sharvara can see I understand.

Kneeling before the blessed, cursed water, I hold my left hand out over its pale surface, easily discernible in the gloom.

"I have something for you," I murmur, eyes open, but it is not the water I see anymore. Instead, I feel the beating rays of the sun, the trickle of sweat, and the burning labour of digging hard, rocky earth. I see the bodies of my brothers, and the body of my lover—the mother of my child. "I have no libations other than my sorrows to give you."

With palm outstretched, I imagine Litti, the goddess of mindlessness, outstretching her hand to take mine in the most caring of grasps to gorge upon my grief.

"And I have something for you, young Haduwas," a faint, melodic voice decrees. I don't open my eyes to see—the images pour into my mind, and to open my eyes would be to blind myself.

A stunning creature stands before me, hands clasped before her in such a casual fashion, only the crown on her brow tells the truth of her station. My heart stomps, once, skipping a beat entirely before galloping wildly. The image disintegrates and I see myself holding the golden fruit. A tendril of once dark hair falls into my line of vision, as bright and white as the milky river before me. Again, the vision shifts, but now, spotting my reflection in a looking glass, a crown, but not the crown of my father. The streak of white hair is still present.

"Do you see?" the voice asks, and I can feel a gentle stroke against the back of my hand. "Do you see what you will become? This is your inchoation."

"Yes," I whisper, eyes still closed.

"You shall give me such gifts in your time as *Lord*. Such...*painful* gifts." Her voice is not unkind, and in fact, her tone strikes me as though she is empathetic to the future she sees in store for me, and I wonder how she knows.

If she is the goddess of forgetting, how does she remember? But then another part of her words sink in.

"Lord?" I ask, confused, eyes bursting open, but the second I do, the image of the goddess and my future is gone. In their place, the milky river comes back into view, and Sharvara, who moved in the time of my vision, sits patiently at my side as he awaits my movement once again.

Standing, I nod and see my goal clearly. Seeing myself succeeding, not only holding the object of my quest, but seeing the crown on my head...

"That was not the crown of my father," I say to no one in particular. I do not expect Sharvara to reply, and he does not. Instead, silence answers me. It holds space for me to come up with the answer, but I do not understand...not yet.

"The time for resting is now over," I declare. "Let us find Upelluri—the god that holds up the heavens. I can rest and rejuvenate when the quest is completed."

I no longer require Sharvara or Askalpusa's guidance through the twisting, carved corridors. Little in the way of design marks the place, and in a way, it is sad. There is so much room for art, for expression, and the restless dead surely have stories to tell and beauty to share.

Urged by this thought, I imagine how I would decorate this place, and, for one, elaborate carvings would decorate every path, and there would be lighting. Torches could easily light the way, and though I suppose the deities of the dead hardly need light to navigate, it would be a nice touch.

Statues, murals, tapestries, and other such decorations would be displayed in the palace, and each gate would have a special depiction—would show the stories of this place.

Vast, cold archways crest high, high above our heads, intended for beings of a much larger scale no doubt, and I remember the stories of my youth, told to me by foreign travellers, about giants and the dread blending of divine and mortal blood. The resulting progeny were of monstrous size and capable of feats beyond both groups from which they had originated. I had seen the bones of such fallen peoples, and truly, they were staggering to behold.

More staggering to behold, however, is the sight in the distance. Even from where I stand, so far away, I can clearly see a single god holding the epicentre of a swirling mass converging above him. How he holds such weight is truly beyond me.

My breath whooshes out, and I am reminded of both Parasuwa's words and Askalpusa's. The one told me to convince him while the other told me to trick him. The latter would be easier, but the former safer—more honest. Steeling myself to what I must do, I breathe in sharply, twice, and then let the breath go.

"Come, Sharvara. Let us meet with Upelluri. He is the only chance I have at succeeding in my quest."

The rocks underfoot give way to deadened, grassy plains. Hunger gnaws at my belly, but I ignore it along with the growing burn of my lungs. How long had it been since I had eaten or slept? Too long, to be sure. Demarcating the silence is the occasional gurgle of my belly and the slow panting of Sharvara at my side. I know the second Upelluri senses my approach because Sharvara halts, and won't move further.

"Come on, Sharvara," I coax, but it's for naught. He refuses to move, and when I look up, I see Upelluri staring daggers at me. Sharvara barks once before lying down, and I realize I must do this part on my own. Even a casual glance into the air tells me Askalpusa too has made himself scarce.

"Who approaches?" Upelluri demands, his voice steady despite the slight shake I detect in his arms.

"I am called Prince Haduwas," I call, head bowed as I approach the god. "I have come to ask a great favour of you, Great Upelluri, Holder of the Heavens and arm of the World."

"In case you hadn't noticed," the god sneers, "I'm a little busy"

"I have freed your brother, Parasuwa."

For a moment, I think the world will end. The god, in his shock, falls to a knee, and the shaking in his arms becomes even more pronounced. Sweat falls in rivulets, down the stark valleys of his neck, chest, and back.

"You did what?"

"I freed your brother from eternal torment. I did it against my better judgement for I don't believe he deserved it. Nor do I believe you deserve your punishment. Would that I would relieve you of that duty, we both know I cannot."

The god does not reply. Instead, he simply stares at me as he waits for me to finish what I had come to say.

"I require a divine fruit, one guarded by your daughters."

He booms a laugh, sharp and staccato, and slowly, gets back to both feet. "You could never achieve such a feat."

"I know," I reply calmly, and again, the god looks at me. Sharp curiosity stares back at me, and a keen intelligence is at work despite his imprisonment.

"Your solution?" he asks, a derisive smirk beginning to grow on his agonized face.

"You will grab it for me."

He shakes his head with a laugh again. “Excellent plan,” he says, his voice a scathing, disenfranchised retort. “Except,” he rolls his eyes, “as we’ve established, I have no replacement.”

“I will stand in your place.”

The statement makes him go utterly still. “You cannot.”

“I can. Not for long, but for long enough. I will do this thing for you, and in return, you will give me the fruit. You will not be implicated.”

“Assuming you can hold it, why should I do this thing for you?” he asks. It is a question of genuine curiosity—spoken from a place deep down.

“How long has it been since you’ve seen your daughters?” I ask, and though his face does not change, I easily see the shift in his demeanour. It has been ages likely. I forge ahead, determined to get beyond his questions. “I have been parted from my son for but a week, and it is agony. To be cleaved so wholly from one’s family is a torture in and of itself. I offer you the opportunity to see them—be with them again, even if for a short time.”

"You present this as though it's of benefit to me, and yet you will walk away with a great treasure."

"Yes," I agree. "Presumably, I shall. But you shall receive a gift too. I will see to it that you get to see your family. Take the time to spend with your family, but you must come back and take this burden for I am not immortal."

Upelluri frowns. "Do you not mean for me to obtain the fruit for yourself?" he asks. "If I gave you the fruit, you too would ascend and become a god. If you're able to hold it while mortal..."

"Alas, it is not my intention to keep the fruit for myself. I am on a quest to prove I am worthy of my throne, and to do so, I was tasked with facing Death herself, forging through her lands to obtain this gift. Eating it is not what I desire. Proving I am worthy of ruling my people is my goal."

A long moment of silence ensues as he assesses me. "You are worthy," he says at last. "I am not certain you understand the true weight of the world. I shall give it to you slowly to make sure you can handle it. If you can, I shall do as you ask."

"Very well," I say, approaching the god. A manic intensity seizes the god's eyes as I approach, and I wonder the last time the god had relaxed. Upelluri is taller than I, and when he stoops, I stoop my head and lift my hands high to brace for the weight of the world.

"Hands lower. You will not be able to hold it the same way I do. It's a personal experience." Lowering my arms so they hover by my head, I allow my palms to face the vortex of swirling matter cascading towards me. Staggering my feet, I assume my warrior's stance, at the ready for whatever battle lies ahead.

"We will start by holding it together," he says, and I nod, gritting my teeth in preparation. He lowers it, and the moment my skin makes contact, an adhesion occurs, and even if I had wanted to drop it, I could not. Gasping for breath, I can't seem to bring in air, and I feel my lungs beginning to collapse.

"Let it in," Upelluri coaches, and for a moment, I don't know what he means. Let it in? Let what in? But then, it occurs to me that the burden of the world might not just be physical in nature. As soon as the thought blooms in my mind, all at once, my head and heart burst open, and the full spectrum of the human condition bombards me. Every life felt at once, the whole scope of their suffering and bliss, bewildering in intensity and life-altering in capacity, I am assaulted in every way a human can be.

Brutalized and adored. Hated and shamed. Tortured and loved. Killed and reborn. Over and over, the cycles pummel me like cresting waves determined to drown me forever in the tumult of the collective sea of souls.

"Let it wash through you. Be one with it. You are it now."

Nodding furiously, I do as he says, and when I allow it in, the pain of it lessens. I am nothing more than a vessel of dualities. Every contrasted thing courses through me, and as the concepts sink their claws in deep, burrowing through every fibre of my being, through my skin, my bones, my very soul, Ubelluri steps out from below the weight of the world.

"I will leave you now. Do not fail."

Panic shoots through me at the idea of bearing this burden alone, but the whine of Sharvara at my side reminds me that I am not alone. Steeling myself hard, I dive deep into myself and halt every thought I have about the experience. Tears well in my eyes, blurring my vision, but my sight is not hindered in the slightest. The place below my neck and between my shoulders burns in agony. There is only fear. Fear and darkness, and my knees are seared with white hot pain. Only then do I realize I have fallen, and struggling, blindly through the darkness, I force myself back up. My eyes are open, and I see nothing. Voices clamber for my attention, laughter, wailing, screaming, moaning, and quieter, pleading, praying, hoping. Still, my eyes are blind. I smell nothing but stale air and cold, sharp wind that pierces the lungs.

Then, a shocking, brilliant light. I know it cannot be death because here, in the Underworld—the home of death—there is only darkness. I see everything. Every marriage and every death. Every failure and every invention. Madness. *Madness. MADNESS.* Loss. Joy. Grief. My soul is split apart and mended, over and over. I smell fire and smoke, and roasting meat. There is cheering, and harmony, divine union. The sensual pleasure of creation and the pain of being cleaved and hacked apart. I feel it all, but like all that came before, that soon ebbs away too leaving emptiness. I sob and laugh hysterically.

My own body weeps in despair, and the true weight of the world hits me. All at once, I am both hot and cold, tired and awake, alive, but also dead. Physically, the weight of the world is no more than a feather, and yet, I tremble with terror just the same.

Twin serpents rise within me, their heads coiling around each other in a terrible dance. My skin flushes hot and my senses scream at me, telling me I need to eat, to sleep, to rest, but to rest is to shatter the delicate balance holding the realms of the mortal and divine apart. To rest is to doom the world to suffer a world they are not yet ready for. As a prince, I never knew starvation or dehydration, but now, as I experience it, I know it better than my closest friends.

The serpents rise, and with it, desires; ones both known and unknown to me.

The burning needs and wants of human existence throttle me, and I want nothing more than to throw this burden away, to fight, to give into my sudden passions and live like a beast without a care in the world, but I resist. I open my eyes, and once again, allow these feelings inside. I pass no judgement over them, instead, letting the waves crest and pass through me. The moment I accept them is the moment, they have no more power over me.

As though testing me, the world changes the scene.

I see Huella, and around me, she dances. Her fingers trail over my chest, arms, and back, and her hair cascades over her shoulders in dark waves. The curves of her body writhe and undulate to music I cannot hear, and when she turns to look at me, it is as it was in life. With high cheekbones and hazel eyes framed with dark lashes, her beauty seizes me. I want to reach out to her, to touch her, to listen to her raspy voice as she takes her pleasure with me, but my hands remain exactly where they are.

She grows closer, and even with eyes clenched shut, I see her still, her phantom fingers stirring my blue-hot embers. "Do you not want me anymore, Duwa?" she asks, lips upon the shell of my ear. Her hands roam under my shirt.

"Do you remember?" she asks, finger tracing the lines of my hips until she's blocked by the fabric of my pants. "Our first time?"

I want to tell her, *Of course I remember,* but the words stick in my throat. How could I forget? I see our union, relive the moment, and time seems to cease to be. It had been my first time with a woman.

In the frame of a blink, time speeds up and she swells; the next blink, I see my son. He has precisely my eyes. We had just been dancing around the fire together, and then those dread horns had blared. I had armed Huella with a knife and told her to get to safety. I can see the path she took, weaving between tents towards the centre of the camp, the river at her side. I see the eyes of the hound in the dark waters before she does. It's more terrible than I could have imagined, and no amount of screaming or pleading will warn her or bring her back. And then, her dead eyes staring up at me in supplication to save our son—to protect our son.

As much as I try not to, my own individual experience overtakes me, and suddenly, the fears of the collective no longer matter—only mine. Gazaza, the tribe's orphan child, with his tear-streaked face laced with fear turns to me, pleading with me to save him, to make everything better, but nothing in the world can save him from life and the horrors that come with it. Not a thousand wishes or ten thousand good deeds, and the agony of that knowledge undoes me. I see my son, Idari, fishing at the bank, pulling his catch ashore, and the reward of a little smile cutting through his grief.

Again, my knees quake, and my words to Parasuwa haunt me. I'd told him I would rather his fate than his brother's. Now, I'm not so sure. I see too much.

Wroth, sorrow, grief, guilt, and shame crowd around me, stealing my breath. Defeat. Failure. The emotions are a never-ending, spiralling pit, but despite it all, I hold onto my goal—my purpose. My itchy cheeks mean nothing when compared to seeing this task through, and my pain means nothing if it means the days keep on coming.

Shifting my stance, not physically, but intellectually, the burden weighs less and less. The setting of a new merestone in my path shows me the true way to hold the weight of the world. Webs beam out of me, strings that uncoil and stretch out away from me in incandescent tendrils. They recede in every direction, and I can see where each string is going, where they lead, and I see each individual I've ever been in contact with in this life and in past ones. I see them all. They are all in various stages of life, and some are successfully going through their lessons, while others are not.

I lean into the feelings, and no longer do they feel like punishments to feel. Instead, I see it as a privilege. Everything passes through me, and no longer do I feel the desire to be numb to the pain. I relish in every burn, in every stab, in every slice, and every freeze. I exalt in every birth, in every death, and in every milestone met. Laughter rings louder, and the sun is dazzling. Colours are brilliant to the eye, and sadness is a balm to the void. Anything is better than the nothing that devours eventually.

I can see it, and before, I would have dreaded its coming, but now, I see the void, and I exist in the knowledge that everything that happens is a gift precisely because it shall end one day, far from this one.

Carrying the weight of the world is a mantle of power, of understanding, and of divine leadership. To hold it and not attempt to change it is the point. To try and meld things into one's own vision is not the point, and to do so, would crush you. Only in subservience can the holder truly wield power. Respecting it, understanding it, and acting accordingly. Abuse would crush, misunderstanding would smother, and to change it would be akin to burning the world to the ground.

I stand taller than ever before, and I now know, even if I do not get the apple, that I am worthy—inherently worthy of leadership, and of power.

Both my mind and the world grow quiet with only the slow trickle of time passing remaining as I calmly await the return of the god. My thoughts move back to Ubelluri, my perception of him having shifted entirely. Before, he was a prisoner with a terrible fate, forced into the cruelest of labours, but now, I see him as a truly divine being doing what must be done. Few can hold up the mantle of the world and be able to both hold the weight, but also interact with their desires and not follow through with them. How many men would try to seize unlawful power when so easily presented to them? How many women would seek to alter their fates?

In a trance-like state, I take up my post with renewed vigor and observe. Burning incense and floral notes waft up to my nose, but when I open my eyes, there is no one there. I sense a presence, but they do not make themselves known, and then, and only then, do I know for certain who is there.

"I understand you," I say, arms reaching overhead, but no longer straining. I stand as easily as if stretching in the morning. She does not appear, or respond, but I know she heard me. Again, I grow lonely until I hear the subtlest of footsteps and a gentle, rhythmic thwapping comes from behind me. It takes me only a few moments to realize what it is.

"You've returned, Ubelluri."

"I almost didn't."

"The thought did occur to me," I admit, "but I didn't give it much credence."

"Why not?" Ubelluri asks, now coming into view. The fruit lands repeatedly in his hand as he tosses it carelessly up and down, like a playful taunt.

"Because," I say simply. "For one, even if you didn't come back, I can manage this. For two, I don't think you're here as a punishment. I think you *like* it here."

"And why do you think that?" he asks, the fruit now utterly still in his palm.

"If I can grow to like it in this short of a period, surely you did. I imagine you felt the loss of it the moment you went away."

Ubelluri sighs. "You're correct, of course. It was wonderful to see my daughters. Beautiful, like their mother. But I yearned to be back here. I did enjoy some rest, though. I can't remember the last time I rested, but I started to feel...guilty." He looks down at the fruit in his palm. "You survived."

"I did," I say.

"Then you must understand how imperative it is that this does not land in undeserving hands."

An icy chill creeps over my spine, and for the first time, I allow myself to think about the quest. The priest had given little in the way of instruction or explanation. He'd mentioned the Sumerian texts and a great library; had he been alluding to the *List of Kings*? My father had been obsessed with that tablet. He'd travelled as a young man to many lands, and he had *seen* one such tablet with his own eyes on a journey to the east. Is that what this is all about? To obtain a fruit of immortality, one would become like the kings of old. It had been an era of peace, where no one fought and no one aged. There had been no famine or sickness. It was not a secret that my father yearned to return to such times, but one question remained—when I return with the fruit, who will keep it? My father, the sitting king, the priest in supposed communion with the gods, or the warrior who earned it? I would have to safeguard it with my life.

"I do," I say, and when Ubelluri looks at me, he nods, his cerulean eyes deep and foreboding. He might not have been Parasuwa, god of foresight, but he did not require the gift to see the dilemma before me. My face must betray my thoughts because he shrugs his shoulders, tosses the fruit one last time, and then takes his place once more under the vortex of swirling matter.

"Take the fruit and go, Prince Haduwas. I thank you for freeing my brother. His truly was a punishment undeserved. You have done my family a great service, and it will be remembered."

Stepping out from underneath the vortex, I grab the fruit from his outstretched palm, and I watch in wonder as Ubelluri stands there holding up the weight with only a single arm and a casual whistle.

"Oh, one last thing," he says, and I turn to look at him. "The white looks good."

I'm confused for only a moment before I remember I had seen a vision—me with a single streak of milky-white hair.

"If you had taken even ten more seconds to figure out how to hold the weight, you'd have been crushed and killed. As it is, that will be a permanent reminder of the stress of neglected emotions. Let it be a lesson to live by."

"I will."

"Goodbye, young prince. Though...I suspect this will not be the last time we meet."

"I suspect it won't," I agree. And then, again, with Sharvara at my side, I walk away.

It's surreal. I feel simultaneously lighter than ever, and yet so incredibly heavy at the same time. In some intrinsic way, I am changed. The very fibres of my being have been rearranged, and I don't recognize myself from the inside. To have been exposed to so much sensation, I am nearly unable to feel anything now.

Something sharp jabs my left shoulder, and as I jerk away, I see the hooked claws of Askalpusa. His head cocks to the side, and he trills lightly—he sees freedom at long last.

"Back to the surface now," I intone, and Askalpusa hoots again, albeit aggressively.

The sharp talons dig in deeper to my skin before he flies up and ahead. The way back is far easier. Not only is it easier to see, somehow, but I also know the way. The lack of food does not bother me, but my thirst is another matter. Every river we pass I must remind myself is not a thing of sustenance, but rather the promise of the darkest, deepest oblivion.

We do not go the same direction as last time. Last time, as Askalpusa had explained it, we had pre-emptively crossed before we should have. Now, we simply loop around the left side back to the entrance we had begun—except...I can feel eyes upon me. Not the eyes of the dreaded troglodytes that dwell on the cave walls looking for scraps of flesh to gorge upon, though I can see the tiny moons reflecting every so often on the walls high above us. Rather, I can sense a being of immense power observing us with the keenest of eyes.

Even so, nothing attempts to stop our escape. It all seems...too easy. Of course, the moment I think it is the moment I sense change. Sharvara senses it at the same time, and the howl he releases—it is loud enough to alert everything in the Underworld of our presence.

"Sharvara, shh," I implore, but it's too late.

In the distance, I can see a form emerging from the darkness, and the hulking body screams in response. The being approaching is larger than Ubelluri and Parasuwa combined. Standing at almost twice my height, the god lumbers towards me with deceptive speed, and I recognize him at once. Ubelluri and Parasuwa's brother, Zari—god of doomed might.

Scrambling backwards, my hand dives into my empty pack. I had lost all my weapons. Sharvara barks while Askalpusa hoots angrily, but the god has eyes only for me—and the fruit still in my hand. I barely have time to shove it into my bag before he charges.

Bracing myself for impact, he pummels into me, but he does not take me down. Our arms lock in a struggle, and we push and pull, trying to topple the other over. His head flies back, and before I can pull away, he sends his forehead crashing into mine. Blood gushes out of my nose as my head snaps back, and the sudden metallic taste of my own blood fills my mouth. Spitting it back into the god's face, I blind him temporarily as I swipe my nose with my forearm before deciding to not fight fair.

Stepping forward, we circle each other, and I get the sense there is madness in this god. He is not all there, mentally. The god does not blink —he just stares, hard, tasked with an objective I do not yet understand. In truth, this god could have smothered me, and though I have sudden strength I do not understand, surely I am not stronger than this behemoth of an ancient god?

I step to the right and he follows. I step to the left and he retreats—always opposite me, blocking my way to the exit of this world.

Furrowing my brow, I approach him directly, and he does the same. I step backwards, but he still continues forward. He moves with an unnatural gait, one that is lopsided like he has an injury that will never heal.

Changing my tactics, I approach his injured side and he immediately shifts to face me with his opposite side.

"I freed your brother," I say, attempting diplomacy first.

"Which one?" he asks, and I shrug.

"Ubelluri and Parasuwa both. Parasuwa has escaped this plain, and Ubelluri, well, I held up the weight of the world so he could visit his daughters."

"Puny human. You could not hold up the weight of the world. You would be crushed."

"I thought so too, and yet, I bore it. I will have this to remind me of the experience for the rest of my life," I say, holding my white streak. "What is it that you are trying to do, Zari?"

"Stop you."

"You've been tasked specifically with stopping me?" The god nods. "I assume you mean to say that Lelwani herself has given you this task?"

The god's nostrils flare. "You are not worthy of saying her name."

I hum as I contemplate the situation. "You say I'm not worthy. I believe I am. You say I'm not strong enough to hold up the world. I did. How about we make a bet, you and I?"

"Bet?"

"Yes," I say, breaking away from my fighting stance to stand straight. "A fair bet. If I beat you in a fight, if I manage to pin you down, you must let me leave."

"Yes, fair bet. You will not do this thing. When I win, you stay here—be my queen's *thrall.*"

A shudder courses through my body at the words—and not one made up of entirely disgust, either. At the beginning of my journey, the idea would have horrified me, but now? The idea is almost...intriguing.

"Shall we shake upon it? Agreement?" I ask, holding out my hand.

The god peers down at me, cocking his head to the side as he assesses my proffered hand. "Trick?"

"No trick," I say, hand steady as I hold it out. "Agreement, yes?"

"Yes."

The god steps forward, and as he takes my hand in his, he squeezes. His squeeze does not stop. Instead, his grip increases, tightening as he tries to beleaguer my hand into submission.

I squeeze back, and the titan's stunned expression causes me to chuckle. "I told you, dear Zari. I am strong."

"Not human," he whines, as I return the favour. His bones crunch beneath my grip, and he howls in pain. Wrenching his hand from mine in a wild arc, he retreats. Had it not been for my reflexes in releasing him, he would have dislodged my shoulder from its cradle.

Now wary of me, frustration emanating from him in waves, he wants it over with. In a move faster than I expect from him, he picks me up and squeezes me, but I squeeze harder. My arms can barely wrap all the way around the giant god, but when I hear the first bone break, I don't stop.

"Do you yield? Have I won yet?" I shout, and he tries harder to crush me, but my ribs seem to be made of the strongest of forged metals while his snap like the wishbones of river fowl.

"I will never yield," he roars, and then I let loose.

"Enough."

The voice is soft—feminine, and again, that phantom aroma of burning sweet wood is all I can focus on. Whirling around, grip loosening, I let go of Zari. The moment I do, his hand wraps around my throat and lifts me into the air. Dangling like the little dolls my sisters used to play with, I make no move to harm the god any further.

The goddess before me is nothing like I had envisioned the goddess of death to appear. In my mind, I had envisioned little more than a corpse ruling over the dead, with rotting, mottled flesh clinging to aged bones and rags covering the body to preserve what little modesty she could salvage. That image could not be further from the truth. With curling hair the colour of golden wheat and eyes bright like spring grass, she stands in utter contrast to her surroundings. Her cheeks bloom with colour, blood coursing through her veins as they do in mine. I had seen her in my vision from Litti.

"Zari, please. Release our guest."

At once, the titan does as she commands, but I barely notice the difference. Her very presence overwhelms my senses, and I realize that she must have been literally following me around the realm the entire time. How many times had I smelled burning florals and wood? I had smelled it when I held up the world, and I had smelled it before too.

Sharvara smells it too because he whimpers and lays down. She smiles sweetly at him and his tail begins to wag. Perhaps Nippa had been correct in believing the hound was hers, but I can't help but truly believe the connection forged between us.

"Prince Haduwas," she says, and when I look up at her, my eyes are level with her thighs, covered and draped in fabric as they are.

"My goddess, Lelwani," I say, averting my eyes to look down upon her feet. She hums, her voice melodic and raspy.

"You have done well down here," she says, looking around her realm. "I was aware of your descent before you even set foot in this place." Her eyes travel away from Sharvara and towards Askalpusa who hides in an outcrop of rock above us, but she makes no moves to recapture him. "You freed many of my prisoners, *prince*."

Taking a moment to stand, I nod. "I did, my goddess."

She turns her back to me and begins walking away. After a moment, she halts, but she does not turn around. "Follow me, prince."

My skin prickles at the sardonically placed title, but I ignore it and stand. Zari looks unhappy at the turn of events, but nonetheless, he allows me to pass, and even though I am surely walking to my death, the only thing I can look at is her hypnotic, swaying hips as they walk away from me.

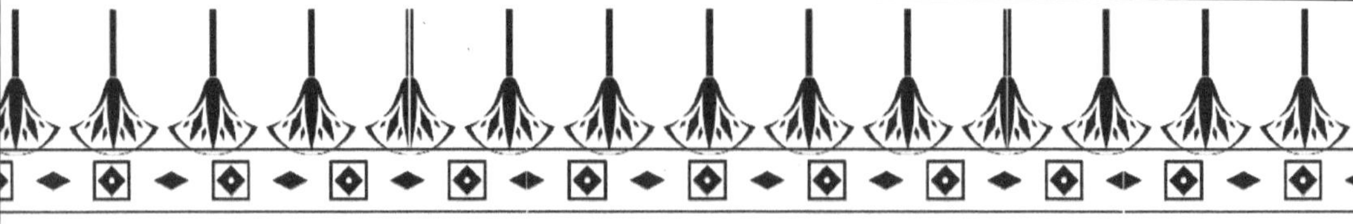

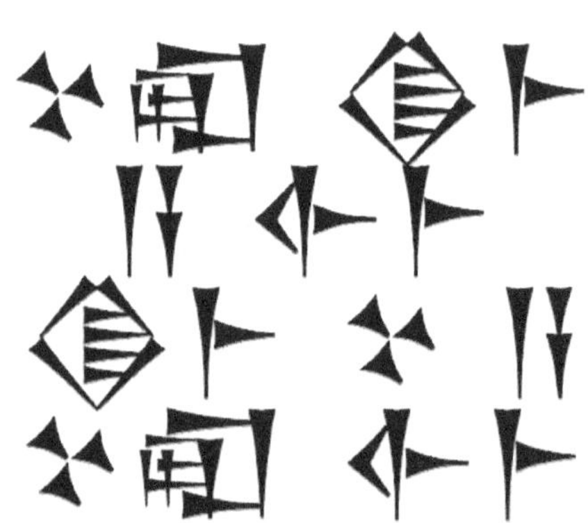

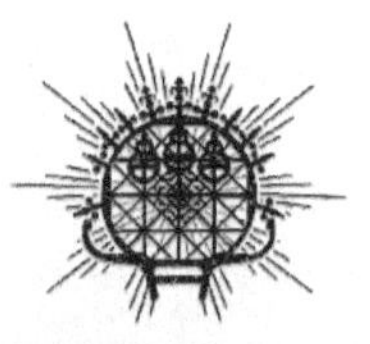

The chains of life fall away,

she stands unbound in power.

Rising steady in her strength.

The bindings are gone.

XVI TABLET

WHEEL OF SELF

It is with great effort that I make myself pay attention to where we are heading. It is, of course, in the direction of the dreaded nine gates to the palace. The myth of it is legendary. It was said Lelwani's sister descended here, just as I had done, and had thought to steal her elder sister's throne. She had been forced to go through the nine gates, as I suspect I will have to. To pass each gate, Šauška had to shed something intrinsic to her. By the time she made it past the ninth gate, she was bare. She wore no finery, nor was she clothed in her fantastic, elaborate clothing. Even her face had been wiped bare of her cosmetic beauty. She had been fully revealed. As the goddess of love, sex, and beauty, her journey had asked her to face what she was beneath the title, and she'd been spit out a husk.

As I approach the gates, my own uneasiness creeps in. The journey through must not be as simple as shedding one's clothes. The point was being bared soul deep. For Šauška, the journey was through the baring of the body and the removal of the trinkets;it lacked depth.

Lelwani must sense my thoughts because she smirks over her shoulder at me. Her gait is relaxed, easy, and her tone conversational. Sharvara licks Lelwani's hand and she, in turn, rubs between his ears. His tail immediately begins to thwap my leg as I walk beside her.

"I see you've been keeping my dog company," she says, and I nod.

"Sharvara has been my saving grace."

"Sharvara?" she intones, and she looks surprised as she looks upon her hound. "Fitting name. He did always have the cutest spots around his eyes." I say nothing to this.

"You know of my gates?" she asks, and I nod.

"They are legendary, after all."

"These gates will test you beyond what even the burden of the world did."

"I found it to be less of a burden and more of a privilege to stand in Ubelluri's place."

"I suspect that's how you're still alive," she replies, nodding slowly. "My sister once tried to break through my gates. She thought she could trick the gates by shedding a piece of clothing at each gate instead of baring layers of her soul." She snorts in derision. "As though she could outsmart sentient stone."

"You killed her as punishment for her audacity."

She turns on me, stopping so suddenly, I am invading her space. She makes no move to put distance between the two of us. If anything, she leans in. Despite my height advantage over her, she feels taller in this moment.

"Did I?" she asks, a razor sharp edge to her tone.

"What happened?" I ask instead. Her gaze lingers on me, darting from my lips to my eyes. Silence stretches and I think she isn't going to answer me when she turns around to keep walking, but then she responds.

"The stone found her unworthy. When the final gate opened, it spat her out like an unsavoury meal. She was dead—as dead as one of us can be at any rate. My only punishment was holding her corpse here instead of allowing her back to the surface—which I eventually did do."

"Through a threat." This time, she smiles, and it's brilliant. My breath is stolen from my lungs at the sight, and she laughs, the sound an unhinged chuckle from a dark place.

"The fates like to make their threats." She whirls on me, planting her palm directly on the centre of my chest. "And so do I."

The world around me shifts and warps, and I am no longer on a path towards the gate. Now, the towering stone stands tall and proud before me, foreboding and ancient. Veins of pallasite with crystals wink in and out of existence within it. Lelwani's palm is warm—and still on my chest. Her expression is pure mirth as she leans in.

"There are gods far older than even I here. Each mountain is a divine being at rest. Their subconscious is what will be testing you. Each gate is bound to a different primordial being. For what it may be worth, I do hope you survive."

Her teeth sink gently into my ear before she is gone again, and a flush of heat bolts through me. Chest tight with sudden emotion, I close my eyes, trying to still my racing heart. Turning around, I face the first gate. Carved with intricate designs and inlaid with precious metals and stones, the twin doors are a sight to behold. Swinging inward on silent hinges, I proceed with utmost caution and care. I sense a shift in the air the moment I cross the golden threshold, and as the gates behind me snap shut with alarming swiftness, I become witness to the grand space before me.

For a moment it appears empty, its cavernous walls blank and ominous. Until suddenly, almost within a blink, the room transforms into a grand library. Row upon row of tablets are placed on shelf after shelf in a dizzying, serpentine loop around the room. Stairs curl around the entire room in a steep ascent, where even more tablets fill every free nook within the recessed walls. Ahead, a raised dais, whereupon, a strange structure stands grand and imposing. There is no one around as I approach, so I take in the mysterious structure with awe. Concentric rings half as tall as the room stand one within the next, twisted into a spherical shape of polished brass. In the candlelit room, the brass gleams, highlighting the ancient runes and glyphs of earlier times. Each ring, smaller than the last, is in varying states of orbit. Some spin fast and others slow. Some oscillate while others still spin smoothly.

On the podium before the display, two tablets with cuneiform script. Inscribed upon the first, a diagram of the puzzle before me, presented by nine horizontal lines of decreasing size down the fire-hardened surface with symbols next to each. On the second, instructions.

"Before you lies the Wheel of Self. Nine rings, each bound to the next,

wait to be turned.

The path is not straight, nor is it simple. The rings are tied to what within you lies.

Force may move them, though wisdom may guide them. Choose your method with care.

One motion disturbs another. One answer leads to the next.

The balance of realms is within your grasp.

What is false, correct; what is undone, complete.

Let the heavens mirror your soul and let your soul mirror the heavens.

Look to the rings for further guidance, for they alone will reveal the truth.

At the centre of it all, the self must be unmade. Only then, may you proceed."

Icy fear trickles down my spine. *What on earth does that mean?*

Gaze returning to the tablet's instructions, I read carefully, my fingers gentle caresses on the hard surface as I keep my place. "The stars shine not alone; the earth rests upon many hands. A single hand will spin the wheel, but more will make the earth whole," I read aloud, though there is no one but the resting god to hear. Lifting my gaze away from the tablets and the spectacle in the centre of the room, I instead focus on the room itself. It's opulent in an overbearing sort of way. Priests often preached about the grand divinity of the gods, but was not Lelwani a great goddess? She did not display her wealth in such a fashion. Only the gods above the earth did this. Only gods of the sun.

With renewed hope, I approach the first of the rings which spins horizontally in a clockwise direction. If I understood the directions clearly, the rings are interdependent. Moving one would create a chain reaction down the line. Each ring has a mechanism: a pulley and lever. The first ring is golden, and upon it, an array of symbols which shimmer with white light. Betwixt the symbols, an inscription, but with the constant rotation of the ring, it moves too fast for me to read it even as I follow it round and around.

With tentative hands, I grip the ring and attempt to hold it in place, to cease its movement, but the second I attempt, the fourth ring begins aggressively spinning the wrong way. As that happens, the second smallest ring begins to topple. I immediately release the thought of physical manipulation, and the rings right themselves to how they had been positioned before I'd started.

Eyeing the lever affixed to the outer frame, I pull it, and the ring starts to lift from a horizontal position to vertical, still revolving, still refusing to share its secrets. It had said the task could be achieved through force, but that wisdom could *guide* them. As the structure revolves once more, I notice a twin set of levers and pulleys on the other side.

Mind moving in furious abandon, I mentally time each revolution, and almost instantly, I discover that not only do I not have time to run to the other side to complete it on my own, the levers have to move at the exact same time to be effective—a feat not possible, at least by me.

Once more, I approach the podium, whereupon, the tablet of instructions sits glibly, mocking my inability to figure out my task. My attention snags on a single line once more. *The stars shine not alone; the earth rests upon many hands. A single hand will spin the wheel, but more will make the earth whole.*

I am utterly alone in this room. Alone...apart from the deity who has created this task and is no doubt observing me this very moment. I could ask for his aid.

"Telepinu," I venture, hoping my voice does indeed carry the strength it requires to speak to one such as a Solar Deity and that Telepinu is, in fact, listening. I wait for several moments, unsure of whether or not my hunch was correct or not. Is the god answering me in some abstract fashion or am I wrong altogether? I try again.

"Telepinu. Are you there?"

I do not see him at first, only the ever increasing shadow dimming the brilliantly lit room. The light wavers as the god materializes. In my mind, a god of the sun and harvest surely was a god that emanated light, and yet the being who now approaches is...lacklustre. His pallor is depleted as though the sun itself steals it from him to sustain itself—a parasite. His youth, his beauty, his drive, all sucked away by the vicious orb in the sky. Averting my eyes as the god approaches, I begin to kneel, but he sighs and stops me.

"There is no need for that now, Prince Haduwas." With stone in my limbs, I rise with a stiffness I've never experienced before. Meeting the god's eyes, I suppress my gasp. His eyes are golden with the hair to match, but there's an underwhelming air about him. While the sun god's followers all wear elaborate robes of gold and vivid colour, the god himself wears an undyed linen shift while his feet are bare. "Not what you were expecting?" he asks, lifting a humourous brow.

"No." He smiles, and the lines on his face show his age despite the fact that he appears physically no more than thirty.

"You have called upon me."

I swallow, hoping this is the right path. "The instructions said there were multiple ways to complete this task." Telepinu says nothing to this, so I continue. "It said one could use force, or one could choose the path of wisdom. I would like to think I am a man who would choose the path of wisdom. The tablet also spoke of multiple hands moving the earth easier than a single pair. Surely the wisest way to solve this puzzle before me is to not do it alone."

"As you say," Telepinu says, nodding. There is grace in his face I hadn't expected. So many of his followers ran so contrary to his being that I wondered what he thought of them and their ways, but then I knew. It was not for him to judge.

"You are wiser than me," I declare. The god...titters.

"If you say so," he responds in a sober tone, as though remembering himself. "It could be said, yes."

"I therefore will ask a single question of you." He awaits my question. "Will you help me solve this puzzle?"

The god's mouth opens slightly, and I feel a brief moment of elation that I have shocked a god before I make myself pay attention. His shock is brief, and in its place, a smile. "Led with wisdom indeed." He nods to himself. "You have passed my test."

"What?" I ask, tilting my head to the side. "I haven't even figured out the puzzle yet."

"In truth, it's not a puzzle but a state of being wrapped in a puzzle, and my 'test', as you call it, was one of balance. This instrument is an Orrery, though different in many respects to an average Orrery."

I stew with this information. "So...the purpose...has not been completed?"

"The puzzle was not the test."

"I see," I say, but I'm not quite sure, I in fact *do* see.

"The puzzle was of course one means to get out of this room, and one could solve it in one of two ways. The first, asking for help to physically and externally alter the positioning of each ring to their optimal levels, and the second, to internally and emotionally alter them. I already know which way you would have solved them. There were also any number of tablets in here that could have been perused for such answers, and any number of things you could have given up as payment for entry."

I eye the thousands of tomes all chained to gilded posts around the room. It hadn't occurred to me to *read* any of the thousands of works around me. Surely *one* of the titles could have identified the task without having to look at the inscriptions on the rings themselves.

"Can they all be done at once? Or must they be completed one at a time?"

"I have never seen all balanced at once before," he replies, "but, seeing as you have balanced all emotions of the world..." He looks to the Orrery which immediately rights itself. "It is done. You asked for help as per the instructions, and instead of fruitlessly toiling, you asked a greater power than you to aid your endeavour. You set aside personal pride."

"One would think," I say, "and yet, doesn't that defeat the purpose of the test?"

"You have paid for passage through the gate."

"You've completed the Orrery for me," I intone, and his eyes hold me captive.

"Have I?" he murmurs, observing the structure once more. I am silent as I watch his gleaming, golden eyes. "I previously said there were only two ways to solve it. I also said I had never seen this Orrery corrected in a single movement. I stand corrected on both counts. Go now, Prince

Haduwas."

He holds out the key to the next gate.

"What would have happened if I had not called upon you?" I ask, and his face contorts into a thoughtful expression.

"Well, I suppose you would have been in here for a long while...until your body perished and your bones turned to dust. Your soul would have ventured to the shores perhaps, or, you'd have been stuck here with only these texts to accompany your bones. It could have been that Šauška's method would have occurred to you, of shedding something as superficial as clothes. When your mind desired collapse, you could have returned to the instructions, desperate to find something you'd missed..."

He titters again as he lifts the stone and shows me the inverse side, which has further instructions on it. My head falls back, and as a groan of despair escapes me, the god begins to cackle.

XVII
TABLET

CHOICES MADE

When my stride breeches the barrier, the gate slams shut behind me. Again, the gate ahead swings open. Gate after gate, I pass through them easily, some citing my kindness and generosity to Parasuwa, and others citing my deed in holding the weight of the world.

At long last, I reach the ninth gate, and apprehension tickles my neck and spine. Beyond, an atrium of white. In the centre, a being of shifting smoke and vapour hovering over a throne of iron. Averting my gaze, I bow and await her judgement. I get the sense she wants me to approach, and as I do, I can feel the cool, vapourous power of Kumrešepa sweeping around the room. I feel her gaze even though she remains featureless to my senses, and it is one heavy with unweighed emotion.

The goddess sits stoically, arms relaxed at her side, but as I approach, her right hand lifts in divine expectation. She does not speak, and I sense that even if I ask her questions, she will not respond regardless of what I may ask. It is the final gate, and the request is clear even without words.

A physical token must be bestowed, but my clothing, homely as they are, will not do. There is only one thing of value on my person, and to give it away is to doom my people—if my father's rule continues that is. My options are few, and increasingly dismal. I can stay here and give the goddess nothing—and die. I can give her something unworthy—and die. Or. I can give her the fruit, the very item I came to this place to retrieve, and fail...as foretold by Parasuwa. My path requires me to fail. To give this up. For if I bring this to the earthly realm, I sense only utter despair for myself and my people. I approach her, and her eyes seem to sparkle. Divine fruit in hand, I toss it up and down a couple of times, feeling the true weight of the fruit before I lightly place it in the goddess's outstretched palm. I clear my throat.

"I offer you the greatest gift I have in my possession. I hope this shall suffice, and I place myself entirely at your mercy."

Bowing my head, I sink to my knees, and await her directive. She says nothing. My knees begin to ache on the stone steps, but still I do not look. Outstretching my hands, I press my forehead to the floor, silent save for my breathing. Still, she says nothing. The only sound is the slightest breeze on my skin; when I finally chance a glance at her, it is only to find she is not there. Panic grips my throat. The thought that it had been not enough plagues me, that I had not been enough...Šauška had been strung up as a corpse until the other gods had interfered, demanding she be returned. There would be no such demands on my behalf if I have failed. Perhaps this is it then. The words of Parasuwa echo in my mind once again: *"You will fail the task, but win the real prize"*.

But what is the real prize? Evidently, it is not the fruit, the very purpose of my initial quest. My hands burn where the fruit had been only moments ago. In its place, my flexing palm. Despite my failure, my heart beats with the steadiest of thumps. No tremor ails my hands, nor does sweat drip from my brow. I feel utter peace with my decision—in fact—I believe it is the correct one. No longer do I trust in the will of my father. Too much venom in his ears—and his purpose? No longer difficult to surmise. Clearly, he wants it for himself.

The kings of old, spoken of in the divine list of kings from that ancient land called Sumer, they'd lived eternal lives in a gilded age of youth, wealth, and health. My father desires to return to this long-gone age through fraudulent means—and that priest, using my efforts to bolster his own rancid reign.

The last gate groans as it opens, and standing beyond, the goddess Lelwani. Her eyes are blazing as she assesses me, gaze traveling from head to empty hand, to my feet, noting all my clothing still in place, and her lips quirk. Her hands are clasped behind her back, and her voice is filled with humour when she says, "So, prince. You yet live."

"It appears so," I reply, hands outstretched at my sides in demonstration. "I have passed your test."

Her laughter is not a light, airy thing. It is a dark simper that promises danger and darkness. The hair on the back of my neck raises, and a shudder passes through me as she slowly encircles me with a single finger on my skin, leaving a trail of heat and shivers in her wake. Her laugh dwindles until she simply stares at me with a smirk.

"Have you."

Without another word, she turns around, and in her palm, the golden fruit I had given up.

The palace we approach is carved stone with great stairs, looming pillars, and high ceilings. It is the image of the temple of Arinna, and I wonder at the similarities. The emaciated bodies of the dead are nowhere to be found, nor any of the other propagated imagery of the "Dread sun goddess of the earth." In fact, there is nothing that marks it as different from the other temples.

Where before I would have felt the physical fatigue, there is hardly a strain on my muscles, even as I keep pace with the goddess scaling the mountain. I sense, rather than see, the smile on her face as she speeds up ever so slightly. Effortlessly, I keep pace. Now, her chin turns in my direction as her pace quickens and a grin cracks on my face.

A flicker of something younger flashes in her immortal face, and I wonder: how long has it been since the goddess of death played? Probably back when she was the maiden above—a being full of life and joy.

I surge forward, as does she, and in pace with one another, we race up the steps. Though the stone be dark, and the sun far away, I've never felt so much light in my life as I race against death herself. She laughs as her arms pump at her sides, her many layers of cloth treading behind her like wings of night. Determination floods me, and it doesn't occur to me that I'm racing a goddess that I have no chance in beating, or even that to challenge the gods themselves, invites both death and punishment. None of these things occur to me, and for once, neither of us wear our titles or responsibilities.

We are not queen and prince, immortal and mortal—we are simply a man and a woman having a good old-fashioned foot race—one steeped with something like a promise of something...exciting. What direction that promise falls, remains to be seen.

My feet seem to fly as they pound on the rocky terrain, sure and steady, and so swift, I barely feel the steps underfoot. I propel myself, and soon, I'm leaping, taking the steps two at a time, three, four steps at a time.

Lelwani is silent beside me, and when I chance a look, she smirks at me and disappears into thin air before reemerging two hundred paces ahead at the top of the steps. Gasping, my momentum falters, and I stumble.

When I reach her, I am huffing for breath, but she is still and silent, and though I have sweat dripping from my temples, not a hair on her head is out of place. Truly divine.

"You cheated," I declare.

"Oh?" she asks, settling onto one hip. "When did we discuss rules?"

"Are you truly arguing semantics with me?" I demand, and she chortles.

“Did you truly think you could win?” she asks, genuine curiosity across her face. After a moment of reflection, I shake my head. “Shame." Her giggle subsides and her serious expression reappears. "If you had, you could have won.”

Turning, she enters through the twin pillars, clearly structural rather than decorative, and again, I am struck by the lack of art, of decoration, of grandeur. It makes sense why there is none, in the land of the dead, nothing can flourish. In the land of the dead, *nothing* can live. And yet...

here she is. More than anything, I want her to live and flourish. More than the kingdom, more than my crown, I want her to have glorious art and beautiful things.

A goddess, a queen, should be surrounded by beauty. The stone walls beg for carvings, and the floors yearn for decorated wovenware. The great atrium desires light, a great ball of flame suspended in the ceiling, both for light and heat as my skin prickles with the cold—and a true throne of power. Eyeing the room, a single chair stands on the raised dais, but like everything else, it is unremarkable.

She says nothing as she steps through a jagged slice in the face of the rock, and I follow her. Inside, it isn't quite what I'd describe as cozy, but it's a great deal warmer. Gesturing vaguely, she sits down and seems to wait to see what I will do. Eyeing the options, I opt for the seat directly across from her. I could have kneeled, stayed standing, sat at her side, or sat far from her. No cushions line the stone, though a natural spring gurgles in the corner in a meandering fashion; the seat is warm, and I can only presume the spring is a natural hot spring, the source of the heated room and stone.

"You raced well," she says, not smiling. Her voice is cool, edged with the same stillness I felt at the riverbank before the souls had tried swallowed me.

"I didn't win."

"Was that the purpose?" A pause. "You kept pace." It's not a compliment. It's a measurement. Her fingers trace the rim of a shallow bowl beside her; it is plain stone, which holds nothing. "And still, you hesitate. As if still awaiting instructions."

"I'm your guest."

"No." Her eyes lift to mine. "You passed the gates. You chose to continue. That makes you something else entirely." Her stare doesn't burn—it freezes, and I feel the temperature drop between us despite the heated room. The way my heart thunders within the cage of my chest is unlike anything I've personally experienced, though I'd felt it through others when I held the duty of Ubelluri. I swallow.

"Then what am I?"

She studies me, and I know I've made an error. She was hoping I'd tell her what I am, not ask her to decide. She has called my indecision and I've responded with more of the same.

"Still waiting for someone to name you," she remarks. "Your father does it. Your gods do it. Even now, you wonder what title *I'll* give you."

I lean forward, elbows on knees, hands open. "And you? What title do you wear when no one is looking?"

She pauses, lips tightening as she shifts in her seat. "None," she says. "That's the only way to keep them from using it." I nod once, slowly. The room feels colder again, but charged. She sets the bowl aside, empty. "You came for something. You left it behind." Though the bowl is empty, it is clear she refers to the golden treasure. She deposits the fruit into the bowl and places it in the centre of the table—a taunt.

"I gave it up," I say, refusing to look any longer at the bowl. No longer is it a temptation to me—not in the way it was before in any case. It represents something I no longer believe, something marred by the schemes of my father and Kammara. The question is not whether I will return with the apple. It is whether I decide to return at all. The proffered apple is an invitation, an unspoken declaration—of partnership.

"Gave it up for what?"

"Because it was the correct thing to do."

"Was it?"

I sit in the silence, something enhanced by the dimness of the cavern and the slow trickle of water between us.

I don't answer her at first, and when I do, it is unrelated as I endeavour to circle around back to it. "Tell me: when I entered that competition set by frauds, I actually *did* climb up that vine of divinity, did I not? *Your* vine of divinity."

Finally, a flicker—an almost smile. "Yes. I granted it."

I tilt my head to the side, staring deeply into her eyes. "Why? My brothers did the same, and my people make a custom of it. To my knowledge, it is a gift so rare to be marked by you that truly, it has never happened."

"Many are marked by me, prince, and always, they *die*."

"And yet, not I."

"Not you."

"Why is that?" I ask, trying to force her to answer without further questions. Now it is her to stew in the silence, though she shifts again, ever so slightly, and it's only a result of my heightened senses that I'm able to catch it. It is only because of how keenly aware of her I am that I even notice the movement at all.

"You're curious," she murmurs. "Curiosity usually leads men to ruin."

"Then ruin me." Now, she *does* smile.

"Sleep before you decide whether you've earned what you came for."

"And what did I come for?" I ask, and she snorts in the most human way.

"Perhaps you'll come up with an answer for that too, prince." She stands up, dismissing me.

"And if I have?" I ask, before she leaves the room.

She levels me with a hard look. "Then you won't need to ask me again."

I remain seated, uncertain whether I'm colder for the distance she placed between us—or warmer, for having seen her remove the mask for even just a moment.

The place is not unlike the chambers I had been given in the land above. It is a cavern set in darkness with a gurgling stream. There is light, though not like the sun. It's like the light of a distant fire, offering little in the way of detail, but enough that my eyes are now capable of viewing what most could not. There are no cushions of comfort, nor stuffed linen wraps filled with feathers or woven blankets to preserve warmth; it's a stark difference from the world I've come from.

All to be found is myself, what I have brought, and the cave that has been provided to me. No food, no drink, and no creature comforts.

Is it required of gods and goddesses to eat? Does a goddess of death require such things? Can she enjoy wine or beer? She knows of such things, in particular, because she blessed me with a slice of her divinity when I drank the gods. Truly, she had reached down and plucked me up from the throng. I *owe* the goddess of death. She has given me a piece of herself, of her divinity. What this means exactly...I do not know.

Does this mean I have powers over life and death too? Am I myself immortal now? Or just...divinely touched for this life?

My questions throttle me, and the longer I sit and think about the choice I have to make, the more questions I have with no answers.

Even though there are no comforts such as what I am accustomed to, sleep comes easily, if not fitfully. In my dreams, I am back in my home of Kuššara, and the scorching day has turned to freezing night. The sun has set upon Kuššara, no longer smiled upon by the revered sun-goddess of Arinna. Gone are the rows and rows of farmers and pockets of herders with their flocks. In their place, silent, swaying stalks of einkorn and trodden trails leading back to the tents, caravans, and huts of their families set up on the perimeter beyond the city walls.

Music can be heard from every direction, interspersed with the sounds of laughing, fighting, and nocturnal activities. The scene shifts, the view getting closer and closer to one tent in particular. Inside, bulbs of drying garlic ward the entrance, and stacked baskets carrying household staples. Stuffed cushions and woven rugs line the floor space while candles exhale flame—the solitary source of light.

On one such rug, a little boy with wild curls plays with a toy while women around him do the day's end's work. One woman organizes herbs, while another busies herself with passing around carved cups, likely filled with beer. One continues fashioning toys with a blade, a pile of completed carvings around her, while another collects earthenware for supper. Some of the toys are for trading at the market no doubt, but some will be given to the child to keep him occupied. Beside him, a teenaged boy, solemn as he stares hard at a flame while his hands idly fidget with the carved bone in the likeness of a stag.

"He's been this way since his mother's death," one remarks. I do not know her face. The one gathering herbs looks up, her hazel eyes tired and knowing, and I find that I do know hers. Nipula. Had her words not chilled me to the bone? Had she not prophesized that I would bury many a thing? Since her words, I had parted from the mother of my child and many a brother. I have buried *myself*. Has her prophecy not struck true? Or am I doomed to bury more and more until there is nothing left to give? Perhaps it is *I* who is damned.

The dream becomes unclear. Images blur and blend together. I see my father on his throne. I see his child queen speaking with the high priest, her father. Again, I see my child, my solemn child who looks so like me it grieves me to see such sadness on his youthful face, sitting on the rug with all women but his mother, and the bone clutched in his hand. Again, I am torn away from the view of my child to see a group of marching soldiers.

Idari. Malinuwa. Soldiers.
Idari. Malinuwa. Soldiers.

They know. Somehow, they know.

Bolting upright, my hair is sodden with sweat, and my clothes cling to my clammy skin. The fruit in the bowl still stares at me, catching the light to throw it back in my eyes.

"You have chosen, then."

Lelwani emerges from the shadows. Her expression is not angry. I blink at her, and when I focus again, she just looks...sad.

"I fear my child is in mortal danger."

She nods, taking a seat across from me. "Children are always in mortal peril. Especially when they shouldn't exist," she says gently. The way my fear seizes me is yet still more powerful than when I held everyone else's fear.

"If there's any chance I can save him, I must do it."

"I understand," she murmurs, pushing the bowl slowly towards me. I tilt me head at the bowl, and then golden fruit within.

"I shall not take such an object anywhere *near* the court. But I have a request to make of you."

Her green eyes, so much like springtime, hold no malice or even confusion. She simply awaits my request. "Anything you ask, and it shall be yours."

I can't even pause to deconstruct her question before the words are out of my lips. She listens intently as I explain my idea, and in answer, her lips twitch before she nods. "Very well. It shall be done."

I think of Askalpusa. "I also desire my friend in the form of the owl to be released into the world above. He desires freedom, and I daresay, he has been trapped below for long enough and punished sufficiently given what has happened to his mother's tree."

"A punishment not of my doing," she says, brows furrowing. "It was my mother. Alas, it has already been done. He walks freely in the land above."

"And Sharvara?"

Her eyes seek mine, and I see a great deal of love for the hound. "Is mine, but I shall allow you to borrow him. You may find that one day, he disappears. He will have rejoined me on this day."

"Thank you," I breathe, and I stand, slowly. It is the first time I have stood above her. I cross around the room to take a knee before her. "Lelwani." I lower my head before her, but as I do, her hand carefully cups my chin to raise my gaze to hers.

"There is no need, Haduwas."

"Not *my prince*?"

"No. Not this day."

Her eyes flick between mine, and she must come to some sort of conclusion because she nods to herself. Her skin is cold, but not in a deathly sort of way. Her hand still cups my chin, and slowly, I reach for her hand. She does not pull away, so I commit, cradling her hand with both of mine. Keeping my eyes upon hers, I bring her hand to my lips. She smells of flowers and sunshine. She smells of hope and life. My lips graze her marble white flesh, and I feel something click into place—some sort of divine understanding.

"You must go," she says, her voice quieter than usual, void of the flirtatious and teasing she had demonstrated the night before. "A child... there is no greater joy."

"You've had children?" I ask, acrid jealousy climbs up my throat with the speed and strength of a demon, though of course she may have. She'd been married before, though no sacred text spoke of children.

“I've never been blessed by such a gift, and I fear I never shall.”

“This will not be so,” I say, sure of it. My inner knowing tells me it shall happen for her.

“I have been cursed to be barren.”

“By whom?” I ask, my voice deadly.

“My first husband...before I killed him.”

“And you know this to be true?” I ask carefully. “You've not...tried?”

“I have not,” she admits, “but curses made by gods hardly fail.”

“Unless made by a weaker god,” I muse, and for a moment, she looks startled.

“Well...I'm definitely stronger than he ever was,” she says, her expression brightening for a moment, but the moment ebbs away and she returns to her melancholic expression. “You must go.”

I nod, finding it increasingly difficult to relinquish my hold on her, though I must. I think of my son, and let go of her hand. You must go now. You must go back whence you came.”

I don't have a chance to ask her what she is apologizing for before I am face-to-face with a wall of stone. Blood marrs the surface, and with a jolt, I realize I am back in my own world, standing at the entrance to the Underworld. Sharvara is at my side and he barks affectionately, knocking me over. I ruffle his fur, his brawn scarcely concealed by the fluff. He barks again, tail wagging, and dog breath wafts in my face as he licks my face with abandon.

“Sharvara!” I protest. “My son is in danger. I must go to him.”

Sharvara immediately gets off me, standing at attention like he truly understands my words. His tail is suddenly stiff, and ears are back. The instant shift in his stature is both impressive and alarming. Sharvara growls low in his throat. He simply turns and trots the way we'd come, and I hurry after him. Not that it's possible, but it seems Sharvara is in an even greater hurry than I am.

Together, we race up the switch-back tunnel system. The steep stairs we'd descended the first time around, feels an awful lot like when I'd raced Lelwani up the stairs to her palace. I'm reminded by what she said: *"If you'd have believed you could have beaten me, you would have."* Another thought surfaces: she'd given me gifts—*her* gifts. She had simply appeared where she wanted to appear. I skid to a stop.

I barely have time to get the thought out when I envision the throne room and appear inside.

XVIII
TABLET

SOUL ETERNAL

There is screaming in the throne room, and it doesn't seem to have anything to do with my arrival. In fact, no one seems to realize I am standing among them though I stand in the centre of the floor. At the dais, the child queen wears an expression of sorrow, while my father upon the throne looks grim. On one side of the room, the priests, and on the other, the court. My brothers and sisters stand in abject horror. My friend, Mutti, weeps openly on the floor, his clothing ripped in grief while Nipula has tear tracks on her face, and a growing welt over her eye where she was obviously struck. She is restrained by guards as she kneels beside Mutti, and other women are in similar positions in a line beside her.

On the floor, a mangled body, so grotesquely abused, I can not visually tell the identity, and yet I *know*. Cold grief washes over me, and in the splinter of a second, I know I have materialized because the screaming from the different parties ceases and gasps of terror echo around the room instead. Shadows billow around me, and I take a single, menacing step forward.

The room seems to disappear as I lock eyes with my father. When he looks at me, he no longer looks like my father—just a man reaching beyond his place. A weak man who is now nothing to me. His lips part as if to say something, a prayer or perhaps a curse? He flounders, and his eyes leave mine to seek out his priest. Kammara, looks faintly green at the sight of me, and he makes a warding mark against me...as though that can save him. His eyes dart to the floor to avoid my gaze, and I return my attention to my father. The soldiers lining the room, including Nippa, whose eyes are wide at the scene, inch closer to the royal couple on the dais.

The room is at a standstill, but at long last, my father breaks the silence. "You are back, my son."

"And not in time, it seems, King Karuwas." A numbness floods my limbs, my head lighter than air, and my limbs heavier than the weight of the world. No longer is the man before me my father. He is something else entirely.

"Were you successful in your divine mission, my son?"

He keeps repeating the words *'my son'* as though they are a placating salve and not the twisting of a spear in my gut. He twists and twists the weapon with every word out of his mouth.

"Certainly," I respond. "Elsewise, I would not have deigned to show my face at court. Tell me of my son."

Gasps erupt around the room, and Mutti's cries pick up once more. Perhaps there had been misbelievers. My brothers and sisters stand in unified, horrified silence as they take in the mangled mess on the floor. I feel something sidle up to me, and when my eyes float to the side to check, I see it is Sharvara.

"We have been brought here to discuss a matter of state," he begins, and suddenly, the room disappears as my eyes stop seeing the room, instead, a veil of darkness befalling me as my rage finally boils over. I see only darkness, and great crashing waves in my ears as water crests on a great and rocky shore.

"Tell me about my son!" I roar, and at the precise moment of my eruption, so too do the walls seem to shake and the floors tremble. My father looks at me now in a way I have never seen before: he is truly afraid of me. *Good.*

"I am now Crown Prince, am I not?" I ask, pulling the golden fruit from my pocket to hold it high. "Look at this great treasure I have won from the depths of the earth!" I cry in a mockery. "It was asked of me to accomplish this deed so I could become Crown Prince, a title I already hold in all but name by right of birth and deed!" The room is silent as I begin to pace. Tremors still rock the room, but no one dares to flee my mounting wroth.

"*'It is a rite of passage for all aspirant kings,'* the king had said. And yet, I ask you, when has *any* other come back and declared such a gift?" The room grumbles with dissonant murmurs, but I continue. "And surely if my *great father* had completed such a task, he would not be *dying* as we speak." I turn to him, and a cruel smile twists my mouth when his mouth drops in shock. "Oh yes, father. I know all about it. You thought you hid your limp? Not well enough, I'm afraid." I turn to the room. "The gods strike where they are angered. Look to his limbs—they bear the weight of heaven's wrath. His foot burns because the gods have withdrawn their favour. The earth rejects his tread. You have all seen it of late.

"He requires this fruit," I say, holding it up above my head once more, "to preserve his life—a life the gods themselves have deemed forfeit. He is not in any of their favour. This priesthood?" I gesture blithely at the high priest and his creatures. "They're not in communion with any god. They have lied! To the king, to me, and to you!"

"The boy has been in communion with the dread goddess of the Earth! Heed him not!" the high priest cries at last, swallowing his fear. "Do not listen to what he says! The gods deemed him unfit to lead us, and his own line has been struck down! Follow him, and you will all live a life of grief too. The king is divine, as he is chosen by the gods! Tell me true that you believe this man more than the word of the gods," he says, gesturing at me with a flippant hand. I change tactics.

"Look me in the eye, *Father*, and tell me you went into the dread underground to retrieve a treasure like this." The demand is out of my lips before the soldiers can take any action, and the room rests like it wants to know too. Again, my father refrains from answering.

"You make no demands of kings, Haduwas," the priest tries, but the room takes no action against me.

"The king can answer for himself," I say, tone artificially light. "You'll notice that he does not immediately say he did, because he cannot. A man who had done such a thing would not withhold a defence. What happens to these great treasures if our line of kings did indeed complete the task as was given to me? Surely having relics of the gods would be a great honour and would not be kept a dirty secret. I posit to you they have never done such a thing. Instead, my father intends to keep this great fruit for himself to usurp my rightful place as is the order and custom of the land. He wishes to rule you in perpetuity. He and this *priest* murdered my child—"

"It was not my doing!" the king shouts in rebuttal, and I silence him with a narrowing of my eyes.

"So he acted without decree and without your knowledge?"

The king pales. He is silent as he contemplates his answer—ever the politician. I point at the bloodied mess on the floor. "That is my blood. *Your* blood. You have kinslayed."

"Haduwas, no! I had nothing to do with this!" my father cries, and as he looks to the high priest, eyes wild and unfocused. The twisted malice on Kammara's face reveals his true character, and slowly, he rises to her feet. He says nothing, headdress swaying on his head as he struggles through the throng.

"He holds the property of the king. Seize it now!" Kammara demands. The warriors look to the king for the final word.

"Then know it is from my cold, dead, hands you shall be prying it from," I say simply, bracing myself even as I hold the fruit. Mutti is dragged to his feet, as are the women, and taken to the edge of the room where my siblings watch with shining eyes alongside the rest of the court. My brothers usher my sisters back, shielding them from the crackling of violence coasting upon the thickening air.

Sharvara rumbles a growl, teeth revealed, and it stalls the line of soldiers pressing in towards us, but only for a moment. All at once, the private militia converges on me, and any time one tries to land a blow upon me, I neither feel it, nor move. Holding both hands tight over the apple without putting pressure upon the fruit itself, I protect it. My arms are seized, and despite the many men trying to pry them apart, I do not budge. It is now a symbol—a symbol of Lelwani, and I will not have this last gift from her be touched by the likes of these men it would be a failure on my part. So, with all the strength I possess, I hold strong.

"Take it, by the gods!" the priest screams, and the men try all the harder. Someone takes a hold of my hair to yank my head back, and my body is wrenched back, and I grit my teeth. Throat exposed, someone tries to slash my throat with a blade, but it's as though my skin itself repels violence. A sickening crunch tells me Sharvara has clamped down on someone, and the answering, tremulous cry tells me just how painful the bite is.

The men move from blades to spears and bow and arrow, but everything thrown simply returns to the assailant. Men go down as fast as they approach, and soon, they all cease, stepping back to keep a wide berth around me.

"How does he not die?" someone murmurs, and the room grows cold as my own resolution grows.

"You may not have entered the realm of the dead, Father," I say quietly, eyes on the floor. Slowly, my gaze rises to meet his own, and again, my cold smile appears. "But *I* did."

Still, the fruit is in my hand, and in one, cruel moment, I lift the fruit to my mouth and take a bite, teeth tearing through tough, textured skin before the inner juices flood my mouth. I do not hear the shouts of the men or of my father. I simply sit on the floor of the palace, casually, and eat the apple in silence. It is but an ordinary fruit, but taking something precious from my father is all I have at the moment. If I allow myself to feel everything in this moment, what needs to be done will not be done. The fruit tastes like ash. It tastes of death and suffering. It tastes like failure.

The room grows quiet as I eat the skin, flesh, and seeds as well for good measure. I grow unfocused as I see yet another snake on the ceiling. It is not real—at least I do not believe it is. Perhaps it's a sign that Lelwani is here with me. Perhaps I *will* die soon. It matters no longer. At my side, my son. In silence, I sidle towards the bodies, see my son and Gazaza both. The guiltless victims of a corrupt governance—children, always.

Sweeping their broken bodies into my arms, I rock them side to side, not to comfort them, but to comfort myself. Reaching, I note the scar on the middle of Idari's bicep from when we'd been attacked by the birds on the road. Something inside me had cruelly hoped this was someone else's child, someone else's grief, and shame floods my veins at the thought. At last, I relax, seated upon the ground with my hands cradling the children in my lap as I just wait to see what happens. Sharvara wraps his giant body around me, his warmth and strength a blessed buffer. I don't bother looking at my father or that scheming priest who now stands at his side. Instead, I focus on the stained blanket, trying not to think about the suffering he endured. Instead, I hold his body, and I think of what I shall do next. The answer to me is obvious.

So deep in thought am I that I do not notice the change in the room. Standing from his seat, the king approaches me. "My son," he croaks, falling to sit on the floor at my side, heedless of Sharvara's warning growl. "My son, please believe me. I know nothing of this, and if I had, I would have protected him!" Lifting my head, I stare hard at my father, *wanting* to believe him. At the wall, cradling a mangled arm, looking so much like Alluwa had after the battle, Nippa. His face is pale and ashen, but whether from remorse or blood loss, I'll never know. My eyes meet his, and I *know* Idari's death was his doing.

"Why?" I demand, but I get no answer. Nippa's eyes plead with me to understand, to forgive him, but how can I when my boy's broken body is before me?

At once, there is a sharp gasp, and I look up to see the priest charging me with an axe in his hands, stolen off a soldier at his side. Before I can let go of Idari and Gazaza, my father bolts to his feet, knocking me aside, and as he does, Kammara hurls it at me in his wroth. Time slows as it hurtles toward my father, and all I can do is watch its trajectory and hold my breath as my father embraces his own deathstroke. My father barely has time to hold his hands out before the sickening thud tells me it claims purchase. His body hits the floor.

"Please," he wheezes. "Believe me." They are his last words. I *want* to believe them.

"My king," Kammara gasps, but the guards who'd been lining the floor descend upon him at once, securing him in unforgiving holds. The room is deadly silent, and all faces turn to look at me. I am their new king, but my grief is too fresh, too raw, too complicated. Still, I clutch my children, Gazaza mine in the way he was a child of my village—mine in the way I had taught him to dance as a father would.

My brothers openly weep, but my sisters just look at me with faces of stone. My eldest sister, Hestuwa, steps forward. Avoiding the blood spilled on the floor, she approaches our father. His eyes are wide and unseeing. Guiding his eyes shut, she brushed her fingers over his forehead. Gently removing the crown from our father's head, she approaches me. Her eyes move to Sharvara, but she approaches slowly, and Sharvara's tail playfully hits the floor at her approach.

"You must let them go," she says, gently. Gathering my courage, I lay them side by side on the floor. Drying blood stains my hands, my clothes, but I take a knee, bowing my head before my sister. The crown of my father lands upon my brow, the metal still holding warmth from my father's head.

"All hail King Haduwas."

The room kneels instantly after my sister, whether through fear or admiration, it can hardly be told. Hestuwa is the first to look at me, and it is with the slightest of smiles, but there is warmth in her eyes. "You must sit upon your throne, little brother."

My gaze moves to the throne, and I, still kneeling in my son's blood, yearn only for the realm of death. The throne is no longer mine. The threat is gone, and yet, I must take a seat. When again I stand, I look for my friend, the most faithful Mutti, and he is at my side in an instant, fleeing from the guard's grasp at the side of the room.

"I'm so sorry," he sobs. "I'm so sorry." It is a broken chain of words and tears, and I can barely understand anything else he says, but I bring our foreheads together in ultimate mourning. I withdraw to take in his face, and it is flushed with tears and anguish. *I cannot ask anything further of him*, I think, and as I think it, my gaze turns to my sister once more. "Hestuwa, can you...?" I trail off, but she requires no further instruction as she begins her own duty as eldest female in the family. It is her duty to care for the dead along with my sisters.

"And our father?" she asks, not bothering to turn her attention away from my son as she approaches, stooping to guard his body. The bloody patches show through the clothing, and my young sisters, Heriya and Dameruwa, appear at her side.

"Give him the burial he deserves." Moving across the floor, I step up the dais, eyes firmly on the throne. The queen quakes like the gentlest of grain in the wind, and I slow my approach.

"Malinuwa," I say gently. "You don't need to see this next part. Please return to your chambers. You have nothing to fear from me." She rises, and when her father reaches for her, she flings his hand away from her to stand closer to me. She says nothing, and yet the fire in her eyes communicates so much more clearly than the spoken word can. Sitting upon the throne of my father, I take a deep breath as I regard the man before me, but he only has eyes for his daughter as she leaves the room.

"High Priest Kammara. You are hereby stripped of all titles, lands, and offices. You and the rest of the priesthood will be tried by the will of the gods in accordance with our sacred laws."

There is an outcry from one side of the room, but when I raise my fist in the air, the sound ceases at once. "The gods know the truth of it. If you were not involved, there is nothing to fear from me. But if you were..." I let the words run rounds through the room, and allow their imagination to do my work. "Take the accused to the secured gatehouse. I will convene with The Pankus on the morrow to decide how to proceed."

When the hall is emptied of the accused, everyone around is now a familiar face. I sit. "There are many things to be discussed," I begin. "Firstly. My men will be released. *Now.*"

My brothers are immediately released, and they approach the seat, all taking a knee. I try to smile, but I'm sure that it just comes off as a grimace. "Rise, my brothers. Your loyalty will not be forgotten." I do not think about Nippa, whose face still lingers at the forefront of my mind. He had been taken alongside the priests. The guards were not likely loyal either, but they would be dealt with too.

"My sisters shall take the bodies of my son and father and prepare them for funerary rites on the morrow. My son will have a burial, as is the custom of our royal family in honour of his life so cruelly stolen." I swallow the growing lump in my throat. "My sisters shall decide how our father shall be honoured. You may begin those preparations immediately." They nod, and together, they depart with the help of some of the household guards to collect both bodies.

"Next, the priesthood. With many crimes afflicting the sect, there will need to be a restructuring and recruitment to ensure there are no gaps or forgotten rites and festivals as we move forward." The nobles, whose names I do not yet know, are eyeing me with varying expressions, some hopeful, and some with irritation. Some more have ambition clear in their eyes, and the thought of marriage for political gain makes me want to dive into the grave with my son. And it is then that I know what I will do. The servants begin to enter the room, and when Kazera sees me, his relief is palpable. I nod at him and he moves in unison with the other servants to clean the floors. His face is stony as he takes in the mess.

"Prince Pasaduwa. Prince Zuwasa. Approach."

My brothers approach and bow before me. "Rise. I would look upon each of you." They do, and my brothers look just as tired as I feel. "Court dismissed." We wait for the room to be empty but for the servants, and with a sigh, I rub my eyes, before looking at my brothers. "Come." Drawing myself up once more, I move behind the throne and peel back the tapestry from behind the wall. My brothers haven't followed. "I'm not going to harm you," I say in exasperation. "You'll notice I did not *kill* anyone even though many in my place would have done so."

"I think they're scared of Sharvara," Kazera calls, and sure enough, Sharvara is sniffing both of them, tail raised, but he soon licks their hands, allowing them to pass and follow me.

"I didn't know this was here," Pasaduwa says, inspecting the tapestry.

"I didn't either until recently. Father brought me here to catch up when I arrived."

My brothers follow me down the chamber my father had once led me down. My footsteps sound more confident than they are, and even the weight of the world had not prepared me for this.

"It's hard to see," Zuwasa says, an edge of petulance leaking into his tone.

"Is it?" I can't remember what my eyesight had been like before. I had not yet tested my eyes in the light of day. When I'd entered the throne room, it had been dusk, where there was no direct sunlight—only braziers and candles and glinting bronze. My first encounter with this tunnel, I seem to recall the smell more than anything, but perhaps that's because I could not see anything and therefore had nothing remarkable to pay attention to. Now, I can see the details in the shorn walls, carved out with symbols and language that even I do not know.

"It is," Parasuwa agrees, and when I turn, I see they trail their hands on the walls to keep steady. The ground underfoot is uneven, but I sense the veins of rock before I step, easily navigating my course. The chamber beyond lights the end of the tunnel mouth, and I feel more than hear my brothers' relief. The floor evens out, and the vaulted stairs to the living quarters reveal the lounges, extravagant cushions, and half filled goblets, which my father had no doubt been drinking before the throne room debacle. The scene has preserved the last peaceful moments of my father, but I don't think my brother's have noticed yet.

Gesturing at the spread, they peel down the stairs with an energy I cannot muster, and as they help themselves to the wine flagons and cheese on the boards, I take my time descending, noting the differences here compared to the land below. It's certainly much darker below, and yet there was an intimacy in the dimness and warmth. Here, it feels staged, orchestrated, and cold.

“I don’t feel much like toasting. Much has been lost today,” I admit, when Pasaduwa hands me my own cup.

“To those lost today,” Pasaduwa says, raising his cup. In silence, Zuwasa and I raise our cups too and drink. Zuwasa reaches for some grapes and cheese.

"So," Zuwasa says, still chewing, "you're king. What are you going to do?" Pasaduwa hits him on the arm, shooting a sideways glance at me as he does, as if to say ‘*he just lost his father and children.*’

I sigh, sitting down on the cushion across from them before resting my chin on interlocked fingers as I stare into a candle flame upon the polished table. "I will rule," I say simply. "I cannot abandon that task, especially not after discovering the rot of the priesthood."

"What are you going to do about Queen Malinuwa?" Pasaduwa asks, holding his cup close to his chest.

"I..." The words fail me. "I lost a son and a father today. Two sons, really. I would not have another life on my hands. If she is amenable, I should like to bring her into the household." I am not met with opposition. "She will be raised with our younger sisters so there will be no unnecessary bloodshed. I will not marry her if the Pankus insists. I will *raise* her. It does not matter to me that she is the daughter of Kammara. She has done no ill to me or this city. This city is divided, and if I am to rule, I need to repair that. To shun the daughter of the priest seems a poor way to mend that, whatever his shortcomings."

"I think she'll agree," Zuwasa says.

"Like she can refuse," Pasaduwa says, and I shrug.

"She could. But I don't think she will. She is not like her father."

Pasaduwa pours another cup and passes it to me. I wonder if they notice my father's glass, but if they do, they do not speak of it.

"She's always been quiet and kept apart from us, so I don't know her well," Zuwasa says. "Kammara never allowed her to be around us." He bites his thumbnail, and Parasuwa nods. "I'm sure our sisters would enjoy having her around."

"Good," I say. "Then that's settled."

The silence that blankets the room is fraught with the tension of unspoken emotion. I cannot handle a conversation about Idari right now. The way their eyes dart around the room makes me wonder if the knowledge that Idari was their nephew has struck them yet, but they refrain from mentioning it. Instead, we catch up, and they fill me in on their lives here. There's a distance between us though that I want to close. The yearning in my heart is an ever-widening chasm. The ones I love seem to vanish. My brothers laugh and regale me with stories of their shenanigans of youth all while I make a tally of everyone I've lost; I doubt my smile reaches my eyes, but if it doesn't, they either don't notice, or, more likely, are kind enough to allow me the space to process.

"Haduwas?" Zuwasa asks, tone shifting, and despite Pasaduwa clicking his tongue in warning, Zuwasa rolls his eyes before turning them on me.

"Yes?"

"What was it like down there?" Pasaduwa eyes Zuwasa with narrowed eyes, but I know he wants to hear about it too when his eyes shift to me and he leans forward expectantly. Nodding, I take a sip of wine, stalling as I gather my thoughts.

"Dark...and peaceful," I say at last. "I faced many trials, but if I had not been tasked with obtaining that fruit, life there would have been peaceful. Nothing is in a rush down there, and everyone I met treated me with kindness." At their raised eyebrows, I pause. "Well, almost everyone," I amend, thinking of .

"Who did you meet down there?" Pasaduwa blurts, and Zuwasa nods like the question had been snatched before he could voice it.

"I met Ubelluri and Parasuwa," I begin, listing them off on my fingers casually, and their eyes bug out of their heads. "I actually *freed* Parasuwa," I admit, and if their eyes were not secured in their heads, they'd have fallen out with how wide they look at me.

"*The* Parasuwa?!"

"*The*," I agree. I pat Sharvara who had curled around my back, and he snorts and shifts, getting comfortable. "I met Litti too. And Lelwani," I add, too quickly though, because Parasuwa tilts his head, eyes assessing—knowing. "I went through her nine gates, each guarded and protected by an ancient one."

"Brother," Parasuwa breathes, eyes on my hair. My hand reaches up to play with the discoloured lock.

"Yes," I say. "This is from when I met Ubelluri. I took his place and held up the heavens for him so he could grab the immortal fruit for me."

"The one you ate? What's it like to be immortal?"

"It was a fake."

"Upelluri tricked you?" Parasuwa asks, tilting his head.

"No," I say, shaking my head. "I asked Lelwani to give me a fake one," I correct, "but I did get the apple. I just surrendered the real one to Lelwani."

"You surrendered it?" Zuwasa looks incredulous, but Parasuwa just looks confused.

"But, if you surrendered the fruit, how are you alive?" he demands. He puts his goblet down a little too loudly making Zuwasa jump, but Parasuwa does not take his eyes off me, expression thoughtful. "Come to think of it, you seemed immune to injury before you'd even eaten the fruit.".

"We have Sharvara to thank," I say, gently combing my fingers through his fur, and Sharvara grumbles sleepily, tail wagging. "I almost died immediately. The river there, where the ferryman carries the souls across...I swam through it and nearly drowned. I was immersed, head to toe—even swallowed some." I think not to mention how I had seen Alluwa and Huella in the river. I gloss over that part, keeping that sorrow to myself. "Sharvara dragged me out of the river and saved my life. I believe that the river had certain properties. I don't know the extent of it, but I can't seem to be physically harmed." My mind drifts to the many times I could have and *should have* died. "That's my best guess. When I had the fruit in my hands, I was close to escaping when I met Zari and somehow, I was stronger than him. That's when Lelwani appeared."

Parasuwa looks at me with pursed lips. "You say her name rather easily, brother." When I don't respond, he forges on. "It's familiar. You do not call her the sun goddess of the earth."

"She is nothing like we've been told."

"What is she like?"

"Have you ever met Nipula? From the old settlement?"

"She was there," Zuwasa says in a hushed voice. "In the throne room."

I swallow hard, and nod. "Yes, she was. Lelwani looks...similar. Her hair is like the sun when it glows gold in the distance, her eyes like the greenest grass after the rains ripens the earth."

"You love her." Somehow, it is both a question, and an accusation.

"I don't think so..." My fingers fidget with the linen of my pants. "I could. She'd be easy to love. But it doesn't matter."

"Did you...?" Zuwasa wiggles his brows, and Parasuwa punches him in the arm.

I shake my head. "No, it wasn't like that. I felt...understood—*seen*. She seemed...interested though." I think back to when she'd bitten my ear before sending me through the gate, and how she'd stared at me when I'd come through the other side. My mind returns to the race up the steps to her palace, and how free I'd felt. When was the last time I'd felt free?

"Lucky you then," Zuwasa says blithely. "You'll at least have a friend in high places when you die then."

"*Can* you die?" Parasuwa asks, a smirk lifting the side of his mouth. Somehow, the grim question lightens the air.

"Probably a natural death," I say, shrugging. "I'm not too concerned about that anymore."

"Are you immune to poison, then?" Zuwasa asks, his eyes bright as though he is contemplating slipping me some to see how I react. "I mean, you said you swallowed the river, right?"

"I'd rather not test that theory."

"No fun," Zuwasa mutters, staring into his swirling wine.

"No fun," I agree. "Now, tell me everything I need to know about ruling this city."

I stand before my people, a keeper of the dead. The crown upon my head, the crown of my father, makes my forehead itchy. I want to scratch it. I want to remove the band and hurl it at the ground. I want to remain in my chambers, to rest, to wallow, and yet, I was spiritually king the moment my father had passed, crowning or not. Duty. It is my duty to stand here, guiding the priests in their prayers and rites over the death of a royal. The fabric on my skin is rough, and the wind ruffles my tunic against my legs.

The people in the crowd openly weep for their dead king. To the public, he had been a fair and just ruler. His decisions had been for the benefit of the people, and trade, commerce, and abundance had flourished all while strengthening our borders and territories. He was a good man. And yet, the feelings churning within me twist my image of him into something unrecognizable. He had *known* he'd been playing with fire. He had put the family in harm's way by keeping the priest so close. I know he'd had his reasons, *know* that if he had shunned the priest or allowed him to become distant, he would lose even the illusion of control, but my heart cannot accept that. My father and son are laid to rest beside each other, and my sisters sing a hymn of grief, their tunics ripped over their left breast in the sign of mourning.

A group of priests who had been cleared of wrong-doing were in attendance for the rites, and they stood in attendance waiting for the right moments to perform their duties.

My mind drifts, and no matter how many times I pull my eyes back to the scene, they just as quickly flit away to observe the cloud formations overhead. There is no message to be found in the clouds, no birds flying in unusual formations. The gods do not make their wills known, and my gaze, in constant motion, seeks a sign, anything, that they are here, but the wind is quiet, the sky is flat and colourless, and I stand before the masses, utterly alone.

The song of mourning rises in volume, and I force myself to look upon my son's shroud. Upon the sacred frame, his and Gazaza's bodies are wrapped in the finest of dyed and embellished cloth with golden bells adorning each corner. My sisters honoured the fallen with grace, first by washing and then by decorating the dead with elaborate cloth. They had done well under the instruction of the remaining priests, and I try to hold space in my heart to be proud of them.

And then the ritual is over. I only know because Pasaduwa's hand lands on my shoulder, pulling me free from my rampant, spiraling thoughts. I don't look at my father, or either boy—not even the earth piling over them. I close my eyes, and I can *hear* it, and that's enough. Too much. *Was there ever a pain such as losing a child?*

"Long live King Haduwas!"

I am no king—not even a prince. Barely a man. I'm something else now. Sharvara trots at my side, and he growls every time someone gets too close. Ahead of all else, I breach the gate flanked by the twin lions. They guard the city with frightful faces and eyes which see too much.

The tents of the common folk engulf the land, but as I look at the scene, it morphs before my very eyes. In my mind, the streets darken with the encroaching of night, and I see the guards cutting through the maze of tents, ducking under awnings, and tearing into tents obstructing their path with terrifying swiftness. I see people drinking and laughing before crying out as they see the royal guard in their midst. I see swords drawn and people desperate to get out of their path. I see someone trying to warn Nipula, but it being too late as everyone within is dragged away from their home and up to the palace where my son would be slain. I see Idari fight fiercely and defend Nipula when she is struck, and three guards converging. I blink the image away.

Now, where the town would usually be bustling with merchants selling their wares and children playing in the streets, it is dead silent—as though they are all aware of the atrocity committed to their neighbour—to the son of the prince. All is quiet on the street, but it is not difficult to mark the path.

There are signs of disturbance from the night last. Curtains are hastily drawn, pots and urns on corners are smashed, and tents have been marked with wicked slashes through the sides. The most damning evidence of all is the plume of pale smoke rising from the outskirts.

The way is clear, and before I know it, I stand before the tent in my dream where the women sewed and carved toys. Upon the ground, nothing discernible, though I imagine any number of the charred lumps could have been Gazaza's toy. The tent had been put to the torch, and the small flames that had been thrust upon the walls had climbed into an inferno, spreading with deadly speed and precision. I know there were casualties without the need for further inspection—the group mourning at the front of the Palacial walls is an obvious enough testament.

Still, I keep walking. I walk past scorched earth and burnt crops. I walk past wild wheat and beyond the reach of the sun. Clouds shield me from Arinna's scorching gaze, and...I feel grateful not to be in her spotlight. No longer am I bothered by my distance from her. She was never my intended devotee, and I'm at peace with this fact now.

From cloud cover to sand-swept cavern, I take refuge in the cool, carved earth. Sharvara whines, circling a spot in front of me and leans his body into mine to remind me I am not alone. Vision blurry, I stroke Gazaza's head, utterly beside myself in grief. The weight of such an emotion when it comes from others is a burden far easier to carry.

With no spectators to my grief, I roar my anguish. Something inside snaps; collapsing to the side, I slam the ground with open palms upon the jagged face of stone, my grief stepping aside for a moment of divine wroth. My nails drag across the stone, collecting sharp sediment. It stings, and I know my fingers bleed, but what is that in the face of such agony? I clutch my hair, tugging at the roots, and lose myself to the rhythm of rocking side to side, face buried in my hands.

Allowing my emotions to sink into the stone, they course through my body and into the ground, whereupon, it shatters the stone in front of me, a web of cracks and a pit. When again I look at my hands, there are no more wounds, and more notably, no more pain in my nails. A part of me yearns for it, to shift the hurt into something physical, but instead, I slump against Sharvara and decide to stop resisting the feeling. I sink into it and allow it to toss me around like a wave of old, the gods throwing everything they have at me, but I simply clutch Sharvara's fur between white-knuckled hands and soak his fur with my tears.

Sharvara whines, and upon my next, wracking breath, he stands to face me, licking the salty tracks on my cheeks. When my shudders don't cease, he backs away from me, and suddenly, I am alone in the cave mouth. The shock of Sharvara disappearing before my very eyes is enough to staunch the flow, but the agony yet pierces me in rolling waves, and it hurts to breathe.

Throat swollen as I hold back the swells of emotion, I am reminded not to do that when the lock of white hair falls into view; slumping with my back against the deepest wall, I curl into myself. The stone is cool to the touch, but I feel nothing.

The refracting light in the distance from the clouds does not reach me, but the light edges into the cave mouth with varying intensity as the goddess tries to reach me. I pull my feet closer to my body as her attempts grow. A faint, sweet smell reaches my nose, and I am struck. Sweet wood and florals. *I know that smell.*

Gazing around, I see no visible sign she is near, but I sense her.

"Lelwani?" My voice cracks, and I clear my throat. "Are you there?" She does not show herself, but I feel a brush upon my mind that simultaneously soothes and stirs me.

'I am taking care of your son, Haduwas.' A choked, muffled sound escapes my mouth, and I clutch at the area. *'He is a wonderful soul.'* I don't hear her words as much as I *feel* them. *'You will reunite. This is not the end, dear Haduwas. I am keeping his soul safe.'*

"Where did Sharvara go?" I whisper, but I know she hears me.

'He did not like seeing you in pain. He came to get me.'

"Is he coming back?" My voice is tentative, and somehow, I feel her arms wrap around me. The scent of her grows stronger, cocooning me, and I can't help but relax into it. The frown between my brow smooths out, and my eyes flutter shut.

"He's coming back."

Freezing, I feel her arms solidify, and I feel a coil of her long hair fall from her shoulder to graze my arm. A puff of breath escapes me, but I say nothing, scared a senseless question or acknowledgement of her being here will shatter the illusion. Her skin is as cold as the stone. Easing my eyes open, I meet her gaze, and she cradles my face, wiping my tears away with her gentle thumbs.

The air is charged, but we don't acknowledge it. "How are you here?" I ask, and she smiles.

"By willing it to be so."

"I need to help my people," I say, and she nods.

"I would expect nothing less of you. The man I know, who freed Parasuwa, stood in the place of Ubelluri, and passed through the nine gates is not a man who would shirk his duty."

I don't speak. I *want* to shirk my duty. I want to bury myself with my son and live in the world below with Lelwani, be at her side, and yet, to be worthy of such things, I cannot.

"One day," she says quietly. "One day. You will return to me. I have seen it."

"In death?"

She shakes her head. "No. In life."

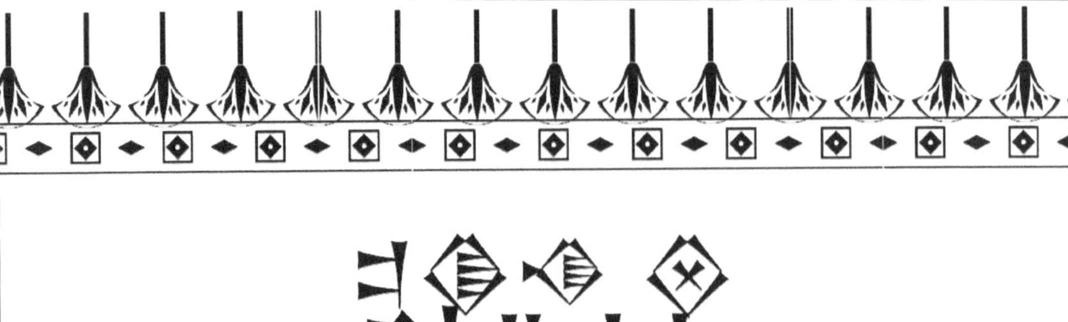

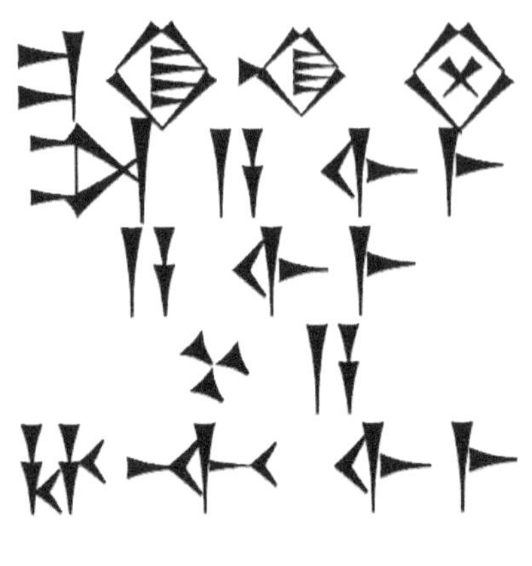

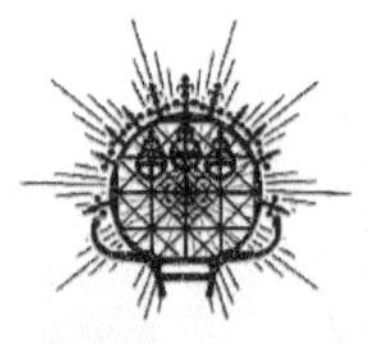

The sickle is in her hand.

The earth is bound.

She makes it a sign of death.

In her hand, the first reaper is made.

XIX
TABLET

SWORD & SALVE
10 YEARS LATER

Reaching across the expanse of linen sheets and silk stuffed pillows, I seek the familiar form of Sharvara, but my fingers encounter only a cold spot where he'd fallen asleep the night before. Blinking, I sit up, finding the bright light of morning has overtaken my quarters, but for all the illumination of day, it does not show my Sharvara.

"Kazera?" I call, and at once, the doors to my chambers open, and he pops his head inside.

"Yes, Haduwas?"

"Have you seen Sharvara?" I ask, bewildered. Kazera frowns, entering the space fully.

"He has not left the room, my king," he says, expression matching mine. "The guards would have alerted me, and they have not."

"Unless they fear my epic wroth," I say, lips twitching. Kazera scoffs.

"I assure you. He has not left this room."

My hand gestures at the room. "And yet, he has."

Kazera bites his lips, and his shoulders lift in discomfort. "Well, Haduwas, he's...well, he's not..."

"Yes?"

"He's not a normal dog, Haduwas. Does he have any...powers? Can he turn invisible or something?" His words strike a cord.

"Not invisible, no." I rise from the bed and snatch a tunic from the cushion at the foot of my sleeping platform and pull it over my head in haste, forgoing my belt altogether. With scarce a look in Kazera's direction, I leave my chambers, words echoing in my head all the while. Sharvara has no powers of invisibility, but he can travel in queer ways... just as I had—once. I had not attempted it since that day my father had sacrificed his life for mine.

"Haduwas!" Kazera follows me through the twisting chambers to the throne room. I had not taken my father's apartments. I had allowed my ward to keep it. For all intents and purposes, Malinuwa is my daughter by choice. She's so very fierce in spirit, reminding me of Huella, a fact which is both sword and salve to my heart. Many of the court had thought I would banish her or, at the very least, send her away in a far away marriage alliance, but I wanted to show the people I was not trying to sow discord among our intermingling peoples. I was trying to unify us, show us that our differences were not insurmountable, and that respect among us was not only possible, but made us all the stronger for it. What better way to prove I had no prejudice than to take the foreign daughter under my wing with no malice, but with love?

The land had never known such peace, and all who called Kuššara home flourished. The farmers, the artisans, the guard, the servants all had food enough to eat and places to call home. All were free to worship as they wished, something that had not been so when my father and the priest, Kammara, had ruled. The gods of my people had not been banned, but any who openly worshipped the gods of the further east had been given sullen looks at the best, denied company, work, or food at the worst. Had my father been aware of the state of affairs? I could not be sure, but I had made it a personal point of mine to be seen among all people, helping the farmers when the season called for it, trading handsomely for wares from the artisans on market days, and led a campaign or two before passing that torch to Pasaduwa, who was much happier to be beyond the walls of the known city to see the wonders of the world.

At the thought of my brothers, I am brought back to my memories of Idari, and the pain of his remembrance still clutches with vicious cruelty at my heart. Kammara, in his banishment, had started a priest settlement named after his patron goddess: Arinna. He had not caused trouble, but I always kept my ear to the ground where he was concerned. Should I hear whispers of encroachment upon his banishment, it would be dealt with.

The throne room comes into view; I still see the blood of my sons and father intermingling on the cracks between stone, and it had taken far too long for the stain to fade from memory and floor alike in the mind of the people too. For me, it's not something I think that will ever fully disappear. Alas, the room is empty, and Sharvara is not in his other spot, curled up at the foot of my throne.

This time, when I close my eyes, I am reminded of my journey in the underworld, where I had asked Lelwani if I could keep him. Her response was fuzzy in my head, like a thought desperately fleeing from me, but when I grasp it and pull it close, I remember.

'He is mine, but I shall allow you to borrow him. You may find that one day, he will have disappeared. He will have rejoined me on this day.'

"He's gone," I whisper. "He has returned to Lelwani."

Kazera had heard the story in its entirety. I had not hid anything from him or my brothers, or from Malinuwa when she had found the courage to ask. *Why now? Why had Sharvara left me today?* The words cycle through me until the words themselves lose all meaning. "Kazera?" I say, and I feel his hand on my shoulder.

"Yes?"

"I'm going to make an impulse announcement. Ready the Pankus."

"The Pankus?" Kazera gasps, eyebrows flying high and jaw falling slack.

"Yes. The assembly of men who can, on a technicality, veto the king," I agree with a smile. I clap my hands twice, before turning to sit on my throne. "I shall wait here. And bring Malinuwa with you."

When the nobles arrive, both my brothers are included alongside the husbands of my sisters in the crowd of high-ranking men of the city. I stand from my throne and Malinuwa stands beside me, hands interlocked behind her back as she chews on her lip. Meeting her eye, I raise a brow and she releases her lip with a small wince before smoothing her expression out.

"What is it, King Haduwas?" Zuwasa calls, breaking the tense silence of the room. The grumbles which had been making rounds cease, and I smile broadly.

"How do you think I am doing as king?" I ask, extending my arms, waiting for an answer.

"You're doing a better job than I would," Zuwasa mutters, and Pasaduwa snickers, as do several men behind him.

"Hear, hear," another nobleman says.

"High praise," I intone jokingly. "Better than my brother. Anyone else?"

"You're a wise king," Pasaduwa says, elbowing Zuwasa who grunts. "You listen to counsel on matters you are torn by, but you also know when not to listen. You are kind, but firm, and you care for all under your rule. I have no complaints."

There are nods from around the room, and I brace myself for the deluge of protests I'm sure to bring upon myself. "Then it would displease you to hear I wish to pass the throne on?" I was correct. The room was not built for such outbursts, and wincing, I paw at my ears which hear more than theirs do, and immediately, the room quiets, their reactions highly attuned to mine. "You call me wise, and yet do not trust my judgement when I tell you of my plans," I say mildly. "I find your words confusing."

"Why?" someone calls, and I nod. "My hound, Sharvara, has left." Silence. They do not comprehend, and I sigh. "Sharvara was a gift from the sun goddess of the earth," I explain. "She told me that one day he would disappear. Today is that day."

"I don't get it," Zuwasa says and again, some men hum in agreement.

"It sounds as though the sun goddess of the earth foretold an event that would happen, and it has come to pass! Why must that mean you leave too?" one man asks, stepping forward.

"I see it as a sign," I say. "What more can I do for this city than I have already done? I do not cling to power for the sake of title. I have strengthened this city, its people, and its bonds, to ensure that when my time had come, the city would be in good hands. If I were to die, you would have no choice but to select one from among you to carry on in my place. However, as you have all admitted to seeing the wisdom of my rule, I had thought I might suggest my own heir: Malinuwa."

Pasaduwa and Zuwasa are among the first to nod, but there is hesitation in the room. "I do not make the choice for you," I say, "but I will make a case for it. Before I was king, she was the queen. She is of this land, she knows of my plans and of my method. Further, she knows the ways of the priests and priestesses, having lived among them for a great deal of her life. She knows the festivals, the words, the rituals, that the ruler must observe. She can read and write. I have taught her all that I know in the matter, and I ask you, who among you has a fiercer heart? My brothers could offer themselves up as candidates, but they won't want to."

"Says who?" Zuwasa asks, goading me, but when I raise my eyebrows and gesture for him to do it, he remains silent. "Alas, I know my brothers too well. They would rather be in the royal family rather than be the ruler. Their talents lay elsewhere."

"But she cannot go to battle!" The outburst is met with more chatter as they discuss. "She cannot represent the storm god, even if she can speak for our sun goddess!"

"That is why my brother, Pasaduwa, will continue leading our armies. He will handle the armies and warriors, and she will handle the city, the people, the gods. They will rule in title side by side, but in action, she will be the law giver, still beholden to the Pankus just as I willingly submit to you." More grumbles, but less pronounced. "Any other objections?"

"Well, Pasaduwa and Malinuwa will have to marry."

"I will not," Malinuwa says, breaking her silence. "And before you speak, hear me. There will be no succession crisis. When Pasaduwa or Zuwasa have heirs, I shall name them without question. In matters of battle, I shall of course defer to Pasaduwa. I will act on his behalf as high priestess in that case, shielding him and protecting our city. In matters of correspondence, of stock, of rites and festivals, I shall have dominion. I shall hold the seal, but I shall not withhold it for any reasonable request."

"And should both princes die before an heir is secured?" someone asks, and everyone turns to him. His face burns scarlet, but he does not retract his question.

"Well, we'd be in the exact situation we are in now," I say brightly, an edge creeping into my tone. Of course, I could have had an heir, but—I block the images from my mind, not allowing the blood to return to the floor. More murmurs. "Why do you want to leave?" the same one who asked what we would do if my brothers died.

"As you know, I went into the underworld to obtain that gift from the gods," I begin, trying to be patient. "When there, I met and aided many gods. I passed through the gates of Lelwani, and saw her true form. Despite the cries of my heart to stay with her, I came back because my people needed me. I could not allow the rot of my father's reign to continue. It was fraught with tension, factions vying for power, and with segregation of my people and customs. I have fixed these issues, and I have paved the way for a smooth transition, one without upheaval or greed, with a worthy candidate. I have done my duty. I don't even know if I can die, and I do not wish to rule like the kings of old, living thousands of years while all whom I know perish. I have been touched by death, and it calls me back. For what other reason would she take my greatest companion if not to draw me back to her?"

The room descends into quiet—one hushed with understanding, and slowly, a few people nod. It spreads through the room, and soon, everyone is in agreement.

"We hear you, King Haduwas," Urappi says, owner of the closest vineyard. He is among the oldest in attendance. "We recognize your request and your solution alike. From this moment forth, let it be known Malinuwa, daughter of Kuššara, supersedes King Haduwas in accordance with the Pankus. Be seated, Queen Malinuwa." Stepping back to watch her, I smile as she turns to the throne of my father, my throne, and seats herself, looking like she was born to it. She is near the same age as I had been when I had first sat upon it, but thankfully for her, they are not in dire circumstances. I fall to a knee before her, the first in the room to do so, but at my display, the rest of the room follows.

"If I may," I say, head still bowed, "I would like to request one last thing, my queen."

"And what might that be?" Malinuwa asks, looking amused.

"A personal favour."

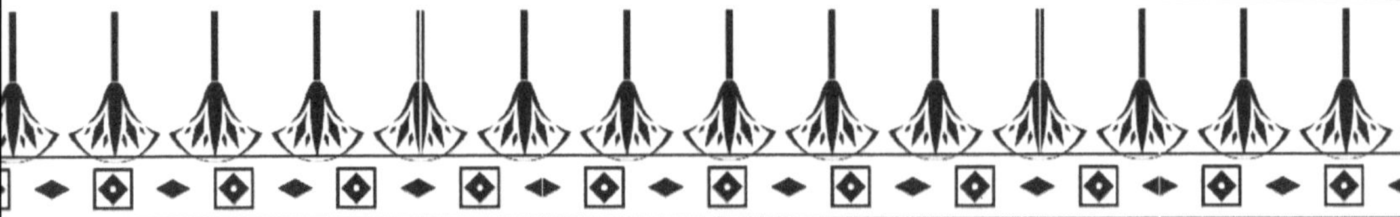

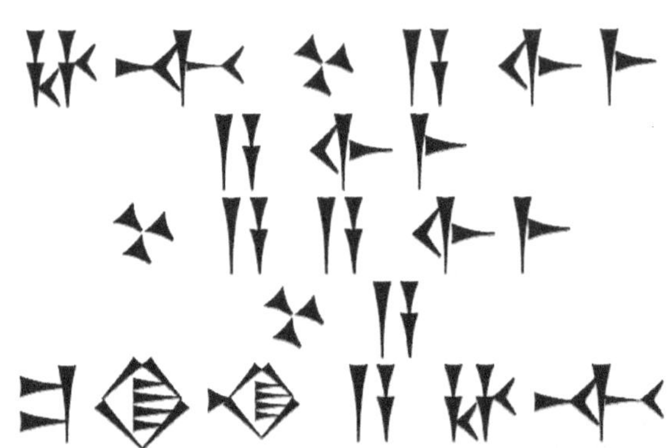

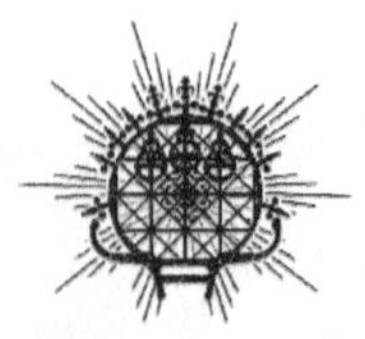

Šauška descends, wary of death's power.

The gates consume her.

The Fates have spoken.

And so Death awaits her match.

XX
TABLET

ROOTS TAKE HOLD

Standing with my horses, Harli, Puza, Kurli, and Marassa, who now share muzzles of sprouting white, I watch the stablehands prepare the horses and chariot. Typically, only two horses are fixed to a chariot, but I am not leaving any behind. Two will be attached to the chariot while the other two will follow behind. The chariot sits upon two wheels, affixed by an axle running between them under the back of the landing. Strips of leather cushion the basin of the chariot, a springy, uneven floor, but after years upon it, I am used to it.

Behind me, the Pankus gathers to watch the procession, and word has spread. Now, even the people beyond the wall have come inside the fortified city to see their beloved king off. Queen Malinuwa stands at my side alongside my brothers, who watch the sun descending towards the horizon. Nipula, the wise woman, smiles at me, and I smile back.

"How do you know she will come?" Pasaduwa asks, voice hushed.

"I have faith," I reply, eyes roving the ground, seeking the right place to strike. I had not used my powers in all these years, not since accidentally destroying the throne room after travelling through shadows. Not once had I kindled the connection that tethered us together, but even now, as I feel inside for it, it waits for me to call upon it, and when I acknowledge it, it ebbs with light and warmth.

'Strike the ground with open palms.'

Exhaling hard, I drop to my knees. So clearly her voice rings in my head, I wait to smell the sweet bark and florals, but I do not detect it just yet. Following the instructions, I lift my hands above my head, and with my heart in my throat, I bring my open palms hard against the earth. Screams and cries ring out above the crackling and breaking of stone. Where my hands had struck, there is now a gaping pit into the earth. Whispers erupt around me, but I can only make out one word that weaves from one mouth to another: *api*, a word which means an entrance to the land of death.

"Malinuwa?" I ask, and though her eyes are trained hard on the hole in the ground, she approaches me with the favour in her hands. Pressing it into my awaiting hand, she pats my hand and stands back with my brothers. Clenching my hand around the stem, I bring the blossom to my nose. The parted, delicate petals reveal a dark pit in the centre which bleeds into a vivid red. It smells of cut grasses, honey, and saffron, and there is not a single imperfection. I had asked Malinuwa to permit me to select a single flower from her gardens; she had held it for me as I'd gotten everything ready.

The smell of the flower nearly conceals the scent of toasted sweet wood and florals, and behind me, I hear an intake of breath as my people behold the goddess from below. Her golden hair is the first thing I see as the light strikes it, making her hair look like it glows. Her gaze seeks mine immediately, and when she smiles, I feel like I can breathe for the first time in over ten years.

"You may rise, Haduwas," she says lightly, still smiling. Standing, I swallow hard and present her with the wild tulip. I tower above her, and my neck strains to look down. Her smile falls, and the panic that claws at my chest makes me want to rewind time, but when she takes the flower with a shaking hand, her eyes water, and I see there is sadness in her eyes, but not a sadness caused by me.

"Do you like it? I selected it for you myself," I say, unsure. Commanding armies, putting the city in order, governing...these are easy things. "If you do not like it, I shall bring you another, and if that's not sufficient, I shall plant you a garden past the gates so you can have all the flowers you desire down below."

"My mother is the goddess of reeds and grain," she starts, but she stops to inhale the rich fragrance from the flower. "I was a goddess born to become root rather than flower. I am buried in the mud, drowning in darkness, not intended to flourish in the sunlight with gentle winds and a face dappled with colour and beauty. That is my sister. She is the beautiful one."

"*You* are beautiful," I say, refraining from alluding to Šauška at all. "You are far more than your function, and *I* see you."

Her startling, green eyes seek the jest in my words, but when she finds none, she relaxes, sniffing the flower once more. Her eyes lift to mine. "And I see *you*." She is draped in inky-black cloth. My servants yet prepare the chariot, now packed with the gifts I had collected over the years in her honour. The chariot bed had been extended for exactly this purpose. Inside, tokens of my affection, including a new tunic dress, embroidered and ornamented with long golden floral patterns up the front, secured with a golden belt with tassels as in the style of my people. Beyond, golden slippers, perfumed oils with damask rose and art. Everything that could not fit upon the chariot would be buried in her honour, and we'd receive it at the banks of the river.

Her eyes land behind me upon my people who watch in awe. Without my noticing, they had all fallen to their knees, foreheads pressed upon the earth as dusk falls. Looking at her, trying to communicate every thought I'd had about her in the past decade with my eyes, I wonder how much of it lands.

Clearing my throat, I bite back the tremulous nerves which course through me. In my hands, a golden artifact: a replica of the golden fruit which had joined our souls together. Her breath hitches, and when I toss it in the air, I wait to see if she will catch it. When she does, I smile, but then it's my turn to have my smile wiped away when from her cloak, she pulls out the real thing.

"Will you join me?" she asks, holding the fruit out with a casual air that is not at all honest. She tries to hide how much she wants this, but I see her. Her free hand knots itself in her tunic, and when I hesitate to take it, her lips tighten a fraction. Stepping towards her, movements slow, I rest my forehead on hers before pressing a kiss to her forehead.

Wrapping my hand around the fruit, fingers overlapping hers, I swallow.

"The yawning expanse of forever is a trial I would only ever want to face at your side."

Her exhale is sharp, but the tense silence is broken by my brother, Zuwasa, who whoops and then grunts as Pasaduwa elbows him hard in the ribs, but the crowd joins in, and soon, cheers from all in attendance. Her fingers tighten around the stem of the flower, and her cheeks bloom with a rosiness which competes with the tulip.

Guiding my hand, she helps me bring the fruit to my mouth, and when I open my mouth to take a bite, teeth parting the rough outer flesh, juices explode in my mouth, sweet and tangy. Her eyes crinkle as she smiles, and she lifts her hand to her mouth to cover her smile.

"What?" I ask, and she shakes her head.

"I've never seen someone eat it like that." I tear my teeth free, chewing on the fibrous innards before swallowing, even the seeds.

"How are you supposed to eat it?" I ask, matching her smile.

"Just the inside. You peel the rind away." Humming, I continue eating it the way I had started, and when I finish, I suck my fingers clean. Her eyes meet mine, and her mouth parts.

"It is done," she says, and when I look upon my people, their eyes are stuck on mine. I hear murmurs on the wind, and I hear one thing over and over: *his eyes. Look at his eyes.* "They are golden, Haduwas," she whispers.

"Come," I say, gently guiding her to the chariot; the servants had finished packing it, and there was room for both of us, but not abreast. Placing my hands on her waist, I lift her up, and a squeak of surprise escapes her. Biting my cheek to prevent the smile from escaping, I step up onto the platform, sealing her inside as I stand at her back with the reins in hand. Flower still in her grasp, I turn to look over my shoulder at the faces in the crowd. I know many of them, and some weep tears of joy while others weep tears of sorrow. My brothers grin at me, but it is Queen Malinuwa who captures my gaze. Her eyes dance between Lelwani and I, and she nods with the smallest of smiles. It is not often Malinuwa, the melancholy child who had grown up to be a stern woman, smiles. My eyes seek to memorize this place.

The wind tastes of smoke, mud, and livestock, carrying the grit of a late spring thaw. The city sprawls as far as the eye can see, with the fortified walls guarded by lions keeping us strong while the farmers nourish us and the vineyards quench our thirst. Traders frequent our roads, and we have become a thriving hub of commerce. I have done my duty as king, bringing prosperity to the lands. We are a people who follow the sun, but even the sun must eventually fall in the face of night. They say the gods built this place, and they must love it, for they've allowed it to rise, nurturing a crown built from the darkest of roots to bloom into the brightest of flowers.

"Let it be known that our King Haduwas rises with the gods!" Malinuwa calls out, her voice clear over the tumult. "We are blessed! This is not the end for King Haduwas. He rises now, a god." My people roar their applause, and when I look down to my bride, I find she is already looking at me. Pivoting within the limited space, she turns to face me, hands gripping my biceps to stabilize herself on the flexible leathers underfoot. Her thumbs stroke my skin, drawing heat to my face; leaning down, I move slowly to allow her to pull away, but she does not, and when my lips meet hers, I am undone.

Eyes shining when I break the embrace, I turn forward, and snapping the reins, I race to bring my queen back home. The horses spring forward, guiding us into the pit of my making, and when Lelwani screams, it is with joy, unadulterated. I had always wondered what the goddess of the sun does when she leaves the skies. Perhaps I would find out.

To be continued in
The Solitude of Hades

FURTHER READING

The following are the sources I was either inspired by, or operating out of the constraints of. The case use of research for a novelist is quite different than the case use for a scientist or historian, and as such, think of this less like "works cited" and more like "works consulted". To preface, I did not directly quote anything within the book, because not only would that be far more "meta" than even this book could handle, I am still writing a fantasy novel. Where I could find sources for things, such as for the purpose of maps or religion or plants and food of the time, I of course included historically factual details where that information could be found, but I would be remiss to say it's historically accurate fiction. I did consult real maps, and I did actually discover the plants and wildlife that were actually in the area in the bronze age, and where relevant, I do make mention of them, such as einkorn, a grain still around today, untouched by modernity (and it is rich and nutty. I know because I made a point to make bread with it, and I highly suggest you make it too.)

In the case of the city of Kussara itself, it has not been found archaeologically. I have invented a structure where, what if that lost city had been found? What documents and tales could have been inside? And I merged that "what if" with another: what if I used the ancient epic as a vehicle for a modern myth set in the ancient world? One where it is inspired by the chthonic deities instead of the Olympians? There are many Greek mythology retellings out there, but I don't think there are many that utilize history and myth and speculation like mine. I'll let you be the judge of that.

Therefore, for my academically inclined readers, I have listed the most potent sources I used for my research below for you should you take interest. I hope you find them as interesting and informative as I did.

Barsacchi, Francesco. "Distribution and Consumption of Food in Hittite Festivals." Manfred Hutter - Sylvia Hutter-Braunsar (Eds.) Economy of Religions in Anatolia : From the Early Second to the Middle of the First Millennium BCE - Proceedings of an International Conference in Bonn (23rd to 25th May 2018) Alter Orient und Altes Testament, no. 467 (2019): 5–19.

Bower, Jody. "Ereshkigal: A New Look at an Old Goddess," n.d.

Breasted, James Henry, Carl F. Huth, and Samuel Bannister Harding. *European History Atlas: Ancient, Medieval, and Modern European and World History.* 10th ed. Denoyer-Geppert Company, 1954.

Cline, Eric H. *1177 B.C.: The Year Civilization Collapsed.* Princeton: Princeton University Press, 2014.

Corti, Carlo."Wine and Vineyards in the Hittite Kingdom: A Case Study of Northern Anatolia and the Southern Black Sea Coast." Aness 51, 2017.

Cotterell, Arthur. *The Encyclopedia of Ancient Civilizations.* First ed. London: The Rainbird Publishing Group, 1980.

Demirel, Serkan. An Essay on Hittite Cultic Calendar Based Upon the Festivals.Athens Journal of History. 3. pp 21-32, 2017.

Durant, John, and Michael Malice. *The Paleo Manifesto.* First ed. Harmony Books, 2013.

Durusu-Tanrıöver, Müge."Now You See Him, Now You Don't: Anthropomorphic Representations of the Hittite Kings." Journal of Near Eastern Studies, 2019.

Forlanini, Massimo. "Forlanini M. 2010 An Attempt at Re-constructing the Branches of the Hittite Royal Family of the Early Kingdom Period." Pax Hethitica Studies on the Hittites & Their Neighbours in Honour of Itamar Singer, 2010.

Ghazaryan, Robert. "Issues of the History of the Early Hittite Kingdom." Bulletin of the Institute of Oriental Studies, 2023.

Giesecke, Annette. *Classical Mythology A to Z: An Encyclopedia of Gods & Goddesses,*

Heroes & Heroines, Nymphs, Spirits, Monsters, and Places. First ed. New York: Black Dog and Leventhal Publishers, 2020.

Gilan, Amir, and Alice Mouton. "The Enthronement of the Hittite King as a Royal Rite of Passage." Alice Mouton; Julie Patrier. Life, Death, and Coming of Age in Antiquity: Individual Rites of Passage in the Ancient Near East and Adjacent Regions, 124, Nederlands Instituut voor het Nabije Oosten, pp.97-115, 2014.

Ginevra, Riccardo. "Myths of Non-Functioning Fertility Deities in Hittite and Core Indo-European." M. Serangeli & T. Olander (Eds.), Dispersals and Diversification. Linguistic and Archaeological Perspectives on the Early Stages of Indo-European, Leiden, 2020, pp. 106–129.

Hoffner, Harry. "'The King's Speech'. Royal Rhetorical Language." Beyond Hatti. A Tribute to Gary Beckman. Edited by B.J. Collins and P. Michalowski, 2013.

Hoffner, Harry. "Daily Life Among the Hittites." Life and Culture in the Ancient Near East. Edited by Averbeck, Chavalas and Weisberg, 2003.

Hundley, Michael. "The God Collectors: Hittite Conceptions of the Divine." Altorientalische Forschungen, vol. 41, no. 2, 2014, pp. 176–200.

Irvine, Scott. *Ishtar and Ereshkigal: the Daughters of Sin.* Winchester: Moon Books, 2020.

March, Jennifer R. *The Penguin Book of Classical Myths.* London: Penguin, 2009.

McMahon, Gregory, and Sharon R. Steadman. *The Oxford Handbook of Ancient Anatolia.* New York: Oxford University Press, 2011.

Mitchell, Stephen. Gilgamesh: A New English Version. New York: Free Press, 2004.

Mouton, Alice. 'Dead of Night' in Anatolia: Hittite Night Rituals. 2007.

Narimanishvili, Dimitri. Mytho-Religious View of the World in the Middle Bronze Age South Caucasus. [PhD Thesis in Archaeology, Tbilisi State University]. The Institute of Archaeology. 2015.

Papi, Angelo. Hittite Paradox.

Peled, Ilan. "Peled 2022 - Contempt in Hittite and Akkadian Literary Texts." The Routledge Handbook of Emotions in the Ancient Near East, 2022.

Quarrie, Deanne. Inanna's Descent to the Underworld.

Steitler, Charles. "Solar and Chthonic Deities in Ancient Anatolia: The Evolution of the Chthonic Solar Deity in Hittite Religion." Presented at the Conference "Theonyms, Panthea and Syncretisms in Hittite Anatolia and Northern Syria – March 25-26, 2022, 2022.

Stone, Damien. *The Hittites: Lost Civilizations.* London: Reaktion Books, 2023.

Tatishvili, Irene, and Levan Gordeziani. "Hittite Funeral Traditions and Afterlife Beliefs in the Context of Hittite Cosmology." Ancient Near Eastern Weltanschauungen in Contact and in Contrast Rethinking Ideology and Propaganda in the Ancient Near East, 2022.

Tatishvili, Irene. "Transformations of the Relationship between Hittite Kings and Deities." Acts of the IXth International Congress of Hittitology (Çorum,1-7 September 2014), 2019.

Torri, Giulia. "Remarks about the Transmission of Festival Texts Concerning the Cult of Lelwani (Based on the Fragment KBo 13.216 + KBo 56.89 (+) KBo 56.90)." E. Rieken, A. Müller-Karpe, W. Sommerfeld, Saeculum. Gedenkschrift Fur Heinrich Otten Anlasslich Seines 100. Geburtstags, StBot 58, Wiesbaden 2015.

Van den Hout, Theo P.J. "Death as a Privilege: The Hittite Royal Funerary Ritual." Hidden Futures: Death and Immortality in Ancient Egypt, Anatolia, the Classical, Biblical and Arabic-Islamic World, Amsterdam University Press, Amsterdam, 1994, pp. 37–75.

Vigo, Matteo. "Plague, Pandemics, and Divine Punishment Among the Hittites." Interdisciplinary Integrated Disaster Administration on Covid-19 Pandemic. 2021.

Vigo, Matteo. "The Use of (Perfumed) Oil in Hittite Rituals with Particular Emphasis on Funerary Practices (2014)." D'Ascoli A. (Ed.), Consumption of Perfumed Oil in the Ancient Mediterranean and Near East: Funerary Rituals and Other Case Studies, (JIIA 01/2014), Pp. 25-37, 2014.

A SPECIAL THANK YOU

So much of this book was made possible by my Kickstarter backers!

Desiree, Cortney Babcock, Ellie from Elle Jackson Narration, Annie (@houseofbooksandboardgames), Patrick Border, Corey Votta, Julia Deutsch, Colleen Heidecker, Tonya Johnson, Cassandra G., Miki Nancy, Dyane MacKinnon, Brandon Ringham, Anne-Marie Puccini, Ryan Tanner, Kenneth Davis, Adalaide Marie, Frank S., Sarah Steenbergen, Samantha Rush, J'aime M., Sarah Maier, Chad Nedzlek, Kathleen Gurski, Katherine Malloy, Nikki Ramey, Tim Stroup, El Johnson, Geo Sag, Kara Roncin, Stephanie De Luna, Brittany H., Mr. A., Sera Z., Liz, Anita Maynard, Charneka Edwards, and Alex Hanley.

This book was always going to exist, but because of you, it became something far more ambitious, tangible, and alive than I could have managed on my own. Because of you, you made special editions possible, prints and overlays real—and not just ideas sitting in my notebook. You unlocked stretch goals that let me build deeper immersion into the world in ways I had never attempted before. You also gave the launch structure. The campaign didn't just fund production; it changed the game in a way I could never have conceived even a couple years ago. When you hold this book and the extras that came with it, you're not just seeing the finished product. You're seeing what your support directly built. They exist because you chose to be part of this at its earliest stage.

Thank you for joining me on this journey, and thank you for taking a chance on this unknown, Canadian author.

ACKNOWLEDGMENTS

Thank you for taking the time to read this book. Your interest, support, and feedback mean a great deal. There are many people I want to thank for their part in bringing it to life.

To my cover design team at Miblart: thank you for your incredible work on the cover, page headers, section breakers, and publishing logo. You helped shape the full visual identity of this book, and I'm deeply grateful for your creativity, care, and attention to detail.

To IRIS Society (Indie Readers Influencer Society): thank you for your support throughout the pre-order campaign, the Kickstarter exposure, ARC distribution, and for helping make the book launch event possible. Your work in connecting books with readers made a real and lasting difference to this project.

To my editors Samantha and Molly, and to my proofreading team at English Proper Editing Services: thank you. Some of you worked with early drafts while others helped refine the final stages. Each step was essential in bringing this book to completion, and I'm deeply grateful for your skill, patience, and dedication.

To the early readers and reviewers: thank you for giving your time, attention, and thoughtful feedback. Your insights helped shape this book in ways both seen and unseen, and I'm deeply grateful for your care and honesty.

To the booksellers, librarians, and members of the reading community: your enthusiasm for new stories and your willingness to champion them make all the difference. Thank you for helping books find their way into readers' hands.

And to you, the reader: thank you for being part of this book's journey. It means more than you know.

ABOUT THE AUTHOR

Amanda L. Rautio is a fantasy author from Banff, AB, with a background in Classical History and English Literature. She began crafting her imaginative worlds at the age of fourteen and continues to weave tales rich with mythology and symbolism. When she's not writing, Amanda enjoys black [decaf] coffee, immersing herself in books, spending time with her pet snakes, and cherishing moments with her supportive fiancé, her very own pillar of Heracles.

To purchase a print edition or special edition, please visit my website:

https://www.themythosmith.ca
Goodreads: Amanda L. Rautio
Instagram: @themythosmith

Please consider leaving a review on your platform of choice.

ALSO BY AMANDA L. RAUTIO

The Fruit of Life & Death Duology

The Tale of Kore (#1)

In the heart of academia, Corey, an ambitious master's student, yearns for a life beyond the confines of dusty books and lectures. Wanting to turn her theoretical research into tangible knowledge, she and her friends recreate an ancient ritual dedicated to Persephone and Demeter in a cave—and it ***works****.*

TBA (#2) *coming soon*

The Hades Chronicles

(a companion series to The Fruit of Life & Death)

The Rise of Haduwas (#1)

The Solitude of Hades (#2) *coming soon*

Non-Fiction:

A Fairytale in the Making: a Guided Journal

This is a book for anyone who believes their life could be a little more magical—with some self-reflection, a little rebellion, and a dash of hope. Start wherever you are. Rewrite your narrative. And remember: even the darkest forests have a way through.

Short Fiction:

The Mirror of the Lost and the Found

(a Short Story Collection)

Defying categorization beyond "short fiction," this collection moves across genres and forms, from the familiar to the experimental. Each piece is a fragment: sometimes anchored in history, sometimes cast into futures unknown, sometimes hovering in the spaces we cannot name.

www.themythosmith.ca

www.ingramcontent.com/pod-product-compliance
Lightning Source LLC
LaVergne TN
LVHW091046080826
845145LV00002B/648